"Next time I spend the night," he said in a low voice, **"I won't sleep on the couch, and we will actually have something to hide come morning."**

Reva shook her head. "You can't...we can't... Last night I made a mistake when I suggested... You were right when you said we shouldn't..."

"I said *not tonight*," Dean said calmly. "I didn't say never. I want you, Reva, but I want you unafraid." He traced a finger across her neck. "When you ask me to make love to you, it'll be because you want me, not because you don't want to be alone."

"I won't ask you for anything," Reva insisted. "Not ever again."

"Yes, you will."

Dear Reader,

The days are hot and the reading is hotter here at Silhouette Intimate Moments. Linda Turner is back with the next of THOSE MARRYING McBRIDES! in *Always a McBride*. Taylor Bishop has only just found out about his familial connection—and he has no idea it's going to lead him straight to love.

In *Shooting Starr*, Kathleen Creighton ratchets up both the suspense and the romance in a story of torn loyalties you'll long remember. Carla Cassidy returns to CHEROKEE CORNERS in *Last Seen...*, a novel about two people whose circumstances ought to prevent them from falling in love but don't. *On Dean's Watch* is the latest from reader favorite Linda Winstead Jones, and it will keep you turning the pages as her federal marshal hero falls hard for the woman he's supposed to be keeping an undercover watch over. *Roses After Midnight*, by Linda Randall Wisdom, is a suspenseful look at the hunt for a serial rapist—and the blossoming of an unexpected romance. Finally, take a look at Debra Cowan's *Burning Love* and watch passion flare to life between a female arson investigator and the handsome cop who may be her prime suspect.

Enjoy them all—and come back next month for more of the best and most exciting romance reading around.

Yours,

Leslie J. Wainger
Executive Editor

Please address questions and book requests to:
Silhouette Reader Service
U.S.: 3010 Walden Ave., P.O. Box 1325, Buffalo, NY 14269
Canadian: P.O. Box 609, Fort Erie, Ont. L2A 5X3

On Dean's Watch

LINDA WINSTEAD JONES

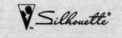

Silhouette®

INTIMATE MOMENTS™

Published by Silhouette Books

America's Publisher of Contemporary Romance

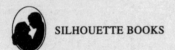 SILHOUETTE BOOKS

ISBN 0-373-27304-5

ON DEAN'S WATCH

Copyright © 2003 by Linda Winstead Jones

All rights reserved. Except for use in any review, the reproduction
or utilization of this work in whole or in part in any form by any
electronic, mechanical or other means, now known or hereafter
invented, including xerography, photocopying and recording, or in
any information storage or retrieval system, is forbidden without
the written permission of the editorial office, Silhouette Books,
233 Broadway, New York, NY 10279 U.S.A.

All characters in this book have no existence outside the imagination of
the author and have no relation whatsoever to anyone bearing the same
name or names. They are not even distantly inspired by any individual
known or unknown to the author, and all incidents are pure invention.

This edition published by arrangement with Harlequin Books S.A.

® and TM are trademarks of Harlequin Books S.A., used under license.
Trademarks indicated with ® are registered in the United States Patent
and Trademark Office, the Canadian Trade Marks Office and in other
countries.

Visit Silhouette at www.eHarlequin.com

Printed in U.S.A.

LINDA WINSTEAD JONES

would rather write than do anything else. Since she cannot cook, gave up ironing many years ago and finds cleaning the house a complete waste of time, she has plenty of time to devote to her obsession for writing. Occasionally she's tried to expand her horizons by taking classes. In the past she's taken instruction on yoga, French (a dismal failure), Chinese cooking, cake decorating (food-related classes are always a good choice, even for someone who can't cook), belly dancing (trust me, this was a long time ago) and, of course, creative writing.

She lives in Huntsville, Alabama, with her husband of more years than she's willing to admit and the youngest of their three sons.

She can be reached via www.eHarlequin.com or her own Web site www.lindawinsteadjones.com.

For my nephew Alan Kimbrel, a true inspiration
and all-around good kid.

Chapter 1

Someone was watching her house. Reva came to a surprised halt, her heart stuttering as she realized what she saw before her.

A man she didn't recognize stood close to the massive trunk of an old oak tree, motionless, his eyes and his unwavering attention on her little cottage. She'd left the kitchen light burning, so it probably looked to him as if someone was home.

All was quiet up and down Magnolia Street. It wasn't yet nine o'clock, but dark had fallen a while ago, shrouding the old houses and thick-limbed trees in quiet night. Sporadically placed street lamps, porch lamps and the light glowing from the windows of homes cast illumination here and there. But Reva had found herself walking in more dark than light. She knew the way well, so the dark was not a problem. But then, she didn't usually see strangers on her way home.

If not for the moonlight, she wouldn't be able to see the

man at all. He was almost hidden in shadow, there beneath the oak tree.

If he was lost in shadow, so was she.

She'd walked home from Tewanda Hardy's after dropping off Cooper at his friend Terrance's, where he was spending the night. It was such a pretty spring evening, much too nice to be driving the mile or so to the Hardy house and then home again. When Cooper had said he was ready to go, Reva had pulled on her Tennessee Titans cap, stepped into her walking shoes and hit the sidewalk.

Good thing she'd decided to walk. She never would have discovered the man spying on her cottage if she hadn't cut through the yard of the main house. She would have walked into her cottage without knowing someone was watching.

For a moment Reva stood very still and studied the man. Even though he was where he shouldn't be, she didn't feel threatened. He was wearing a *suit,* for goodness' sake, and definitely didn't look like any burglar she'd ever seen. He didn't look around to see if anyone might be watching, didn't display any signs of nervousness. Instinctively she knew he wasn't a threat to her. Indecision bubbled inside her, making her stomach clench. Her instincts had failed her before. She really shouldn't start trusting them now.

While she watched, he backed away from the tree, did a quick about-face and walked off.

And straight toward her.

Reva had a couple of choices, but she needed to make her decision now. Run. Hide. Confront.

The man who'd been watching her house jerked his head around to stare in her direction. Okay, too late for hiding. He had long legs; she couldn't outrun him. All her neighbors were elderly. Screaming for help would eventually get the sheriff here, but would not do her any good in the coming minutes.

Reva searched the ground quickly, her eyes landing on a three-foot tree limb that had been trimmed from the Bradford pear but not yet taken to the street for pickup. She stepped to the side, dropped down and grabbed the limb, then stood and prepared herself for confrontation, the only choice she had left.

"Hi," he said, his voice calm and even.

Reva relaxed, but she did not drop the branch. "Hi. What the hell are you doing skulking around the neighborhood?" She didn't want to point out that she'd caught him watching *her* house.

"I'm not…" He hesitated. "Was I skulking?" His face was mostly in shadow still, but she could see his reaction. A reluctant half smile transformed his hard face. "I can see how it might've looked that way. I'm renting a room across the street. Just got in an hour or so ago, and I wanted to have a look around." He moved forward and offered a hand. "My name's Dean Sinclair."

Reva stepped back. Maybe he was telling the truth, maybe not. She wasn't about to drop the tree limb and shake his hand, even if he did sound normal and reasonable, and was dressed in a suit, dress shirt and tie. She wasn't going to give him her name, either.

As she retreated, he came to a halt. His half smile faded. "You're not going to hit me with that stick, are you?" There was a hint, just a very slight trace, of something dark in that question. The gut instinct she rarely trusted made her glad she hadn't dropped her makeshift weapon.

Crime in Somerset was practically nonexistent, unless you counted littering and the occasional offense of loitering. And trespassing, Reva thought as she narrowed her eyes. Not exactly a heinous crime, but still, something

about this man set her teeth on edge. The fact that she'd
caught him spying on her house didn't help matters any.

"Not if you don't give me a reason to," she answered.

Casual as you please, the man crossed his arms. So why
was she so sure there was nothing at all *casual* about this
man?

"There are some great old houses in this neighborhood," he said, his voice soft and deep. "I was just walking around, checking them out. I'm interested in nineteenth-century architecture."

"You can actually see the details of that architecture
better by daylight," Reva said sharply.

"Like I said, I just arrived in town." He shrugged his
broad shoulders. "I couldn't wait to have a look around.
Do you live close by?"

"No," she said. "I'm just walking around in the dark
admiring the architecture."

That response got another half smile out of the stranger.
Dean whatever. He definitely didn't look like a criminal,
but he didn't exactly look harmless, either. Beneath that
suit he was physically fit. She could tell by the way he
walked, the way he held himself. There was no softness
about him, unless you counted the voice that was slightly
touched with a Southern accent.

Reva was always wary of the opposite sex, especially
men like this one. This Dean fellow was hard, cocky and
not where he should be. *Architecture my ass.*

"I'm leaving," he said, taking a step back. "I would
say it was nice to meet you, but you never did tell me your
name." He paused, but she did not fill in the blanks for
him. "And I can't see your face," he added, dipping his
head to one side as if that might help. "Not with that cap
shadowing it. But if I ever see an overly suspicious woman

walking down the street carrying a big stick, I'll be sure to say hello.''

Reva hefted the limb in her hand, making sure her grip was firm. Was he flirting with her? Impossible. She decided not to respond at all.

"Sorry if I gave you a fright," Dean said.

"You didn't give me a fright," Reva insisted.

Dean nodded, apparently not believing her for a moment. Could he hear her heart thudding all the way over there? Or did he detect the tremor in her voice?

"I guess I should save my examination of the town for daytime hours from now on. I didn't know they rolled up the sidewalks so early here."

"Now you know," Reva said sharply.

"Good night, ma'am," he said with a tip of his head and a quick turnabout. Reva watched as he walked across the yard, across the street and directly to Evelyn Fister's front door. She glanced down the side driveway of the three-story house where Dean claimed he was staying and caught sight of the rear end of a strange car parked there.

Okay, so maybe he'd been telling the truth. Maybe.

She carried the Bradford pear limb with her as she walked toward home.

Stakeouts were not Dean Sinclair's favorite part of the job. Sitting for hours, days, sometimes weeks waiting for something to happen was a tedious but necessary part of being a deputy U.S. marshal. Despite a good night's sleep, this stakeout was already getting on his nerves, and he and his partner, Alan Penner, had only been in Somerset, Tennessee—population 2,352—for thirteen hours.

Alan, who'd been on duty while Dean slept, stood up as Dean exited his bedroom of their rented apartment. He was obviously tired after more than six hours at his post.

Once thin and wiry, lately Alan had been sporting a paunch, evidence that his wife was determined to keep him well fed. A couple of years older than Dean, his dark hair showing a few new gray hairs at the temple, Alan was still on the green side of forty. By a few months.

Their new residence wasn't actually an apartment; they'd rented the entire third floor of a house that had been built about 1820. Everything squeaked, squealed and needed to be painted. Still, the place had a kind of quaint charm.

The main room on the third floor had been referred to by their landlady as "the upstairs parlor." The furnishings were older than the ancient landlady herself, and a few of the upholstered pieces had a distinctly musty odor. But it was clean and as close to Miss Reva's, the restaurant across the street, as they were going to get.

There were two bedrooms, one on each side of the parlor, a bathroom down the hallway, and rooms they would not need or use across the way.

Stretching and turning away from the telescope situated on a tripod near the lace-curtain-covered window, Alan twisted his thin lips. "One person has entered the house this morning."

"Already?" It wasn't yet 8:00 a.m., and the restaurant situated in the old house across the street didn't serve lunch until one.

"Yeah. She didn't look at all like Pinchon, though. She was maybe five feet tall, white-haired, weighed about eighty pounds, and she's probably ninety-three years old." Alan yawned and shuffled toward his own room for a few hours' sleep.

The lens on the telescope Alan had been manning was aimed unerringly at the antebellum house on the other side of the street and one house down. Dean sat in a chair before that telescope, his gaze trained on the large white house. The subject of this stakeout, one Reva Macklin, actually lived in the guest house behind the structure, which had been converted into a popular restaurant. They could only get a partial view of the guest house from this vantage point. The north side porch of the main house and a couple of trees, in full leaf in an overly warm May, got in their way.

Which was why Dean had ventured out last night, only to get caught by a local woman armed with a big stick. He smiled at the memory. All he'd been able to see well were her legs, and she'd had great legs. Shapely, long and smooth.

He'd seen her legs and heard her voice, and those two things alone had been enough to stay with him through the night. Long legs and a slightly husky voice that had crept under his skin from the moment she'd asked him what the hell he was doing skulking around in the dark.

"Think he'll show up here?" Alan asked with another yawn.

Dean dismissed his dreams of a woman he would probably never see again. He was here on business, and his business was fugitive apprehension.

Eddie Pinchon had been serving a life sentence before escaping from prison in Florida two days ago. A quick glance at Pinchon's record showed that the man was capable of anything and everything. He was violent, occasionally smart, greedy and a little bit crazy. He could appear to be perfectly normal one moment, then do something no sane man would even think of. Killing a man who'd double-crossed him on a drug deal in the middle of a fast-food restaurant while dozens of people watched was definitely crazy.

Dean glanced at the picture they'd pinned to the wall

by the window. The eight-year-old snapshot had been blown up several times, so the texture was grainy. Still, it was more than clear enough. Reva Macklin had been Eddie's girl for almost two years before his arrest. In the only picture they'd been able to find, she was smiling widely, obviously happy. At nineteen she'd been a bleached blonde, wore too many earrings in one ear, too much makeup and a blouse cut low enough to advertise her natural attributes. She was definitely not Dean's type; she was one step away from being downright tacky. But in spite of all those things, she was quite pretty. Beautiful, in a rare kind of way that couldn't be completely hidden by her too-blond hair and her too-red lips. Yeah, Pinchon would come here. Reva Macklin wasn't the kind of woman a man like Eddie left behind without a second thought.

There were other agents working on this case, keeping an eye on Pinchon's family and acquaintances. Most of them were in Virginia and North Carolina, where Eddie had spent much of his life. Maybe the escapee would be foolish enough to go see his mother, or his cousin and business partner, or his drinking buddies. Then again, maybe not. He had to know the authorities would be watching and waiting. But could he turn his back on a woman like this one?

"Yeah," Dean said softly. "He'll be here."

Alan didn't immediately retire to his room, but leaned against the doorjamb and sighed. "Connie hates these things."

Connie was wife number two for Alan, and it looked as if they were going to make things work. They'd been married six years, had two kids—a boy and a girl—and Connie was all Alan talked about when they were away from home. After a few days Dean got damned tired of hearing about Connie and the kiddies. Alan was so happy these days, so domestic. Every now and then, Alan's domestic bliss got downright annoying.

"What about what's-her-name?" Alan asked brightly. "The brunette. Penny, Patty, Pansy—"

"Patsy," Dean said sharply.

"Patsy," Alan said, as if he hadn't remembered the name of Dean's latest love interest all along. "Is she ticked off? Again?"

"I wouldn't know." Dean's voice remained flat. "I haven't seen her in three months." And they hadn't had much of a relationship for at least three months before the final break.

There was a moment of telling silence. "Thank God," Alan finally said with a long, expelled breath of relief. "She was such a…well, I hate to use the word bitch, but really, what other word is there? I'm glad you finally got smart and dumped her. All she ever did was complain. You're never home, you're home too much, we can't make any plans—" Alan stopped speaking abruptly. "Wait a minute. Three *months*. You dumped her three months ago and you didn't tell me?"

Dean continued to study the house across the street. "Actually she dumped me." Not that he'd cared by that point. Their relationship, if you could call it that, hadn't been good for a very long time.

"Ouch," Alan said softly.

"Don't you need to get some sleep?" Dean asked, anxious to let this tired subject go.

"In a minute." Alan moved closer, his steps surprisingly soft on a tightly woven rug. "You know what your problem is?"

Dean sighed. "No, but I imagine you're going to tell me."

"You're all about the job," Alan said in a kind voice.

"So are you."

"Not anymore."

Out of the corner of his eye, Dean saw Alan shake his head. "I love the job. I don't want to do anything else, ever. But not knowing how to leave it behind at the end of the day cost me my first marriage. These days, when I go home, I leave the job outside the door. If I didn't, I would have found myself tossed out of marriage number two years ago."

"Yeah, well, you're a saint."

"No, you're the saint, buddy-boy," Alan countered. "You have a real Boy Scout complex. Save the world, save the family, take care of everybody and his brother. And all the while, you do everything by the book. Didn't you ever ask yourself what about me? What about my needs?"

Dean glanced at his partner. "Have you been watching *Oprah* again?"

Alan blushed. "Just a little. And that new psychologist she has on every week is a pretty smart guy."

"Go to bed." Dean returned his attention to the telescope, listening to Alan's retreating footsteps. It was going to be a long damn stakeout if his partner insisted on dissecting Dean's personal life along the way.

A woman rounded the antebellum house across the street, her stride slow and easy, and Dean shifted the telescope in her direction. For a split second her face was hidden by a low-lying limb, the leaves dancing this way and that in a soft morning breeze. All he could see was the swish of a full yellow skirt that hung well below her knees, the gentle swing of an arm. And then, two steps later, Dean saw her clearly.

At first glance, he was certain this woman was not Reva Macklin. Her hair was a soft dark blond and had been pulled back into a thick ponytail. Her dress was loose-fitting and simple. She wore little, if any, makeup. But he focused on the face, on the shape of her nose and the curve of her cheek, and with an unexpected thump of his heart he realized this was her. She'd grown up since the picture on the wall had been taken, and she'd discovered a touch of class along the way. She was not what he'd expected, but the woman walking through the grass with a serene expression on her face was definitely Reva Macklin.

She had changed remarkably, but she remained beautiful. Had she always been graceful, or was that new? It was impossible to tell from a photograph if she had always carried herself this way. A photograph only revealed so much. Reva Macklin was more than beautiful. She carried herself with elegance and possessed a femininity that might make any man's mouth water.

Yeah, sooner or later Eddie Pinchon would show up in Somerset, Tennessee. Dean and Alan would be waiting.

The kitchen was in chaos as usual, but it was the kind of organized chaos Reva was accustomed to.

Most of her employees were older women. Tewanda Hardy was in her thirties, and Nicole Smith—a kindergarten teacher who only worked summers and Saturdays—wasn't yet twenty-five, but the others were of another generation. They were gray-haired, spry and between the ages of sixty-one and seventy-two. Some of them helped with the cooking, others served as hostesses. A few worked only one day a week, others worked four or five. They all thrived on doing what they did best: cooking, cleaning and telling old friends and tourists tall tales of life in this small Southern town and of the exciting battle that took place just outside the city limits—in 1863.

"Did you hear?" Miss Frances said as she worked the

biscuit dough. "Evelyn has rented her apartment to two men from out of state. They come from Georgia, I believe she said."

Reva's ears perked up as she recalled the man she'd met last night.

"Really?" Miss Edna said as she peeled an apple that would become part of a huge pot of stewed apples she'd prepare later this morning. "Are they tourists?"

"Evelyn wasn't sure," Frances said in a lowered voice. "The gentlemen wouldn't say exactly why they'd come to town." She pursed her lips in disapproval. "We have so few tourists who actually stay here in Somerset, especially in the spring. Though there is that nice couple who comes here every fall to watch the leaves turn. Most tourists prefer the hotel out on the highway or one of the isolated cabins, especially the younger folks. It's very odd, if you ask me. I can't believe Evelyn would rent rooms in her house to strangers who won't even tell her why they're here."

"Well," Edna said, leaning in close but not lowering her voice, "she does need the money. And she sleeps with her daddy's shotgun beside her bed and she knows how to use it, so I feel sure she's safe."

Gossip was another pastime Reva's employees enjoyed. And two strangers in Somerset? This was definitely juicy gossip. Reva decided not to tell them she'd met one of the strangers last night. It would too soon become a part of the gossip, and she preferred to keep a low profile, when possible.

"Perhaps we should have a word with the gentlemen this afternoon," Frances suggested. "Just to be sure everything's on the up-and-up."

Reva smiled as she cleaned and chopped the okra in

front of her. No matter who or what Dean and his friend were, she had to feel a little bit sorry for them.

"Maybe one of them will come calling on Reva," Edna said with a sly smile. "Evelyn said they were handsome young men, though one of them has a bit of a potbelly. Nothing horrible, like that rascal Rafer Johnson," she added quickly. "Just a healthy sign that he's been eating."

"He's probably married," Frances observed wisely.

Edna scoffed, "Then why would he move to town in the company of another man?"

The two older women's eyes met, and they were silent for a long moment. "You don't think…" Frances said in a soft voice.

"Surely not," Edna said, and then she pursed her lips.

"Two attractive men, living together, suspiciously silent about why they're here and who they are…"

"When did they arrive?" Reva asked, knowing the answer. If Dean had been telling the truth, that is.

"Last night," Frances said.

Reva laughed. "Why don't we give them a chance to settle in and meet everyone before we make any rash judgments?"

"She's right, of course," Edna agreed. "And there is the possibility that the one who doesn't have a potbelly might come calling on Reva."

"No, thank you," Reva said sharply. Men like Dean didn't *come calling,* and even if they did, he wasn't her type. She didn't have a type!

"Would you prefer the man with the potbelly?" Frances asked. "Is that why you won't date Sheriff Andrews? I know he's asked for permission to call on you several times, and you always refuse. I had no idea you were looking for a man with a little more meat on his bones. Sheriff Andrews is not a small man, by any means, but he's certainly not soft in any way. If you'd like, we can keep taking him food at the station until he grows a nice little round tummy of his own—''

Reva laughed. ''No! Please, no. Why can't you ladies just accept the fact that I don't want any man to come calling on me?''

''It's not natural,'' Frances said.

''I wish I had a man.'' Edna sighed. ''I miss having someone to talk to in the evening, since my John passed away.''

''I miss the sex,'' Frances confided.

''Well,'' Edna said with a wicked smile, ''your Billy Joe never was much for conversation.''

The two women laughed, and Reva quietly excused herself from the kitchen.

The women who worked for her had changed all her notions about growing older. They had fun, they enjoyed life. Oh, they battled arthritis and they moved more slowly than they used to, but they embraced life and enjoyed every minute.

But try as they might, they had *not* changed her mind about men. Pot belly or no, Reva was finished with the opposite sex. She didn't need a man, didn't want one, which was why she'd sent every small-town Romeo packing during her three years in Somerset.

She leaned against the wall in the hallway just outside the kitchen, wiped her hands on her apron and closed her eyes. Would they ever give up their efforts as matchmakers? Her life was good now. Settled. She was content. She didn't want to go back, not a single step. Since she had horrible luck with men, she was better off without one. A man would turn everything upside down, and as for love, there was no such thing. She'd believed herself in love once, but it had been as elusive and fragile as a soap bubble. And when that bubble had burst, she'd been terribly lost.

Never again. Absolutely, positively, never.

Edna and Frances continued to share their suppositions about the men who'd rented a space across the street. As their ideas grew more and more outrageous, Reva almost felt sorry for the newcomers.

He didn't like this; he didn't like it at all.

The cars had begun arriving before noon. They parked on the street in the shade of ancient trees, as well as in a gravel parking lot on the far side of the house.

Miss Reva's was more popular than he'd imagined.

People milled about in the yard, studied the flowers, rocked and swung on the wide front porch. They came and they kept coming. He couldn't see the side parking lot nearly well enough to suit him. Eddie Pinchon could drive up to the side door and Dean wouldn't see a thing.

At fifteen minutes to one, as the crowd continued to grow, Dean made up his mind. He grabbed his suit jacket from the back of the chair and pulled it on. No one else at Miss Reva's was so formally dressed, which meant he'd stick out like a sore thumb, but he couldn't conceal his pistol if he left the jacket behind.

He didn't run, but his trip down two flights of stairs was fast. He was ready to make his escape, but his landlady, Mrs. Evelyn Fister, stepped into his path without so much as batting an eyelash. He had to put on the brakes to keep from mowing her down.

''Mr. Sinclair,'' she said sweetly, ''where are you off to this afternoon?''

''I thought I'd grab a bite to eat,'' he said, moving to step around her.

She was quicker than she looked to be and moved with

him, so that she remained between him and the front door. "My kitchen is fully stocked. If there's anything you can't find there—"

"I thought I'd eat out," he interrupted.

She blinked, twice. "Out? Where? There's a bakery downtown, Louella Vine's place. The sign out front reads Somerset Bakery and Deli, but everyone calls it Louella's. She's a good cook, I suppose, but all you can get there are sweets and sandwiches. Why, you have to drive all the way to the interstate to get anything decent."

"What about the place across the street?" he asked. And why wasn't Reva Macklin's restaurant considered decent?

His landlady laughed. "Sonny, you don't just drop in at Miss Reva's. You have to have a reservation. Let's see, you might be able to get a space for next week. That's not too long to wait. In the summer and the fall, when the tourists swarm all over the place, you need your reservations at least a week in advance."

Reservations? Somerset was a one-traffic-light town. It was barely a blip on the radar. Everyone knew everyone else, and you had to have *reservations* to get into Reva Macklin's restaurant?

"I can see you're confused," Mrs. Fister said with a tight smile.

"A little," Dean confessed.

"Well," Mrs. Fister said as she took Dean's arm and led him onto her own front porch, "it's rather interesting." From the porch, they could see the crowd that continued to arrive. The patrons were dressed in various ways. Shorts and T-shirts, colorful sundresses, the occasional prim Sunday dress, jeans and neatly pressed button-up shirts. "When Reva came here a few years back, she was determined to make that old place a success. I'm not sure why she chose Somerset, but I suspect it had something to do with the price of the house. We're a bit off the beaten path, and real-estate values have been dismal the past thirty years or so.''

''I can imagine.''

''In the first year, Reva managed to build a respectable business. Nothing spectacular, not at first, but the woman does know how to cook.'' That last was said with pride from a woman who obviously thought this the greatest compliment. ''It was the newspaper article that really got things rolling.''

''Newspaper article.''

''Some hotshot from Nashville came through and ate at Reva's, and he ended up writing an article about the experience. A few months later, there was the magazine article...*Better Homes and Gardens.* That was almost two years ago, and since then you can't get a seat at Miss Reva's unless you have—''

''A reservation,'' Dean finished.

Mrs. Fister consoled him by patting his hand. ''You can walk on over there and ask to be put on the waiting list. They do occasionally have a no-show.'' She cut him a wary glance. ''Not often, but now and then. You might get lucky.''

A quick look around would be enough. If Eddie Pinchon was there, Dean would recognize him. All he needed was a moment or two to eye all the patrons.

Dean walked across the street well aware that his landlady watched. This was why he hated stakeouts in small towns; not that he'd ever participated in a stakeout in a place anywhere near as small as Somerset. It was impossible to hide in a town like this one.

Yet at the same time...it was the perfect place to hide.

Was that why Reva Macklin had come here? Was she hiding?

An older woman with her hair in a tight bun greeted him at the door as the couple she'd been speaking to walked into the restaurant. She held a small book in her hand. "Good afternoon, young man. May I have your name?"

Sonny from his landlady and now *young man*. Dean was beginning to feel like a twelve-year-old. "I don't have a reservation," he said.

The woman pursed her mouth and glanced down at her list. "Well, that is a problem. Would you like to make a reservation for next week? I believe we have a seat available on—" her eyes rolled up momentarily as she pondered "—Wednesday and Friday."

Dean started to tell her to forget it. He could mill around, look at the patrons, watch those who arrived at the side parking lot.

And then the smell hit him.

He took a deep breath. "What is that?"

The lady lifted her pert nose and inhaled. A smile broke over her face. "Fried chicken, stuffed peppers, mashed potatoes and gravy, biscuits, fried okra, fried squash, stewed apples, broccoli and rice, creamed corn, green beans and fudge pie." She leaned in close. "I made the pies today. And the stewed apples."

"Next week will be fine," Dean said as his stomach growled. "Wednesday."

She turned a few pages in her book and poised her pencil above a new page. "And your name?"

"Dean Sinclair. I'm staying across the street."

The old woman's head lifted slowly, her eyes sparkled, and she did not pencil in his reservation for the following Wednesday. "Well, now, isn't that interesting."

Chapter 2

Reva no longer needed to act as hostess at one of the tables in her restaurant. The ladies who worked for her took care of that duty, joining the guests for a meal and telling them all about the history of the house and the town. That was just as well, since Reva had always been more comfortable behind the scenes. People loved her restaurant, and the food she served was always well received. These days she made a tidy profit from her cookbook, as well as the restaurant.

But no one could eat this way every day and not pay a price.

The guests were being seated when Edna burst into Reva's second-floor office. "There you are. Thank goodness!"

Reva could not understand Edna's excitement at finding her; she was always in her office at one o'clock.

"I hate to ask it of you," Miss Edna said graciously,

"but could you possibly take my seat this afternoon? I have table two."

Reva rose, setting aside her menus for the following week. "Are you all right?" Edna rarely missed a meal. She was one of those lucky people who *could* eat like this every day and show no ill effects. Her health was fabulous, with a cholesterol count the envy of many younger women, and she never gained a pound.

"I have a bit of a headache," Edna said softly. "Nothing to be concerned about, but an aspirin and a short nap sounds pretty good right about now."

"Of course." Reva did not consider herself as entertaining as her employees, who knew so much about this area and its history. Still, there had been a time when she'd performed hostess duties six days a week. She'd always done and would continue to do whatever was needed to make this place a success.

"Lovely." Edna took Reva's arm as she left her office. "I did squeeze one extra customer in," she said absently as they walked down the stairs. "He looked very hungry, and I just couldn't make myself turn him away."

"An extra?"

"There was plenty of room," Edna whispered. "Table two is really the largest of all the tables, you know. Well, except for table four, which can seat as many as thirteen, as you well know. Still, table two is certainly large enough for one more hungry young man."

But…an extra? Edna was usually such a stickler for the rules. If you have no reservation and there's no space available, you eat somewhere else, thank you very much.

"Be nice to him," Edna said as they neared the room where table two was located. "He's our new neighbor." With that she released Reva's arm and very quickly disappeared out the front door.

Well, crap.

Reva stood in the doorway and watched as two young waiters placed heavy platters and bowls laden with food on the large lazy Susan at the center of the oversize round table that usually seated ten. Today it was set for eleven. She quickly sized up the patrons.

Three seated couples were obviously tourists. They ranged in age from about thirty-five to sixty-five. Sandals, shorts, T-shirts and the surprised way they stared at the wealth of food being deposited on the table gave them away. A family of three, regulars who drove up from Alabama at least once a month, smiled in anticipation as the food was placed before them. Sharon Phillips and her husband, Doug, sat on either side of their only child, shy, nineteen-year-old Tracy.

The tenth guest, the man Reva had very nearly accosted with a Bradford pear limb last night, was seated next to the chair that had been left empty for her. He wasn't ogling the food as the others were.

He was looking at her.

Oh, Edna would pay for this! This was a blatant, annoying and absolutely unnecessary attempt at matchmaking. The extra guest was handsome and hungry, and it was certainly no mistake that he'd been seated next to her. Headache, indeed. Reva resigned herself to enduring the meal without ever taking her revenge. How on earth could she scold a woman old enough to be her grandmother?

She crossed her fingers and prayed that Dean wouldn't recognize her. It had been dark last night, and her hair had been tucked up under a cap. Even though she shouldn't feel guilty—the man *had* been snooping on her property— she would feel better if the subject never came up again.

"Good afternoon," she said, smiling as she entered the room that had once been a music parlor. A few antique

instruments were used as decoration in the room, as well
as a few pieces of the original furniture. One of the waiters
stood nearby the large round table, in case a platter or bowl
was ever in danger of being emptied.

"Reva!" Sharon Phillips smiled widely in welcome.
"What a treat. Why, we don't see you often these days."

"I'm afraid Miss Edna has a headache. I'm not nearly
as entertaining as she is, so I hope you will all bear with
me." Reva lowered herself into her chair. Dean sat to her
left; one of the tourists, a woman with bright-red hair, sat
at her right.

The patrons filled their plates as the lazy Susan turned
slowly, stopped for a moment and then moved on only to
stop again. Reva suggested that everyone at the table in-
troduce themselves as the food drifted by. She took a little
bit of everything herself, as the dishes spun slowly past,
very purposely not looking at the man beside her. She
didn't look even when they reached for the biscuits at the
same time and his hand brushed hers. Briefly. Very, very,
briefly. And still, there was a spark she could not deny.
No! There could be no spark of any kind.

As she'd suspected, the three couples were all on vacation. Two were retired, and the other couple was taking
two weeks to drive through Tennessee and Georgia. Her
Alabama regulars introduced themselves and raved to the
others about the food and Reva's cookbook.

And then it was *his* turn.

She had avoided looking directly at the man at her side,
but it was impossible to ignore him. He looked out of place
in his dark suit and striped tie and spotless white shirt.
Reva had a feeling it didn't matter what he wore; Dean
was not a man to be ignored. He had a solid, undeniably
strong presence. There were moments when she had to
force herself *not* to look his way.

She told herself he was probably married. Handsome and nicely built, he was not the kind of man who was normally unattached. Women swarmed over men like this one like bees on honey. There was no wedding ring, though, she noticed almost absently, but that didn't mean anything. Not really.

She had a feeling he was not often truly uncomfortable; he was the sort of man who insisted on being in complete command of his life. But this afternoon he was tense, wound so tight he looked as if he was about to explode. Everyone else was smiling, chatting, enjoying themselves.

If he was so uncomfortable, why was he here?

"Dean Sinclair," he said. It quickly became clear that he didn't intend to share anything else about himself. Reva found that rude, since the others had all mentioned where they were from and what they did when they weren't on vacation, but Dean seemed to think the mere mention of his name sufficient.

Fine with her.

But of course, it wasn't fine with anyone else.

"Where do you live, Mr. Sinclair?" Sharon asked.

He glanced at the woman who had asked the friendly question. And hesitated. Reva found herself watching him as she awaited his answer. Good Lord, the man was more than a little gorgeous. He had one of those square jaws that looked as though it had been sculpted in stone, a perfectly shaped nose, nice lips...and killer blue eyes, slightly hooded. Last night she had not been able to tell that his eyes were blue—they'd been standing too far apart, and it had been too dark. Thanks to the dark and the distance, apparently he had not recognized her. Thank goodness.

This was a man with secrets, she thought, as he hesitated in his answer. A man who could turn a gullible woman's world upside down. But Reva was no longer a gullible woman foolish enough to fall for a pretty face and a hard body. Some lessons only needed to be taught once.

"Atlanta," he said after a pause that lasted a moment too long.

"What are you doing in Somerset?" one of the retired men asked. It was clear to everyone that Dean Sinclair was not on vacation.

Again, he hesitated. "I'm thinking of opening my own business here."

Reva stared at him. "What kind of business?" Sharply dressed businessmen did not come to Somerset on a regular basis.

He looked at her, really truly *looked* at her. His eyes met hers and he took a deep breath. Good heavens, he almost smiled. He gave her that same half smile she'd seen last night, as if he were reluctantly amused. "I'm a contractor, a handyman specializing in updating and repairing older houses. I've always had an interest in nineteenth-century architecture."

So much for hoping to go unnoticed. What had given her away? Her fingers twitched slightly, her throat constricted. Maybe she was reading too much into his smile and he didn't recognize her at all.

Then again, what did it matter? Yes, it had been an embarrassing moment, since she'd threatened him and he'd apparently been innocent of any wrongdoing. But he had been where he should not, well after dark. She had no reason to be embarrassed.

A contractor! Reva forgot all about Dean's fabulous eyes, his sculpted jaw, his wedding-ring-free hand and her own unnecessary chagrin. Instead, she thought of the rotting banister upstairs, the crumbling brick in the old kitchen fireplace and the sagging back porch. "Really?"

"I'm not sure we'll locate here," he said quickly.

"We're just taking a few days to visit the place. Get to know the town and the people."

"We?" Perhaps there was a wife, after all.

"My business partner made the trip with me."

Reva gave the man a real smile. "You'll have to bring him with you for lunch one day. I'd like to meet him." The partner must be the one with the potbelly. Goodness knows Sinclair didn't have one. His entire body was likely as hard as that jaw.

An unexpected ripple shimmied up her spine. She pushed the reaction down, forced it from her mind. Edna and Frances were not right. She *did not* need a man.

Especially not one like Dean Sinclair.

"Do I own *what?*" Alan was not yet completely awake. He squinted and leaned toward the window, where Dean sat.

"You know, tools," Dean answered. "A hammer, a screwdriver, maybe a drill."

Alan shook his head. "Why?"

Dean kept his eye on Miss Reva's, even though the last of her customers had left a little while ago. "I paid a visit to the restaurant while you were sleeping." And he was still obscenely stuffed for his trouble. It was like going to your grandmother's house and being overwhelmed by all the choices laid before you. He'd eaten too much.

Everything had been perfect. He couldn't remember the last time he'd eaten such a fine meal. It didn't help matters any that neither of his sisters-in-law or his sister, Shea, were what one could call great cooks. Holidays were always interesting, but no one fed him the way Reva had. And Patsy's idea of eating at home had included a delivery of some kind.

"It was great," Dean finished.

"Okay," Alan said, not sounding at all surprised. "What does that have to do with my tools?"

"They put the customers at these big tables," Dean explained, "and the first thing they did was have everyone tell who they were and where they were from and…what they did."

"Hi!" Alan said in an overly animated voice. "I'm Deputy U.S. Marshal Dean Sinclair, here to keep an eye on your hostess in case her felon of an ex shows up."

"Not likely," Dean grumbled. "She was sitting right next to me." He remembered Reva Macklin with an unexpectedly sharp intensity. Her hand had brushed against his once, and it had been nice. Much nicer than it should have been. She was soft and warm, fragile and strong in that way some special women were.

And she was lovely, far more beautiful than her old grainy picture or the too-brief sight of her through a telescope. No picture or long-range glimpse could do justice to that flawless skin or the sheen in her hair or the depth of her dark-brown eyes. And the way she smelled—like cinnamon and strawberries and soap—was still so real he could close his eyes and…

"So?" Alan prodded. "What did you tell her?"

"That I'm a handyman."

Alan guffawed. "You?"

"It's not that funny."

"Yeah, it is. You don't fix your own car when it breaks down. You live in an apartment and have never even had to mow your own yard, much less fix anything. Face it, you are definitely not mechanically inclined. Do you even know what a hammer looks like?"

"Of course I do," Dean snapped. "It's not that ridiculous."

"Yeah, it—"

"I was caught off guard," Dean interrupted. "Besides, she was the one who caught me snooping around last night."

"You mean *legs* is Reva Macklin?"

"Yep. I knew it the minute she opened her mouth. She's got this husky voice." The kind of voice a man did not forget. "Since I'd already told her I was checking out the architecture, I had to come up with something that made sense. My brother-in-law's a contractor and he fixes up old houses. That's one thing Somerset has in abundance—old, creaking, falling-down houses in desperate need of repair. It was the first logical explanation that came to mind." Dean glanced over his shoulder. "You're my partner, by the way."

"Great," Alan said flatly.

Dean couldn't get Reva Macklin off his mind. She wasn't what he'd expected. Eddie Pinchon was crude, a lowlife if ever he'd met one. What on earth had a woman like Reva ever seen in Eddie? He glanced at the old picture of another Reva. Either she'd changed in the eight years since that picture had been taken—in the seven years since Eddie had been sent away—or she was putting on a show. Was she that good an actress?

Dean was adept at reading people. Lies didn't get past him and he could spot a phony a mile away. The Reva he'd met today was no actress. She'd been friendly without sharing too much of herself, maintaining a professional distance without coming off as a snob. She possessed a quiet gentility that was the hallmark of a real Southern lady.

Again he glanced at the old photograph of another Reva.

"If you can get access to the house as Reva Macklin's new handyman, you can plant a bug or two," Alan said thoughtfully.

"We don't have a court order."

"Unofficially," Alan said quickly. "And if you could plant one in the guest house…"

"No," Dean answered. "Not without authorization."

Alan shook his head. "We can't see every entrance to that big house, and we can barely get a glimpse of the guest house from here. There are only two of us on this detail! Pinchon can walk in any time he feels like it, and if we're not looking in the right place at the right time, we're screwed."

Dean knew Alan was right, and still he didn't like it. His partner gave him a hard time about being such a stickler for the rules, when some other agents broke them without a second thought. He wanted to catch Pinchon, but he didn't want to compromise his standards to accomplish the task.

"Give it a couple of days. Miss Macklin's got a good, steady business here. She's not going anywhere. If Eddie does show up, we'll get him."

"I still think a bug is the way to go," Alan grumbled.

Dean stood. He and Alan would never agree on this point. "I'm going to walk to town," he said. Since "town" was three blocks of redbrick buildings half a mile down the road and the path was shaded sidewalk the entire way, it wasn't exactly an arduous expedition.

"Bring me something to eat," Alan said with a yawn.

It was nice to get out of the house. The streets were quiet now that all of Reva's customers had left. Dean was rarely subjected to such serenity. It was so quiet he could hear the breeze in the trees. His pace was slower than usual, as if to hurry would be wrong in this place.

Even downtown, with its small shops and quaint old buildings, was slow-paced. The everyday necessities were all right here. A small grocery, a dress shop, a barbershop and a beauty parlor. And a hardware store.

An hour and too much money later, Dean headed back to his temporary home. The bags he carried were heavy, but he figured he now had everything he needed to get started. In his shopping bags were a couple of pairs of heavy denim pants, a few cheap T-shirts, work boots, thick white socks, a baseball cap—and a hammer.

He'd looked at the selections and asked himself, *What would brother-in-law Nick buy?* That had made the process quick and easy. Everyone he'd talked to had wanted to know who he was and why he was in Somerset, and he'd given them all the same explanation he'd given Reva Macklin.

He was Somerset, Tennessee's newest handyman, and he'd never in his life so much as driven a nail.

One of the bags he carried contained supper for Alan. He had stopped at the Somerset Bakery and Deli, which was situated just past the beauty parlor and was really not much of a deli at all. They offered lots of baked goods and a few sandwiches. The small place closed at three o'clock, so he'd barely gotten there in time. The somewhat plump woman behind the counter, who had introduced herself as Louella Vine, had been delighted to see him. Maybe business wasn't so good and every customer was a pleasant surprise. Then again, maybe she was just one of those exceptionally outgoing women who never met a stranger.

The sound of pounding feet alerted Dean to the fact that he was about to be run down. He glanced over his shoulder to see two little boys, one white and blond, the other black and half a foot taller, gaining on him fast. Dean stepped to the side of the walkway, giving them room to pass.

They didn't.

"Hi!" The little blond boy practically skidded to a stop at Dean's feet. "Who are you?"

The taller child stayed behind his friend, quiet and watchful.

Dean glared at them both. "Don't you know better than to talk to strangers?"

"Are you strange?" the blond kid asked, wide-eyed and not at all perturbed by Dean's tough manner.

"No."

The little boy grinned, shooting Dean a decidedly disarming smile. "My name's Cooper. I know everyone who lives on this street, but I don't know you. This is Terrance," he said, jerking a thumb back at his friend. "He's my best friend. We're in the first grade." Each sentence ran directly into the next in childlike, breathless fashion. "Last year we were in kindergarten, that's when we got to be very best friends, but I've known him all my life. Almost all my life. As long as I can remember, anyway. But we just got to be best friends last year. Last year we were just little kids, but now that we're older we're still best friends."

The kid talked a mile a minute. When he stopped to take a breath, Dean asked, "Do you live on this street?"

"Yeah!" Cooper answered.

Great. "Well, Cooper, my name is Mr. Sinclair. I'm new. Now run along and don't talk to strangers." Dean resumed his walk toward home. Cooper and Terrance did not "run along" as instructed.

"Do you have any kids?" Cooper asked.

"No," Dean answered curtly.

"That's too bad. We need some more kids in Somerset. We have a T-ball team, but it's not very good. We could really use a good first baseman. Why don't you have kids? Don't you like kids?"

Dean bit back a brutally honest, *Not really.* "Kids are fine, I guess." *As long as they're not mine.* "I have a niece and three nephews."

"Will they come visit you sometime?" Cooper asked.

"Probably not. Besides, they're too young to play T-ball."

"Oh," Cooper said, sounding dejected at the news.

Dean thought about his growing family for a moment. Shea's Justin was two and a holy terror. All two-year-olds were holy terrors, right? Boone's little girl, Miranda, was not yet a year old, and she was spoiled rotten. Absolutely rotten! She had Boone wrapped around her little finger and had since the moment she'd come into this world.

Clint's twin boys were still at that wriggly, wrinkled, useless age. Infants. Why on earth did people insist that they were so cute when, in fact, they resembled big, pale, squalling bugs?

Dean had taken one look at the tiny babies, who had arrived almost a month early, and had told Clint to give him a call when the kids turned into humans. So he wasn't a warm and fuzzy uncle. The world had plenty of warm and fuzzy without him. Especially now that his siblings were all married and making families.

Somehow the kids had bracketed him, Terrance on one side, Cooper on the other. Terrance was trying, very diligently and not quite secretively, to see what was in Dean's bags.

Fortunately he was almost home. "What about you?" he asked Terrance.

The kid jumped back from the bags as if he'd been caught snooping. In fact, he had been. "What?"

"Are you anxious for more kids to come to town?"

The boy gave the question a moment of serious thought. "Not really. I have my best friend Cooper and my second-best friend Johnny, and two brothers and my mama and my daddy. That's enough," he said, sounding satisfied with his young life.

"Smart boy," Dean said in a lowered voice.

"But we could use a first baseman," Terrance added thoughtfully.

Dean came to a halt. "This is where I live," he said, wisely withholding the *Shoo* that wanted to leap from his mouth.

"This is Miss Evelyn's place." Cooper looked at the old house and nodded his head. "Don't eat the sugar cookies," he said in a quiet voice tinged with horror as he delivered the dire warning.

Dean was about to ask why not? when he was distracted. Reva Macklin had stepped outside. She walked in the shade of the trees that lined the sidewalk. So why did she look as if she carried the light with her? She was sunshine and cinnamon, strawberries and…heaven help him, this was the kind of woman who could work her way under a man's skin and make him crazy. She walked toward him, and for a moment, just a moment, Dean didn't see anything else. Dangerous. Very, very dangerous. She didn't dress provocatively. In fact, she was clothed to suit this town. Quaint. Old-fashioned.

He couldn't take his eyes off her as she crossed the street. She walked straight toward him, hair released from the thick ponytail she had worn earlier to fall past her shoulders. It wasn't curly, but it wasn't completely straight. It waved. It caught the little slivers of sunlight that found their way through the thick foliage of the trees.

A lesser man would have dropped the bags and drooled, but not Dean.

She gave him a brief, sweet smile, and he wondered what would happen next. Why was she here? Maybe something in her house needed his immediate attention. Faulty plumbing. A rotting board or two. Maybe a loose stair. So he wasn't any good at repairing anything—he was willing to try.

It crossed his mind briefly that maybe Reva was approaching him for a much more personal reason. He barely knew her; there was nothing personal between them. And yet—

"Cooper Macklin," she said sharply, turning her attention to the child. "You're late."

"I had to stay after school."

Reva reached their side of the street and crossed her arms as she stared down at Cooper. "What was it this time?"

"I was just trying to help Mrs. Berry," he explained. "She was reading us a story, but she had it all wrong. I have that book and I *know* she wasn't telling it right."

"Cooper!" Reva said, sounding properly horrified.

"I was trying to *help*," he explained passionately. "But she just didn't want me to help. She wanted to tell the whole story wrong."

"I stayed, too," Terrance said in a soft voice that managed to cut through the tension. "So Cooper wouldn't have to walk home alone."

Dean was taken aback. That was putting it mildly. His reaction was physical, as well as emotional. His heart pounded too hard, his mouth went dry. He looked from Reva to her son, from Cooper to Terrance and then back to Cooper again.

First grade—that meant the kid was six years old. Blond hair, blue eyes, dimples. Fearless.

Cooper Macklin, Reva's child, was Eddie Pinchon's son.

Chapter 3

Reva closed her eyes and shook her head. "Cooper, how many times have I told you—"

"This is my new friend, Mr. Sinclair," Cooper interrupted in an overly bright voice. Her son was a master at changing the subject, and had been since the age of three. "He doesn't have any kids, so he's probably lonely. We should ask him to have dinner with us. Tonight!"

Reva avoided looking directly at Dean Sinclair. There was nothing quite like being put on the spot, and she hadn't yet decided how to respond to Cooper's unfortunate suggestion.

"You're always telling me to have good manners, Mom, and inviting Mr. Sinclair for dinner is good manners, right?" Cooper's innocent blue eyes remained wide and hopeful.

"I'm sure Mr. Sinclair has plans for dinner," Reva responded calmly.

"I bet he doesn't," Cooper said, turning his eyes up to their new neighbor. "Do you have plans?"

"Well…" Sinclair began.

"Pleeeze!" Cooper whined. "I want you to tell me about your niece and all those nephews, even if they're not old enough to play T-ball."

"Thank you for the invitation, but I don't think I can eat another bite today." Sinclair glanced at Reva. "I ate too much at lunch."

"Dessert, then," Cooper insisted. "You could come over and have dessert with us."

"Don't annoy Mr. Sinclair," Reva said.

"I'm not annoyed," Sinclair replied.

She made herself look at Dean Sinclair. He still wore the shirt and pants to his conservative suit, but the tie and jacket had been discarded. The top button of his shirt was undone, the sleeves of his shirt had been turned up and rolled away from his wrists. There was something about a man's well-shaped neck that could be fascinating in the right circumstances. It was so different from a woman's neck, so solid and strong. And a man's nicely muscled forearms could be just as interesting. Just as tempting.

Reva mentally shook off her unexpected fascination. She'd spent seven years steering clear of men; why did this one stir something long-untouched in her? It was just chemistry, she supposed. That sort of thing did happen, or so she heard. What else could it be? She didn't know Dean Sinclair, not at all. He was handsome, but he certainly wasn't the only good-looking man she'd seen in the past seven years. Their eyes met, and for a moment it seemed that he was just as disconcerted as she was.

"The fudge pie was very good," he said.

"Oh, we're not having pie for dessert tonight," she said. "Do you like strawberries?"

Was it her imagination or did the innocent question catch him off guard? Something in his eyes changed. Sparkled a little, perhaps, as if he was surprised.

"Strawberries," he said softly. "Love 'em."

"I'm making strawberry shortcake tonight."

He nodded.

Reva glanced down at Cooper and his more tranquil friend. "Y'all run on home. Terrance, your mother is going to be worried about you. She made y'all an after-school snack half an hour ago."

"We better go before she starts to get mad," Terrance said, and then he and Cooper both ran for the restaurant, after a quick glance both ways on the quiet street.

"Terrance's mother works for you?" Sinclair asked.

Reva nodded, turning her attention to him as soon as the children entered the house and slammed the door behind them. "Tewanda Hardy. I couldn't run the place without her." She took a deep breath. "Look, about dessert—"

"Don't feel obligated," Sinclair interrupted. "Kids seem to have a way of putting their folks between a rock and a hard place," he added with a half smile.

It was her chance to walk away, to play it safe. To turn her back on the only man who had made her feel this way in years. Just as well. Nothing could come of her attraction to him. She didn't need the complication of Dean Sinclair in her life. All she had to do was smile and walk across the street, and the danger, the awkwardness, would be over.

The chance came and went. "You're welcome to come," she said. "If you'd like."

"Strawberry shortcake," he said. "What red-blooded man could turn down an offer like that?"

"I really would like to talk to you about your plans," Reva said. Why did the way this man said *strawberry* send a chill up her spine? "Goodness knows I could use a handyman around the house. If you do decide to locate your business here, I can throw a lot of work your way."

"So, it's actually a business meeting you're suggesting."

Sounded good to her. Safe. Distant. "Seven o'clock. You can bring your business partner along if you like."

He shook his head. "He's not very sociable."

She turned on him and headed for home. In the middle of the street, she spun around to face him again. He hadn't made a move toward his own home. He still watched her. "And Mr. Sinclair—"

"Dean," he said quickly. "Call me Dean."

"When you come to my house for dessert, Dean, please don't wear a suit."

Once again he was without his weapon. As Dean walked past the antebellum home that had been transformed into Miss Reva's, he tried not to worry about the fact that he'd been disarmed. Reva had asked—no she'd *ordered*—that he not wear a suit tonight. And there was no way he could conceal his pistol while wearing jeans and a John Deere T-shirt that fit snugly across the chest. Even the ankle holster added a too-obvious bulge with every step. That, too, had been left behind.

Still, if Eddie arrived in the middle of strawberry shortcake, he'd be in a heap of trouble.

Somehow Dean didn't believe that Eddie would arrive while he had dessert with Reva and Cooper Macklin and discussed his bogus business plans. Tonight's dangers did not call for a weapon.

But there were dangers all the same.

Alan had laughingly told Dean, as he'd dressed for the evening, that he needed to get laid—but not here and not while he was on the job. That was a recipe for disaster. If Dean really and truly wanted to quit being a deputy marshal and become a handyman, sleeping with Reva Macklin would be a good way to start.

So she was pretty, and sexy in an old-fashioned way, and she smelled great. Just because he was attracted to her, that didn't mean he had to make a move.

Like she would let him make a move. The only reason she'd repeated Cooper's invitation for tonight was that she was in desperate need of a hired man for odd jobs around her old house.

As he knocked on the door of her cottage, he asked himself, How desperate?

Dean shook off the inappropriate thoughts as the door flew open. He steeled his resolve for nothing; it was Cooper who answered the door.

"Come in!" the kid said, throwing the door open wide.

Dean stepped inside. The cottage was of the same era as the main house, but was smaller. Cozier. The furnishings were more modern, though Reva had managed to retain some of the old Southern charm. Filmy, white curtains, an old, well-cared-for rug with a pattern of cabbage roses, fat furniture with afghans tossed across the backs, all of which made the place inviting, comfortable.

Reva swept into the room from a short hallway. "Hi," she said, smiling. She'd changed clothes, too, and now wore faded blue jeans and a pink cotton shirt. Her hair was pulled up and back again, so that nothing, not a single curling strand, interfered with the perfect lines of her face.

"We'll eat in the kitchen," she said, motioning for Dean and Cooper to follow her.

Cooper skipped along and Dean followed, pursuing Reva and the kid and the aroma of strawberries and coffee. His landlady made terrible coffee, but if Reva was as talented at brewing coffee as she was at everything else, he was in for a treat.

The kitchen was bright, more modern than the main room of the guest house, and decorated in a fresh-looking white and pale green. The appliances were all fairly new, the tile floor spotless. Overall, the atmosphere was cluttered but clean. It was the kind of room a person could live in, warm and friendly in an indefinable way. It reminded Dean of Shea's kitchen, though goodness knows his sister had never been able to cook.

A small round oak table was situated to one side, an area much cozier than the dining room he glimpsed through the doorway beyond that table. Places were set, along with three huge pieces of strawberry shortcake, two cups of coffee and one glass of milk.

Cooper quickly jumped into his seat—his usual, Dean surmised—leaving Dean and Reva seats that faced each other. Good. Sitting next to her at lunch today had been more than enough strain for one day. Here, with a table between them, he wasn't likely to accidentally brush her leg or her arm, or see much too clearly and closely the rise and fall of her chest as she breathed. Across the table was good.

Before Dean had a chance to lift his coffee cup, Cooper began, "Mama says you fix things. What kinds of things? I have a remote-control car that's broken. Can you fix it? And last year, when I didn't know any better, I accidentally ripped the head off one of my favorite action figures. Can you fix that, too? Terrance has a dinosaur that used to talk, but now it just makes funny noises. Can you fix that?" He never paused long enough for Dean to answer.

"Cooper," Reva said sternly, but with a touch of a smile that softened her interruption. "Eat." She cast Dean a quick, apologetic glance. "So," she said to him as she forked up a small piece of strawberry shortcake. "What do you think of Somerset so far?"

"It's very nice," Dean said honestly. "And very different from Atlanta."

Reva laughed lightly. "It is that. You should know, before you get yourself in too deep, that there are definite drawbacks to living in a small town."

"Such as?"

"You can't get away with anything here."

Dean wondered just for a second if his ruse had already been discovered. "Like trespassing after dark?"

She didn't respond to his reminder of last night, but she did blush. "It's tough to hide anything in a small town. If you sneeze, three offerings of chicken soup, homemade of course, arrive within the hour. Anything and everything you say will get around town before sunset, if it's at all interesting. There are no secrets here."

"I'm sure there are advantages to living in a small town," Dean said.

Reva smiled. Soft and contented, her face was transformed by that smile. "Of course there are. If you sneeze, three offerings of homemade soup arrive within the hour. By sunset, you know anything of importance that happened that day." Her dark eyes softened. "There are no secrets here."

It struck Dean like a thunderbolt that if Eddie Pinchon was headed here, Reva had no idea he was coming. She wasn't the same woman she'd been seven years ago when Eddie had been sent to a Florida prison and out of her life. She was innocent and good... Dammit, this would never do. Should he tell her everything? Now?

"What's a telecarpenter?" Cooper asked exuberantly.

Dean turned his gaze to the kid. So did Reva. "What?" Dean asked.

"A telecarpenter. That's what my teacher said I should be when I grow up. But I don't know what that is. She said I'm…I'm tenacious. I don't know what that means, either."

"Tele*marketer*," Reva said with a grin.

"Is it good? Mrs. Berry wouldn't tell me. I don't know if I want to be a telecarpenter. I mean, a telemarketer. I want to be a baseball player. Or a tax man."

Dean almost swallowed his coffee the wrong way. He sputtered slightly before asking, "A tax man?"

"Yeah! I can make everyone pay their taxes. Maybe I would rather be a telemarketer, but since I don't know what that is—"

"Cooper," Reva interrupted. "For now, let's just stick with wanting to be a baseball player. That's a perfectly normal ambition for a six-year-old."

"Okay." Cooper, who had almost finished his strawberry shortcake and milk, began again to ask Dean what he could fix. Bicycles, toys, sports equipment. It seemed this town really was in need of a handyman.

And then the kid, who had a charming streak so wide that it took some of the sting out of his constant chatter, asked to hear all about the niece and the nephews that Dean had mentioned that afternoon. Dean relaxed. Finally, something he could talk about that was not a lie.

Reva sent Cooper off to get ready for bed, and she and Dean stepped out onto the porch. They each held a cup of hot coffee and headed for the rocking chairs.

It was almost dark, but a trace of the day hung in the sky, and lamplight from the parlor sliced through the thin curtains and onto the porch. May was such a lovely time of year here. Warm, but not yet hot. Cool in the evenings most days.

Dean sat and stared out at the lush expanse of green lawn between the main house and this one.

With Cooper out of the picture, Reva felt a moment of impulsive bravery. "Why are you really here?" she asked.

Dean started a little, but not so much that he splashed coffee on himself.

"I told you—"

"You told me part of the story. I just wonder why a man who's more comfortable in a suit than he is in jeans and a T-shirt would come to a small town to become the local Mr. Fixit." There was definitely more to Dean Sinclair than he was telling. She'd already warned him; there were no secrets in a town like Somerset. She wanted to ask him what, or who, he was running from, but it was much too early for such a deeply personal question. "You bought a hammer at the hardware store this afternoon," she said. "Screwdrivers, a box of nails, glue, work clothes and a hammer. I can explain away everything else if I try hard enough, but what kind of contractor doesn't already own a hammer or two?"

He didn't look at all guilty. "You were right about living in a small town. I buy a hammer, and word is on the streets before the sun goes down."

Reva found herself smiling. "I warned you." She really should send Dean Sinclair packing and wash her hands of him once and for all. The only thing she needed in her life less than a man was a man with secrets. "You don't have to tell me—I'm just curious."

Dean sat a few feet away, swaying gently. The old rocking chair squeaked faintly. His hands were wrapped around his coffee cup. There should not be anything at all stimulating or arousing about this moment. So why did her heart act this way? Why did a sensation she had forgotten flutter in her stomach?

"I wasn't always a handyman," Dean finally said. "I guess I'm just looking for something new. A lifestyle less stressful than my old job."

"And what was that old job?" She had to know. If anything were to come of this—and it wouldn't, she told herself, it couldn't—there could be no secrets about his past. No bombshell waiting to be dropped. Her heart couldn't survive that kind of shock again.

Good heavens! Reva took a sip of coffee and took her eyes off him. Dean Sinclair, a man she barely knew, already had her worrying about her heart?

Dean took a deep breath. "Law enforcement," he said. "I was in law enforcement for years."

It was not the answer she'd been expecting. The news startled her. Reva held her breath for a moment. Her fingers trembled, very slightly. Not so much that he would see of course. She had gotten pretty good at hiding her feelings. At least on some days and from some people.

A moment passed and she relaxed. She had nothing to fear, not from Dean Sinclair or anyone else. "Really?"

"Really," Dean answered softly. He stared at her, obviously waiting for a response.

"I understand that can be a very dangerous business," she said. Of course it was dangerous. Cops carried guns, she knew that. Again, her fingers quivered.

"It was never the danger that bothered me," he said.

"What was it, then?"

Would he answer? This was getting very personal, considering that they'd met just last night. He'd been skulking; she'd threatened him with a hefty stick. She didn't know him; he didn't know her. What were they doing here?

"Sometimes I feel like I'm running around in circles," he said. "We win a few battles, but we never win the war. It goes on and on, and it can wear a man d hours on end, you give the job everything you've got, and in the end…'' He shrugged his shoulders. ''Sometimes you win, but too often the bad guy gets off on a technicality, or serves a few months and then ends up back on the streets.''

''Sounds frustrating.''

''It is. And the divorce rate is brutal,'' he added.

''Are you?'' she asked, almost immediately regretting her question. Talk about too personal!

''Am I what?''

''Divorced.''

He shook his head. ''Never married. I came close a couple of times, but…here I am, thirty-five years old and never married. You?'' he asked.

''Me what?'' Her heart climbed into her throat.

''Divorced?''

''Never married,'' she said softly. Would he walk away now? There were still lots of men out there, even in this day and age, who had a huge problem with an unmarried woman having and raising a child alone. She'd done the best she could for her son, and she wouldn't change anything, but she didn't want to see a condemning or disappointed look in Dean's eyes.

She didn't get one. Instead, she got one of his half smiles. ''Maybe we're the smart ones.''

She returned his smile. ''Maybe.''

Reva took a deep breath and allowed herself to enjoy the moment. The quiet night, the company. She liked Dean; she had a feeling he liked her. Nothing could come ⸢f it, but still the feeling was nice. She allowed her mind ⸎⸍ a moment, to imagine what might happen if ⸎⸗at came between them.

⸎⸗⸍m. and no one but she would

When Dean rose to leave, Reva stood and took his empty coffee cup. Her fingers brushed his; the contact was brief and electric, as it had been that afternoon at lunch when they'd both reached for biscuits at the same time. When he thanked her for the dessert, she told him anytime, but refrained from the invitation to come again tomorrow night. And the next. And the next.

Dean didn't kiss her, but he thought about it, she could tell. He definitely thought about it. Blue eyes went to her mouth for a split second. His lips parted, his gaze cut to the side, and then he offered her an awkward good-night.

As Dean walked away, Reva called after him. "What are you doing tomorrow morning?"

He spun in the grass. "Nothing."

"Come look at my loose banister? I really need to get it fixed."

He grinned. "I can try out my new hammer."

The lights in the room at the top of the stairs were out, the upstairs parlor dark so no one would see Alan and his telescope at the window.

"You look ridiculous, you know," Alan said without turning as Dean entered the room and closed the door behind him.

"No, I didn't know."

"John Deere?" Alan scoffed.

Dean glanced down at his T-shirt. There hadn't been a lot to choose from at the hardware store. Truth be told, he'd forgotten what he was wearing while he'd called on Reva Macklin.

And that was what it had been—a social call. A pleasant evening. The start of something unexpected.

"She doesn't have anything to do with this," Dean said as he crossed the room. "I think we should tell Reva who we are and why we're here, and ask if she's heard from Eddie since he escaped. She could help us.''

Alan turned slowly. ''Have you lost your mind?''

''No, but—''

''Well, something fishy is going on here.'' Alan ran the fingers of one hand through his hair. ''You know better. Tell her? Ask for her *help?* No way. She could call Eddie and warn him that we're here, and then he'd go under so deep we'd never find him.''

''She wouldn't do that,'' Dean insisted softly. ''She doesn't know where Pinchon is, I'm sure of it.''

Alan leaned back in his chair and grinned. ''Hellfire. She's grabbed you by the nuts, hasn't she.''

''Of course not.''

''She has, I can see it. Dean Sinclair, I never woulda thought it of you. Be realistic. *Think.* You believe that because Reva Macklin is pretty and can cook and has long legs and that sexy voice you keep talking about, she can't possibly be involved with someone like Pinchon. That makes no sense. Has she been making goo-goo eyes at you?''

''Of course not,'' Dean said, while he remembered the way she had looked at him once or twice.

''She has,'' Alan said confidently. ''A pretty woman bats her lashes at you and makes you think she might keep you warm at night, and all of a sudden she's Little Miss Innocent.''

''Reva's not the same person she was seven years ago.''

Alan snatched the photograph of Reva from the wall and waved it at Dean. ''This is the woman you're talking about, Dean. Yeah, she cleans up nice. She's got herself a good gig here in Somerset and she's not about to blow it by showing the people here what's she's really like. But *this* is her.'' He shook the photo at Dean. ''She was an eighteen-year-old cocktail waitress when she met Eddie, working in a sleazy bar thanks to a fake ID. She moved in with Pinchon two weeks after they met. She was never charged with a crime, but you know damn well if she was living with Eddie for almost two years, she didn't stay clean."

Dean's heart sank. "She's changed..."

"People don't change," Alan said in a calmer voice. "You know that as well as I do. Reva Macklin was Eddie Pinchon's woman for a damn long time. She's the mother of his child. If he comes here, she'll shelter him and feed him and take him into her bed without a second thought. She'll fall for his pretty face all over again, if she ever fell out, and she'll protect him from anything and everyone. She'll hide him from us. She'll put herself between us and Pinchon, and I don't have to tell you which side she'll be on."

Dean didn't want to believe it, but he'd seen the scenario play out that way too many times.

"You're thinking with your johnson, bud. Don't feel bad. We've all been there."

Alan didn't mean to be harsh. He was a friend, and he'd been through a few crises of his own. He certainly wasn't accustomed to watching Dean Sinclair have second thoughts about his job. Dean didn't make mistakes; he didn't follow his gut over logic, or lust after a woman because she smelled like strawberries. All his life, he'd been the one to think things through thoroughly, to compose a mental list of pros and cons before making an important decision. And he always thought with his brain, not his johnson.

"I tell you what," Alan said in a calmer voice. "I understand how you feel. Patsy left you high and dry, what, three months ago? Drive to Nashville and have yourself a hot time. You can be back here by sunup, and I promise you, everything will look different. Everything. Especially Reva Macklin.''

Dean took the picture from Alan and studied it. Yeah, it was her. Brasher, younger, wilder, but it was Reva. He had seen her smile a couple of times today, but not like this. Not wide and free and…joyous. The girl in the picture was full of unbridled joy.

Maybe Alan was right, and Dean was drawn to Reva because she was beautiful and sexy and he was alone. Did he need a woman in his bed so badly he'd see something that didn't exist so the truth wouldn't get in his way? He didn't think so, but he couldn't be absolutely sure. He couldn't trust himself, not with this.

He gave up on the idea of telling Reva everything.

But he didn't drive to Nashville.

Chapter 4

Familiar sounds and smells drifted from the kitchen, but this morning a new element had been added to the chaos that was Reva's everyday life. Sporadic sounds of hammering, creaking wood and occasional mutters that might be curses also found their way to her office.

Reva lifted her head when the door to her office opened. Tewanda stepped into the room, closed the door and leaned back with a wide smile on her face. Tall, dark and regally gorgeous, Tewanda had a tendency to reinvent herself every six months or so. Her hairstyle and clothing changed dramatically with each incarnation. At the moment she was in a brand-new tailored stage. Her black hair was cut close to her head, her slacks and shirt were fashioned in an almost mannish style that only accentuated her curves. Nothing Tewanda could do to herself would ever make her fade into the woodwork.

"There's a good-looking man on the third floor and he's playing with your banister."

"Only you could make that sound wicked," Reva said, setting aside the checkbook to give her friend and employee her full attention.

"Sweetie, that man definitely has wicked possibilities."

The last thing Reva needed to think about was Dean Sinclair's wicked possibilities.

"How's everything in the kitchen?"

"Miss Edna and Miss Judith are arguing over how much pepper to put in the squash casserole, and Miss Frances keeps slipping out of the kitchen to sneak up the stairs and take a peek at your young man."

"He's not my young man!"

"That's not what I hear," Tewanda said suggestively.

Reva sighed and leaned back in her chair as her friend walked closer and propped herself on the edge of the desk. "He's not mine, and he's not exactly young, either."

"Young is relative," Tewanda said wisely.

Tewanda had the perfect life, it seemed. Her husband of more than ten years adored her and took her frequent fashion changes in stride. They had three beautiful, well-behaved sons. Terrance was the youngest of the Hardy boys. Nothing rattled Tewanda, not even Cooper, who spent the night at her house often.

Sometimes Reva felt a twinge of jealousy as she watched Tewanda go about her perfect life. *I don't want an adoring husband*, Reva insisted silently, *but I would love to be able to provide that kind of home for Cooper. A stable man who'd be a good father figure, a man she could have more children with, a brother for Cooper, maybe a sister or two.* Deep inside she knew that would never happen.

"He is cute," Tewanda said in a lowered voice, "but I swear, Reva, that man of yours is *not* well acquainted with a hammer. I only watched for a couple of minutes, I promise, but it was kinda like watching Russell struggle with his math homework.''

Russell was Tewanda's eldest child. A few months ago he had insisted that the fourth grade was just too hard.

"Dean is new at this," Reva said. "Give him a chance."

Tewanda pursed her lips and hummed. "Already defending the man, I see. Well, well. Sheriff Andrews is not going to be happy about this new and interesting development."

Reva sighed. "The sheriff has nothing to say about my life!"

"But he surely would like to." Tewanda waggled her eyebrows.

Reva looked down at the checkbook again. She'd much rather balance her checkbook than talk to Tewanda about Ben Andrews or Dean Sinclair. "You'd better go check on the squash casserole," she said. "I have checks to write that need to go out with today's mail."

"Fine," Tewanda said as she stood and headed for the door. "Brush me off. Send me away without a satisfactory report. When you need someone to keep Cooper overnight so you can entertain your handyman wanna-be..." She paused, then turned to grin at Reva. "Shoot, you know you can call on me. Anytime."

"I'm not—" Reva began.

"Don't argue," Tewanda interrupted. "I'd say it's about time you showed a little interest in seeking out male companionship. It's just not natural to live for years without a man in your bed."

Reva lifted her chin. "How do you know I've lived for years without a man in my bed? I might have a very exciting love life away from the restaurant."

Tewanda grinned widely. "First of all, you're blushing

beet-red. You don't lie well, at least not to me. Secondly, this is Somerset, sweetie." She raised a hand to her chest. "If a man had been anywhere near you, I would have heard about it. Face it, there's nothing exciting about your life, and the only love in it is for Cooper. And thirdly, speaking of your adorable son, in all the years I've known you, Cooper has never said a word about there being a man in your house. Until this morning when I walked the boys to school, that is. I understand your Mr. Sinclair came over for dessert last night."

Reva rested her forehead on the desk. What she'd said to Dean last night had been true. There were no secrets in a small town. "Strawberry shortcake, that's all it was. I swear."

"Mmm-hmm," Tewanda said as she walked out the door, closing it softly behind her.

Reva finished writing out the checks. She went over the menus for the next week and glanced at the possible recipes for her new cookbook. Her first cookbook had been selling very well, and people were already asking for more.

Every now and then the sounds from the third floor distracted her. Was Dean really that terrible at being a handyman? Maybe Tewanda had been exaggerating. No man was bad with a hammer.

Was he?

When she couldn't stand waiting anymore, Reva slipped out of the office, turned left and climbed the stairs as quietly as possible. Her shoes were flat and soft-soled, and the long skirt of her cream-colored dress swished quietly.

Unfortunately it was impossible to be completely quiet when a number of the steps had a tendency to squeal.

She caught sight of Dean staring at her through the railing. He sat on the floor of the third-story hallway, hammer in hand, and watched her approach.

"Who's skulking now?" he asked with a smile.

"I guess that would be me," Reva said as she finished the climb without attempting to be quiet.

"Usually when I hear creaking steps, I glance up and see a gray head peering around the corner," Dean said.

"Miss Frances." Reva sat on the top step. A couple feet of space and white slats marred by peeling paint separated her from Dean Sinclair. "I just wanted to warn you, customers will start arriving soon, so you'll have to take a break until this afternoon."

Dean glanced at his watch. "It's not even noon. You serve at one, right?"

She nodded. "People come early to walk in the gardens or explore the house or just sit on the porch and rock. Hammering and cursing kind of ruin the atmosphere."

"I didn't think anyone would be able to hear me," he explained. "Sorry."

"Sounds carry in these old houses. Don't worry about it." She glanced beyond Dean. "If I can get the third floor in good shape, make sure the railing is solid and safe and remodel the rooms, we can open this area up for customers, too. I was thinking of making a couple of the old bedchambers into sitting rooms or small parlors. I could even entertain small parties up here once everything is finished."

Dean carefully laid his hammer down on the floor. He didn't look the part of handyman, though he did try. His hair was cut too precisely. The jeans and boots were too new. The T-shirt, advertising the downtown hardware store, didn't sport a single stain or rip.

And his face...he should have a five-o'clock shadow to make him look less respectable.

"Are you hostessing a table today?" he asked.

Reva shook her head.

"Good," Dean said in a lowered voice that sent chills down her spine. "Have lunch with me."

It was after one by the time Reva climbed the stairs to the third floor again. The dull roar of conversation, the clink of silverware on plates, the occasional trill of laughter, all were muted here at the top of the house.

Dean took two heavy plates from Reva's hands and carried them into the bedroom where a pitcher of iced tea and two glasses already waited. He felt a moment of awkwardness, but dismissed it quickly. There was no bed in this bedroom, just an antique dresser, a few old cans of paint in one corner, a piece of strangely shaped furniture Reva called a fainting couch, upholstered in faded burgundy velvet, and the small table where he and Reva would have lunch.

It was the perfect opportunity to feel her out, to see what she might have to say about Eddie Pinchon. What Dean really wanted was to talk about other things and make Reva laugh, but that wasn't why he was here.

Why did he have to continually remind himself that he was in Somerset on business?

The plates were filled to capacity. Roast beef today. More vegetables, fluffy biscuits.

Once the plates had been deposited on the table, Dean held out Reva's chair. For a moment she seemed to be surprised by the gesture, but finally she sat. Dean took the seat across from her.

They spent a few minutes talking about the food and the weather, and then there came that moment everyone dreads. It was a first-date kind of awkwardness, an uncomfortable silence that begged to be broken.

"So," Dean asked to end the silence. "Have you always been in the restaurant business?"

Reva lifted her head and gave him a decidedly suspicious look. "For the past six years."

"How did you get into it?"

She smiled, no longer openly suspicious. "Shortly after Cooper was born, I went to work for an older man who had a small restaurant that was on its last legs. Donald had expected his sons to go into the family business with him, but they had plans of their own. He'd had a round of bad managers and was about to lose everything. He hired me and let me run the place as I saw fit, and I was lucky enough to make the business profitable again."

Dean scooped up a forkful of corn pudding that was so good it should be illegal. "I don't think luck had anything to do with it."

Reva smiled. "Donald made me a partner. The business expanded, and eventually we sold and made a very nice profit. I took that money and came here."

Here, when she could have opened a successful restaurant anywhere in the world.

"And before that?" he asked. "What did you do before Cooper was born?" This was Reva's opportunity to come clean, to tell him who she was, what she had been, explain how she had changed.

He'd known her two days, and still he expected her to explain. There were two kinds of people in the world. The honest and the dishonest. To Dean's way of thinking, there was very little, if any, middle ground. Shea accused him on occasion of being inflexible. He preferred to think of himself as sensible and uncompromising.

"What about you?" Reva asked, playing with her carrots as she ignored his question. "Have you always been in law enforcement?"

He nodded. "I suppose."

"You look like a cop," she said. "The way you carry

yourself, the sharpness in the eyes. I'm sorry, Dean, I know you're looking to make a change in your life, but I just can't see you as a handyman.''

Neither could he. ''I can change,'' he said. ''People *can* change, you know. They can turn their lives around, become someone or something else. All it takes is a little motivation.'' Something like a kid. Had that been Reva's trigger for change?

''I suppose,'' she said in a soft voice.

He took a few more bites, and so did she. An uncomfortable silence settled between them again, and then Reva asked, ''Did you always want to be a cop? When you were a kid, as you got older, did you always know who you were? Who you would be?''

''Does anyone ever really know?''

''You just seem so…so certain of yourself. I never was,'' she confessed. ''I've always questioned every decision, every turn in my life, wondering if I was doing the right thing. But you, you look like the kind of man who never made a mistake.''

''Everyone makes mistakes.''

''I suppose.'' She fidgeted a little. ''You still haven't told me anything about yourself. Come on. I told you all about my adventures in the restaurant business. What can you tell me about Dean Sinclair?''

''I don't want to talk about myself,'' Dean said. ''I want to know about you. Where you come from, what you like, what you want from life. Tell me all about Reva Macklin. I want to know everything.''

A few minutes ago she had blushed prettily and smiled. Now her face went white. ''There's nothing much to tell. Do you like the squash casserole? I think it might have too much pepper.''

"It's fine," he said abruptly. "Everything's wonderful."

Reva laid her fork on the table, pushed her plate away and stood. "I really should check on the customers," she said, her voice too fast. She didn't look at him, but kept her eyes on the table, on the floor.

"I'm sorry." Dean stood. "I shouldn't have—"

"Finish your lunch," Reva said as she hurried to the door, all but running away from him. "I'll see you later."

She tried to appear calm, but the creak of the stairs told him that she was still running when she hit the first floor.

What on earth had she been thinking? There was no room in her life for a man, any man. She'd known that all along, but Dean had driven the point home when he'd started asking questions. If she got involved with him or anyone else, eventually the question she dreaded hearing would be asked.

What about Cooper's father?

Tewanda had been right; she was a terrible liar. Keeping secrets was one thing, telling an out-and-out lie was another entirely. She blushed, she stammered. No lie detector device was necessary. So what would Dean Sinclair, or any other man say when he asked about Cooper's father and she told him the truth?

Cooper's biological father was a murderer serving life in prison. Eddie had definitely had more than one personality. How else could she explain the fact that he could be charming as hell one minute and a raving lunatic the next? He'd hidden the lunatic from her for a long time, but when she'd discovered that side of him...

Reva shuddered as she walked past the hardware store. When Dean had started asking questions, she'd run from him, hit the sidewalk and started walking. Fast and determined and away from temptation. No matter how much she thought she might like Dean, no matter how attracted to him she might be, she knew nothing could come of it. Nothing.

She stepped into Louella's, naturally drawn to food at a time like this. Reva didn't eat when she was upset, but there was something comforting about the smells of a bakery or a well-run kitchen. Sure enough, a tantalizing aroma teased her. Louella had made something with cinnamon in it. Reva wasn't hungry, but she could certainly use a cup of coffee and a quiet place to sit.

Two other customers were having lunch in the small café, a man and a woman she didn't recognize. They sat together in a far booth and ate sandwiches. Tourists, most likely. Those who worked in the downtown area usually ate early, between eleven-thirty and one. Louella's lunch rush was over.

Louella stepped up to the counter and gave Reva a wooden smile. "Why, good afternoon. What can I do for you?"

"Coffee," Reva said.

"I'm rather surprised to see you out and about at this time of day," Louella said as she poured a cup of coffee.

"I needed a breath of fresh air," Reva explained.

A moment later she had her cup of coffee, fixed just the way she liked it. Cream and sugar. She paid, then took a small table so that her back was against the wall and she could face the window. From here she could see everyone passing on the street. Not that she actually expected Dean to chase her down. Though if any man would, it was Dean Sinclair. He didn't look like the kind of man who gave up easily.

She should've hit Dean with the limb she'd plucked from the ground that first night, maybe whacked him across the knees. He'd leave her alone then. He'd think she was a crazy woman, and he'd steer clear. He wouldn't look at her the way he sometimes did, as if he saw something in her that no one else saw.

Reva shook her head and took a sip of the coffee. No, there was no *as if*. Not with Dean. Not with anyone. She'd been an idiot to think otherwise, even for a moment.

"Busted," Dean said as he walked into the apartment he shared with Alan.

"What happened?"

"Damned if I know." He tossed his bag of tools aside and plopped himself down on a fat, soft chaise. "I guess I moved too fast. I asked too many questions and made Reva antsy. One minute we're having lunch and I'm trying to find out what she knows about Eddie, and the next she's bolting from the room."

"Busted, indeed," Alan said softly. "Just as well."

Dean glared at his partner. "How's that?"

"You were getting too close, she's too pretty, and you really should have made that trip to Nashville." Alan sat back in his chair and thrust his legs out. "Now you know."

"Now I know what?" Dean snapped.

Alan shook his head slowly. "Man, she wouldn't have run if she didn't have something to hide."

It was true enough. The innocent didn't run. They stood there with wide eyes and got caught in the crossfire on occasion, but they didn't run. What was Reva afraid of?

And yeah, she had most definitely been afraid.

He liked her and had all along. Dammit, he didn't like people on sight. He got to know them, weighed their good and bad points, took his time. But from the moment he'd caught sight of Reva's legs, he'd been insanely attracted to her. Maybe Alan was right, and all he really needed was to get laid.

Not on the job. And not with a woman who might very well be up to her pretty neck in the mess that had brought Dean to Somerset, Tennessee.

The last thing Dean needed in his life was a woman to take care of. Make that a woman with a child, and he would be in double trouble. All his life, he'd taken care of his family. They were well past grown, now, making babies and homes and living their own lives.

So why did he have the urge to run to Reva and make her tell him the truth? She should trust him enough, even though they had just met, even though he couldn't guarantee that she was not still involved with Eddie Pinchon in some way.

His life was black and white and always had been. Reva...Reva was caught up in shades of gray.

A faint knock on the door interrupted his sour musing. Alan jumped up and ripped the old picture of Reva from the wall, then expertly covered the telescope with an afghan he grabbed from nearby. That wasn't enough to properly disguise the telescope, so he placed himself between the mechanism and the door, and posed casually. Dean opened the door on a spry Miss Evelyn, who carried a silver tray bearing lemonade and cookies.

''Good afternoon, boys,'' the elderly woman said as she walked into the room. ''I thought you might like a little refreshment on this warm afternoon. Cold lemonade and my own special sugar cookies.''

Dean remembered Cooper's whispered warning. ''Thank you,'' he said, taking the tray from her and setting it on the walnut side table. ''That's very thoughtful of you.''

Alan nodded and said his thanks, but he didn't move. If

he did, the old woman would see the afghan-covered telescope. And no matter what they said to their landlady to ensure her silence, the word would be out. As Reva had said, there were no secrets in Somerset.

"Well," Miss Evelyn said with a pursed-lipped smile, "it's the least I could do."

Dean tried to gently direct the old woman to the door. "I'll bring the tray and glasses down to the kitchen when we're finished. I hate for you to climb these stairs any more than you have to."

She resisted his assistance, remaining glued to the spot. "Oh, it's no bother. Climbing the stairs is good exercise. And I love to cook! It's such a joy to feed a couple of healthy, hungry men. Why, Mr. Fister used to adore my sugar cookies."

"I'm sure we will, too," Dean said as he tried to steer his landlady to the door. At least he had her on the move. She was a wiry one, though, and slipped right past him. "You know," she said as if a thought had just occurred to her, "I have a fence out back that is in urgent need of repair. The gate is off the hinges, and several slats have fallen. It needs to be painted in the worst way."

At least now he knew why she had climbed to the third floor bearing refreshments. "If we decide to locate our business here, we'll be sure to look the job over and give you a quote."

Mrs. Fister pursed her lips. "Well, since you were working at Miss Reva's this morning, I assumed you were open for business." She cast a glance at Alan. "And goodness gracious, young man, you never leave the house! It isn't right for a grown man to be so shy."

"It's a curse," Alan said with a straight face.

"I'm sure it is." Finally the old woman headed for the door. "You need something to keep you busy. You can start work on the fence this afternoon,'' she said as she stepped into the hallway.

Dean closed the door and turned to find Alan already making his way to the silver platter.

"Maybe we're in the wrong business," Alan said as he reached for a cookie.

"Wait," Dean said, "Cooper said…"

Alan raised a cookie to his mouth and took a big bite before Dean could say more. Immediately he made a face, though he did choose to continue to chew rather than spit the bite out.

"…not to eat the sugar cookies," Dean finished.

Alan swallowed and reached for the lemonade. "I think I know what killed her old man." He took a long drink. "Isn't there supposed to be *sugar* in sugar cookies?" He took another long drink. "Cookies aren't supposed to have a bitter aftertaste, are they? You could have warned me a little sooner," he said accusingly. "Or thrown your body between me and the cookies. What kind of partner are you?"

Dean found himself smiling. "What are we going to do with them? We can't eat them, and if we send them back downstairs, the old woman's feelings will be hurt."

Alan stared at the silver platter for a moment, and then he grinned. "Mail them to one of your brothers."

"I like my brothers."

Alan's grin turned evil. "Mail them to Patsy."

"No!"

"Well, for God's sake, we've got to mail them to somebody! They can't stay here!"

"Myron Troy," Dean said, naming the deputy in the Atlanta office who'd screwed up a case Alan had been on before he'd been partnered with Dean. Alan was always talking about getting even with Troy; this could be his chance.

"You're a genius, Sinclair," Alan said reverently. "An absolute genius. I am suitably impressed."

Movement beyond the window caught his eye, and Dean walked past Alan to look out. Curtains parted, telescope moved aside so no one would see it in the light of day, he stood there and watched as Reva Macklin walked down the sidewalk toward her restaurant. Most of the guests had departed by now. Only a few loitered, walking in the gardens, sitting on the porch.

Whatever had sent her running from him, she'd recovered. She was calm, in control, as elegant and beautiful as ever. Her hair was down, and it danced over her shoulders as she walked. The great legs were hidden beneath the long skirt of her dress. Too bad. He wanted to see those legs again, and he had the feeling he might never get the chance.

Reva should turn her head this way at least once. She should look up to see if he was here, if he watched her as she walked home.

She didn't.

Busted.

Chapter 5

She'd managed to remain single and content for seven years; she could certainly ignore the annoying flutter that danced in her stomach when Dean Sinclair came too near. Especially if she made sure he never came too near.

It was simple enough, Reva decided. She'd considered firing him, but that wouldn't work. He'd still be close by. He'd probably be more persistent than ever! So she gave him odd jobs and then made sure she was busy elsewhere. When Dean worked in the big house, she found something to keep her busy in the cottage she called home. When she needed to be in the restaurant for one reason or another, she assigned him a chore in the cottage or in the garden. The yard was filled with ancient, majestic trees, and there were several large limbs that needed to be trimmed. George, her usual yard man, was too old to handle anything bigger than the three-foot limb she'd almost attacked Dean with on his first night in town. Dean was certainly capable of handling the larger limbs that needed to be trimmed. Then there was the garden fence and the drainage problem around back. The constant drip in the cottage's kitchen sink. And the third floor of the big house.

In this way, she could control Dean's whereabouts during the daylight hours at least. As long as she didn't have to look at him all the time or worry about turning around and finding him right there under her nose, she was fine.

For five days, she'd managed to keep Dean busy and out of her hair. Oh, he did try to corner her now and then, but she always had other places to be. It was all part of her well-laid plans. She made sure all she had was a minute to reject whatever offer he presented. Lunch, dinner, a walk to town. She found a reason to refuse his overtures. Eventually he quit asking.

Reva loved Sundays in Somerset, and had since her first weekend in the small town. There were three downtown churches, which seemed like a lot for a sparsely populated place like Somerset. But the pews were always full on Sunday. People came from the surrounding area, from farms and isolated homes outside Somerset's city limits, to attend services. After the sermons, which varied in tone depending on the denomination of one's choice, there was often a picnic or a potluck supper. There was a real sense of community on Sunday in Somerset. A real sense of peace.

Reva had known little peace growing up. She hadn't exactly had a Norman Rockwell life. After her stepfather had died and her mother took off for parts unknown, she'd met Eddie. He'd swept her off her feet, offered the stability and love and sense of family she craved. And she had fallen for him hook, line and sinker.

On the night they'd met, she'd been working in a bar serving drinks. Not exactly her dream job, but it was the best-paying job she had been able to find at the time. Eddie had come storming into town with his big smile and his blue eyes. He'd talked to her for a while, buying drinks and leaving huge tips, calling her over to his table when there was a lull. On that one night, in a matter of hours, he'd managed to reach inside her and understand what she wanted. What she needed. Over a period of a couple of weeks, he'd wooed her with the promise, spoken and un-spoken, of everything she wanted from life.

He'd sucked her in, and she'd been so gullible she'd fallen for every line. Once he had her where he wanted her, he'd insisted that she quit her job. She had. He'd in-sisted on knowing where she was every hour of every day. She thought that meant he loved her. Eddie had often talked about how they'd be married one day. With sweet words and a winning smile, he'd painted a picture of the life she'd craved for as long as she could remember, of a picket fence, a husband who adored her, the children he said he wanted.

But reality was very different from the picture Eddie painted. He had hidden much of his life from her for al-most two years, telling lies, keeping her isolated and ig-norant. Looking back, she realized that she should have known things were not as they should be. She should have asked questions and then insisted on answers that made sense. But she'd been so afraid. Afraid of losing the only stability she'd ever known, afraid of throwing away that picture-postcard life Eddie promised. By the time she'd realized who Eddie Pinchon really was, it was too late. He'd sworn he would never let her go.

That was Eddie's idea of love. He hadn't ever loved her; he'd owned her.

Older and wiser, Reva was determined that no one would ever own her again. When she was tempted to spend time with Dean, get to know him, give him a chance, she remembered that.

Cooper skipped ahead of Reva along the shaded sidewalk that led toward home. The air smelled of spring, of gardens in full bloom and last night's rain. For a moment she forgot her past and the muddled present, and focused on the future.

Cooper was the future. He would grow up here in this lovely town where no one would ever know who his father was. He'd have friends and neighbors who adored and respected him. His mother would love him the way she had never been loved, and he could grow up to be a tax man or a baseball player or a telemarketer—whatever he wanted to be.

A chill crept up her spine. She'd told Dean that there were no secrets in a small town, and yet here she was keeping one of her own. A big, scandalous secret. No matter what, no one could ever know that Eddie Pinchon was Cooper's father.

"She's guilty as hell, you know that," Alan said.

Dean turned to glare at his partner. He'd been watching Reva walk along the sidewalk, trying to decide if she'd run from him if he walked down to the street and pretended to accidentally be in the same place she happened to be. He hadn't moved, because he was pretty sure she would run.

"Reva doesn't like me. That doesn't make her guilty of anything."

"She liked you fine until you started asking too many questions." Alan shook his finger in Dean's direction. Dean had a deep, primal urge to break that censuring finger. He didn't. "She knows something and she's not telling."

Dean wasn't so sure that Reva was as guilty as Alan believed her to be, but he did know that something strange was going on. One minute Reva had been smiling at him, and the next she'd run from the room. Since then she'd gone to great lengths to make sure they were never in the same room for more than a minute or two.

"Maybe she just doesn't like me."

"How is that possible?" Alan deadpanned. "Women take one look at you and their pants fly off. I've seen it happen a hundred times. Okay, I haven't actually *seen* it happen, but you know what I mean. They get this hungry look in their eyes, and sometimes they salivate and—"

"Alan, shut up." Dean turned his back on his partner and watched the street again. Reva was cutting through the grass, heading for her little cottage. Cooper skipped energetically ahead. "You haven't even spoken to her."

"I prefer to study my subjects from a safe distance. It's less messy that way."

Dean tried not to squirm. He usually preferred "less messy" himself.

"I'll bet Eddie called her," Alan said softly. "That's why she did a U-turn where you're concerned. He's coming to town and she knows it. At the very least, she knows where he is."

"I don't think so."

"If you'd planted a bug in her house, we'd know for sure one way or another," Alan said sharply. "God knows you've had the chance, especially since you've apparently taken on the job of handyman full-time."

Dean didn't respond. They would never agree on this subject. He wasn't about to plant an illegal bug in Reva's home just to satisfy Alan's, and his own, curiosity.

"I spooked her," he said. "It has nothing to do with Pinchon."

"I still say a quick trip to Nashville will cure all your ills."

Dean wished for a moment that he could agree with Alan. He wished his dilemma was that simple. Unfortunately the problem was more complicated than Alan knew.

It wasn't that he didn't want to sleep with Reva. He did. Badly. But even more persistent was the urge to watch over her, to make sure Eddie Pinchon never got near her or her son. It was the Boy Scout complex Alan accused him of having, Dean imagined, though he had never before felt quite this way.

Reva Macklin was trouble. Big trouble. The best thing he could do, for himself and for her, would be to call in another team to take over this stakeout. Twelve hours, maybe less, and he could have someone else in place.

But he wasn't going to call anyone else in, not now, not tomorrow—not until Eddie Pinchon was in prison where he belonged and Dean knew that Reva and Cooper were safe.

This was definitely getting messy, and that meant trouble.

Big trouble.

Finally a chore he could handle. Cutting the limbs he'd trimmed from Reva's trees into three-foot pieces so they could be taken to the street to be hauled away was mindless, easy work. He didn't have to know about plumbing, electricity or paint for this chore.

It was hot, sweaty work, though.

In a way, it was a shame to cut any growth from these old trees, but some of the limbs had begun to split on their own and were a safety hazard. A few had been damaged by a spring storm that had come through a few weeks back; others were simply victims of time.

This week was progressing much like the last one. Reva told him what needed to be done and then disappeared. She rarely looked directly at his face, never looked him in the eye. He still benefited from being employed by the owner of the best restaurant in this part of the state, perhaps in the entire state, but it was always one of Reva's employees who brought him lunch a little after one and ice water or iced tea several times during the day. The little old ladies seemed delighted to feed him. Reva's friend Tewanda just shook her head in obvious despair and muttered something unintelligible that did not sound complimentary as she walked away.

He'd gotten a lot of the work done this morning, before the Miss Reva's crowd began to arrive, and then he'd taken a long break. One of the older ladies had told him that the chain saw was not a comforting sound for the guests, so he'd found quieter work in the garden for a while and then had eaten his lunch.

It was now after three in the afternoon, and he was working on the limbs again.

May could offer cool days, even in southern Tennessee, but today was not one of those days. Sweat dripped down Dean's face, tickled his back and soaked his John Deere T-shirt.

Physical activity wasn't his thing, unless you counted the occasional workout in an air-conditioned gym to stay in shape. His brother Clint was the one who was never still, and Boone had been known to go for a run for no good reason, though not on a regular basis.

But chopping wood and hauling it to the street? Dean didn't own a house; he lived in an apartment. For just this reason.

But given the circumstances and his increasing frustration, he found the exertion unexpectedly soothing.

Dean was surprised to see Alan stalking across the yard, cell phone in hand, white paint from Miss Evelyn's fence spattered across his own John Deere T-shirt and brand-new jeans. Dean lowered the chain saw and grinned.

"Do I look as ridiculous as you do?"

"No. You look a lot more ridiculous than I do." Alan lifted his hand. "Where's your cell phone?"

Dean glanced over his shoulder. His phone sat on top of his toolbox. With the chain saw operating, he'd obviously not heard it. His smile faded. "What's up?"

"We're out of here," Alan said. "Thank God. This has been the most bizarre assignment. So long, Somerset. And none too soon."

"They have Pinchon?"

Alan shook his head and lowered his voice as he came near. "No. But he was spotted last night at his cousin's house in North Carolina. The police moved in, but they were too late. Pinchon escaped out a window and disappeared into some nearby woods. But—" Alan shook his finger "—the cousin is spilling his guts. We know where Eddie's been and where he's heading." He glanced back toward the big house. "The cousin didn't even mention Reva Macklin."

Dean sighed in relief. It was almost over. Almost, but not quite.

"You go ahead," he said. "I'll stay here until Pinchon is in custody."

Alan shook his head slowly. "We're to join the others in North Carolina tonight. Eddie has a meeting scheduled with one of his old cohorts, according to the cousin."

"Which he may not keep, knowing his cousin was arrested and could very well talk."

Alan wiped a paint-spattered hand across his face. "This

detail has been called off, partner. We're out of here. Story over.''

No. Nothing was over, dammit. This should be easy; he should be grateful to be out of here. He wasn't. ''I'll stay on my own time.''

For a moment or two, Alan glared at Dean. ''I should've driven you to Nashville myself,'' he said in a low voice.

''This doesn't have anything to do with my nonexistent sex life.''

''Of course it does.''

''I have a gut feeling this isn't over, that's all.''

''So, you're going to take vacation time to baby-sit for Eddie Pinchon's—''

''Don't say it,'' Dean cut in, knowing what was coming.

Alan covered his face with his large, paint-stained hands. The man was annoying at times, spoke his mind when he shouldn't, didn't know when to back down…but he was a good partner. Dean would put his life in Alan's hands without a second thought.

''Fine,'' Alan said, dropping his hands. ''I'll keep you posted on the Pinchon situation and you…you be careful.''

''I'm always careful,'' Dean said with a grin.

''I used to believe that,'' Alan said as he turned away. ''Right now, I'm not so sure.''

Reva was ready to go home, but Dean was still out there, hauling the wood he'd cut to the street. She would have watched carefully and timed her trek so that her contact with him would be minimized, but she couldn't do that, not this afternoon.

Somewhere along the way, Dean had taken off his shirt. It was criminal for any man to be so tempting when he was dirty, sweaty and half-dressed. He looked too good, and no matter how certainly she knew it was wrong, she longed for a closer inspection. No, she couldn't take the chance that they might end up face to bare chest.

Reva stood at the kitchen window and watched as Dean loaded up the wheelbarrow with tree limbs.

"Nice view," Tewanda said as she walked up behind Reva, a teasing lilt in her voice.

"It's kind of disgusting," Reva said, trying to keep her demeanor cool.

"Yeah. That's why you've been standing here watching for the past twenty minutes, because the view is so disgusting."

Reva turned to her smiling friend. She would try to make up some other reason for lingering at the window, but she knew better than to lie to Tewanda. "He does have rather interesting muscles."

"That he does," Tewanda said, glancing over Reva's shoulder. "You could take the poor man some iced tea or a glass of water. Something. Wouldn't you like a closer look at those muscles?"

The truth, spoken so bluntly, made Reva shiver. "No," she said quickly.

Tewanda crossed her arms and sighed. "What am I going to do with you? You obviously like the man, but for the past week you've been treating him like he has the plague or something. Now, it's not entirely your fault. If he was any kind of a *real* man, he'd hunt you down, kiss you till your knees went weak and make mad passionate love to you on your desk."

"My desk?"

"Okay," Tewanda said with a wave of her hand. "The recamier in the south parlor, if that's more your style. Or right there on the stairs, like he just can't wait to get you to someplace soft and easy. It's not the exact place that's important. You get my drift."

Unfortunately she did. "I'm not interested in getting involved." Not with Dean, not with anyone.

"No kidding," Tewanda said softly. "I have to tell you, Reva, I don't get it."

Reva turned her back on Dean, completely and totally. "I can't get involved with a man. Cooper is everything to me. He's my life. Nothing else matters."

"But—"

"We've had this discussion before, when you tried to convince me to date the sheriff," Reva interrupted. Tewanda was no dummy. She had figured out all on her own that Reva steered clear of men because she'd been burned by Cooper's father. Reva hadn't offered details, and Tewanda hadn't pushed. Friends knew when to push and when to step back.

Usually.

"Fine," Tewanda said sharply. "Tall, blue-eyed and studly is not permanent. You don't want a man hanging around. That doesn't mean you can't sleep with him."

"Tewanda!"

"Sex is a fine thing, Reva, a fact you have obviously forgotten. You're only twenty-seven years old. It's just not natural."

"I can't just…just…"

Tewanda leaned in and laid her hand on Reva's shoulder. "Yes, you can," she whispered. "If you want," she added quickly. "I wouldn't ever suggest that you do something you're not comfortable with. But, Reva, you're lusting after studly, and he certainly appears to be willing. Sleeping with a man doesn't necessarily mean sharing your life or your secrets with him."

"I can't," Reva said softly. "I don't… It's just not…"

"Sorry I said anything." Tewanda grinned, but without

her usual vigor. ''I just hate to see you twisting in the wind like this.''

Reva nodded and didn't even try to argue that she was not twisting in the wind.

Like a good friend, Tewanda changed the subject. ''Picnic after church on Sunday.''

''I remember,'' Reva said with a sigh of relief.

''Are you going to participate this time?''

''I don't know.''

Tewanda shook a long finger at Reva. ''You'd better. Last time, there were a couple of people who were very put out that the most famous restaurant in town didn't offer a lunch for raffle.''

In small towns, even Somerset, there were always a few residents who were very quick to get their noses out of joint over nothing.

''Besides,'' Tewanda added, ''how will it look if my best friend doesn't participate? I'm in charge of this spring's fund-raising event.''

''Fine,'' Reva said. ''I'll put together a picnic to raffle off.''

''We need that new roof.'' Tewanda shook her head. ''Every dollar counts. Last time you packed a box lunch for the raffle, we got twenty-five dollars for it!''

Reva watched while her friend and number-one employee fixed a huge glass of iced tea. ''I'm taking Cooper home with me. He and Terrance have a project to work on. Want him to spend the night?''

''No.'' She didn't want to be alone, not tonight. ''I'll walk over and pick him up later. What time?''

''Let him stay for supper,'' Tewanda said. ''You're welcome to join us, too.''

''Thanks, but I'd better not. I have a ton of paperwork to do. Might as well take advantage of the quiet.''

Tewanda nodded, understanding too well. "You can pick Cooper up around seven."

"Sure."

Tewanda turned and handed the cold glass of tea to Reva. "I'm going to collect the kids and get out of here while you take this out to studly. You don't have to sleep with him if you don't want to, but it would be very poor manners to let the man get dehydrated while he's working in your yard. What would the neighbors say?"

Reva turned, iced tea in hand, and watched as Dean returned from the street and began loading the wheelbarrow again.

Her stomach fluttered as Dean lifted a particularly heavy limb and the muscles in his arms and shoulders strained nicely. After tossing the limb into the wheelbarrow, he swiped a hand across his face. He looked so determined, so…tempting. For seven years, she'd managed to get along just fine without being tempted, but Dean was different.

The last thing she needed was to come face-to-face, day after day, with a man who was *different*. Somehow, some way, she was going to have to convince Dean not to settle here in Somerset.

Chapter 6

A frantic phone call from Cooper at six-thirty had the boy begging to spend the night with Terrance. They hadn't finished their project, Russell had promised to help the younger boys after supper, and a breathless explanation of all the reasons Cooper needed to spend the night at the Hardy house ended with a long, loud "Pleeeeeze?"

Reva gave in, packed a bag and walked to Tewanda's to drop off Cooper's things. There had been a time when she'd not allowed her son to spend the night at the Hardys' on school nights, but since Tewanda assured her all the boys behaved well and were in bed and asleep on time, she made occasional exceptions these days.

It wouldn't be fair to make Cooper come home simply because she didn't want to be alone. It was good for him to play with the other boys, and Tewanda's husband, Charles, was a good husband and father who occasionally took all the boys out for a rousing game of catch. Charles was the coach of Terrance and Cooper's T-ball team. They had practice tomorrow afternoon, a game Thursday night. If the kids finished their project on time, Charles would probably spend a little time going over strategy with the six-year-olds. And then he'd have them doing push-ups on the living-room floor, and the kids would giggle as Charles acted like a demanding drill sergeant.

After she'd dropped off Cooper's things and kissed him goodbye—much to his chagrin, since all three of the Hardy boys were present—Reva had walked home, taking her time, letting her mind wander as she walked. She didn't allow her mind to wander too far or to slip into territories best left unexplored. But she did glance into the driveway of Miss Evelyn's house as she passed. The car Dean and his friend had driven to Somerset was gone.

They could be anywhere. After this afternoon's awkward encounter when she'd spilled iced tea all over the poor man, the two newcomers might be gone for good. Her heart skipped a beat. Just as well, right?

For a moment, just a moment, Reva considered Tewanda's outrageous suggestion. She could sleep with Dean without ties, without telling him all about her past. It was tempting in a completely selfish way.

The problem was, she couldn't separate sex from love. The act and the emotion went together, and she couldn't imagine having one without the other.

Eddie had been the only man in her life, in her bed, and she had loved him. She'd been young, foolish and blind, but for a while she had loved Eddie with all of her gullible heart. In the end, his betrayal had twisted her inside out. He'd destroyed her world, taken away everything she'd believed to be true and right. If not for Cooper, she might not have survived.

Which was reason enough not to fall in love again. Ever. Another betrayal, another heartbreak, would have the power to destroy her. She couldn't fall for any man and let him make her believe in a love that didn't exist.

She had a feeling Dean would be much too easy to fall for.

Alan had taken the car and the telescope with him, leaving Dean basically stranded here in Somerset. He didn't mind, not at the moment, though he did miss the telescope when night fell.

Dean sat at the window and looked out on the dark, quiet street.

Until now, he and Alan had taken turns staying up late and getting up early to keep an eye on Miss Reva's. Each night had been as boring and uneventful as the last. So why was he so reluctant to go to bed?

For a while, much longer than was necessary, he sat in a chair at the window, watching the big house across the street. All was dark and quiet, and would remain that way until early tomorrow morning when Reva's employees began to arrive. So why couldn't he let it go?

Maybe Alan was right, and Pinchon was in custody— or soon would be. But then, why hadn't he called? Dean knew darn well that as soon as Pinchon had been apprehended, Alan would be happy to let Dean know he no longer had any reason to remain in Somerset.

It was near eleven when his cell phone rang.

"Sinclair."

"We missed Pinchon," Alan said tersely. "You were probably right. He must've known his cousin would talk and changed his plans."

"Are you coming back?" Dean asked, his eyes remaining on the dark house across the street.

"If you need me, I can swing it. Personally I think I can do more good here."

Dean thought about the offer for a minute. "You stay where you are. Keep me informed."

"You know I will."

Alan didn't have to say that Dean's insistence to stay in Somerset was *a bad idea*. He'd already made his opinion on the matter very clear.

They ended the call, and Dean gave serious consideration to finding his way to bed. It had been a long day. Muscles he hadn't known he had ached. The only high spot of the day had been when Reva brought him a glass of iced tea. She'd walked across the lawn like something out of a fantasy, dress swaying as she approached, shape enticing, walk sexy as hell. When she'd come near, she'd looked directly at him, blushed, tripped over her own feet and doused him with cold tea. The tea had felt good.

Watching Reva lose her hard-won cool had been even better.

Alan was convinced she was a scheming liar; Dean was just as convinced that she was an innocent caught in the crossfire.

Out of nowhere, a flash of light in the night caught his attention. Dean stood abruptly and leaned closer to the window. He held his breath. There it was again. A flashlight beam in a dark window of Reva's restaurant.

And Pinchon's whereabouts were unknown.

Dean grabbed his weapon from the end table by the window and tucked it into his waistband, then he left the house as quickly and quietly as possible. As a stair creaked beneath his step, he hoped Mrs. Fister was a deep sleeper. The last thing he needed was the old woman turning on all the lights in the house and following him outside to see what was going on. She would, too, shotgun in hand.

He ran across the street, staying in shadow and keeping his eyes on the window where he had seen the flash of light. Outside the restaurant, all was quiet. He checked the front door. It was solidly locked. Without making a sound, he slipped around to the side of the house. The rarely used doors there were locked, as well.

Listening for sounds of an intruder, he stepped onto the back porch. When he saw the door hanging open an inch or two, he drew his weapon. The pistol fit comfortably in his right hand as he edged toward the kitchen door.

Adrenaline pumped through his veins in a familiar way, but he didn't panic. Panic was a good way to end up dead or to shoot someone who just happened to be in the wrong place at the wrong time. Dean remained calm, but he listened carefully and searched the corners of the moonlit kitchen as he walked into the house.

All was quiet. The old house had a life all its own, and at the moment it seemed to be sleeping. During the day it was such a lively place, with Reva's employees, her customers, the kids after school. At night the house was eerily silent and still.

Something upstairs creaked. The house settling? Or the footsteps of an intruder?

Dean had worked in the restaurant long enough to know his way around, even when he hit pockets of blackness where no moonlight shone in. He found nothing on the first floor. He was working his way to the stairway when he again heard a noise from upstairs. A shuffle. A creak.

Gun in hand, he crept up the stairs with his back to the wall and his eyes peeled for movement above and ahead. If he stayed close enough to the wall, the steps didn't creak. He'd discovered that in his days repairing this old house. Whoever was up there wouldn't hear him coming.

It wouldn't have been all that difficult for Eddie to find Reva. There had been articles written about her restaurant. All Eddie had to do was type her name into an Internet

search engine, and the articles would pop up, complete
with the address of Miss Reva's.

Like it or not, he had to consider the possibility that
Alan was right. Maybe Eddie had called Reva days ago
and she'd been waiting for his arrival. They were upstairs
right now, hiding in the dark. She loved the bastard still,
and she would do anything to keep him safe.

At the top of the stairs he caught sight of a shadow at
the end of the hallway, the dark outline of a person very
prudently entering one of the bedrooms. No flashlight, this
time.

Again Dean stayed against the wall as he crept down
the hallway. He listened to the intruder slinking around in
the bedroom, noted by the sound of the footsteps where
the person was located. Dean stopped outside the door, his
back to the wall. The prowler—Eddie Pinchon or a com-
mon burglar—had made a circle of the room and was
heading back toward the hallway.

Dean slipped the pistol into his waistband, freeing both
hands. Judging by the sounds in the house, there was a
single intruder, and from the profile Dean had gotten a
glimpse of, the prowler was small and unarmed.

As the prowler exited the bedroom, Dean made his
move. He made a grab in the dark, found his mark in a
too-slender wrist and twisted a delicate arm behind the
intruder's back.

The scream that followed was brief, the voice familiar.
Immediately Dean released his captive and stepped back.
Reva.

She didn't run from him or toss accusations his way,
but spun on Dean and attacked with fists and feet. Blows
landed on his chest, his arms, his shins. Reva was a tiny
thing, but she put all the strength she had into her attack.

"Whoa, hold it. It's me," Dean said as he did his best

to deflect the blows. Reva either didn't hear or didn't much care.

He grabbed her again, by both wrists this time. "Stop it," he ordered in a low voice. When she continued to struggle even though he had her effectively shackled, Dean pressed Reva against the wall and held her in place with his hands and his body.

With his length pressed against hers from shoulder to knee, she didn't have much room to fight. Reva stilled, until her only movement was the rise and fall of her chest as she breathed. He could release her now. She knew who he was; she no longer fought. But he didn't let her go. He kept his body close to hers, his fingers around her wrists, and took a deep breath of his own.

All around them, the house remained dark and dormant. Moonlight through the window at the end of the hallway illuminated his hand on Reva's, the curve of her cheek, the curve of her shoulder. He had dreamed of this. Reva was soft, yielding, her gentle body fitting against him just so. She was so much a woman she robbed him of his usual control. He responded to her scent and the sensation of her body against his, growing hard. Surely she felt that response. Their bodies were so close…

"What the hell are you doing here?" she asked in a low, husky voice.

"I thought someone had broken in."

With her wrists in his hands, he could feel the rapid beat of her pulse. She grew suddenly warmer, and when she breathed her breasts, caught beneath the thin fabric of her pajamas, brushed his chest.

"I heard a noise," she said softly. "A crash in the kitchen. I thought maybe one of Mrs. Gibson's cats had crawled in through an open window again. I just wanted to chase it out."

A cat? "Where's your flashlight?"

"I didn't bring one. I don't need a flashlight to find my way around this house at night. I know this place like the back of my hand."

"You didn't turn on a single light," he said in an accusing voice.

Reva sighed, then seemed to relax. "No, I didn't. Mrs. Logan is a light sleeper, and if she started asking questions about what I was doing in the restaurant at nearly midnight and it came out that there was a cat in the kitchen, I don't have to tell you what kinds of rumors would get started."

She was worried about her neighbors' gossip. Gossip that might hurt the restaurant's reputation. Was she also worried about what people might say about them? Is that why she'd been so diligently pushing him away?

Who was he kidding? There was no *them*.

But there could be. He lowered his head slightly, closed his eyes and inhaled. How could she smell so good even now? In a primal way, her scent had always aroused him. From now on he would know Reva in a dark room, with no words, no touch. No woman had ever made him feel this way, no woman had ever roused the beast in Dean Sinclair.

Reva did just that. Without artifice, without seduction, she woke something within him. Something dangerous. He leaned in for a kiss. He needed Reva's mouth on his, just once. And he needed that kiss now. She held her breath. The house remained still.

She had been chasing him away for days, but right now her body didn't push and fight. It relaxed. It called to him in a way no voice ever could.

Downstairs the kitchen door squealed, a step sounded on the back porch. With a curse, Dean dropped his hold on Reva and turned away. He ran, not bothering to muffle the sounds of his steps on the stairs this time. The kitchen door hung wide open, and beyond there was nothing to see but moonlit night. There were too many pockets of complete darkness, and no clue as to which direction the prowler had taken. Dean ran onto the back porch, searching the grounds in all directions. Nothing.

He heard Reva behind him, spun around to find her standing in the doorway. Legs again. Her pajama top was thin and sleeveless. The matching bottoms were very short. She wore no shoes, and her hair had been pulled back into a ponytail at the nape of her neck. She was beautiful in moonlight. No—gorgeous. And at this rate, pinning her against the wall so she'd stop hitting him was as close as he was ever going to get to her. The moment upstairs had been fleeting; it seemed unreal even now. His chance to kiss her had come and gone, and he'd missed it, thanks to a very real intruder.

Reva stepped onto the porch, her eyes never leaving his face.

"Someone was in my restaurant."

"Yeah." Probably not Eddie. Pinchon wouldn't have run without a fight. "Do you have problems with break-ins in the area? Vandalism? Petty theft?"

She shook her head. "No."

"We'll call the sheriff, file a report, and tomorrow I'll put sturdier locks on all the doors." He tried to ignore what had happened upstairs. He tried to dismiss the way he'd responded to her, the way he continued to respond. "I can stay here in the restaurant tonight if you'd like, just in case—"

"You have a gun," Reva interrupted. At the moment she looked oddly fragile.

"Yeah."

She swayed on her feet, and Dean reached out to steady her. "I hate guns," she whispered.

Dean insisted on walking with her to the cottage, then searching all the rooms when he discovered she'd walked out without locking the front door behind her. He wouldn't listen to her when she explained that most people didn't lock their doors in Somerset, that no one had slipped into the cottage in the few minutes she'd been gone.

Her eyes kept drifting to the gun stuffed so casually into Dean's waistband. It had been a long time since she'd seen one so close. Sheriff Ben Andrews often carried a weapon, but it was always tucked into a massive leather holster so that she couldn't actually see it. And she expected the gun to be there when Ben came around. She had the chance to steel herself before facing him, and it. Dean's gun was a surprise, and without a holster to disguise the harsh metal lines, it was so very real. She couldn't ignore it.

Dean's gun wasn't exactly like the one Eddie had threatened her with, but it was close enough. Too close. Her stomach turned over. No. She would not throw up. Not here, not now.

Not until Dean left.

"I'm fine," she said when he walked toward her.

"You don't look fine," he said.

A dull roar settled in, deafening and disorienting. She tried to appear calm, steady, perfectly normal. Otherwise, Dean would never leave. "I'll call the sheriff in the morning," she said. "There's nothing he can do tonight, anyway. It was probably just a kid."

Dean cocked his head and his brow wrinkled as he studied her. "Are you okay?"

She read his lips, since the roar in her ears drowned out

everything else. The gun was right there, tucked into his waistband. Cold, metal, hot, dangerous... She stared at it.

When he reached out to touch her, she stepped back.

"You have to go," she said. It had been a long time, but she could still feel the muzzle of Eddie's gun pressed to her temple, her cheek, her mouth. Her tongue. She remembered the way Eddie had laughed when she'd started to cry. Cooper had already been growing inside her, but she hadn't told Eddie, not even when she'd been sure she was going to die. She could never tell Eddie about the baby. If he wouldn't let her go, he would surely never let a child get away.

Dean started to talk again, but she couldn't make out the words.

"Go," she said. "Get out." Her eyes were pinned to the gun. "You can't be here."

He said something else she could not understand. Her response was, "You have a *gun.*"

Dean stepped into the kitchen. A moment later he was back. No gun. Not that she could see, anyway. The roar began to subside.

"The pistol scares you," he said gently.

Reva nodded. "I'll be okay." That assurance sounded so weak even she didn't believe it.

Dean took her arm and led her to the couch. He made her sit, and then he sat beside her. Close. Too close.

"Where is it?" she asked.

"On top of the refrigerator behind the bread box," he answered. "Honey, it's not going to hurt you. I know how to use a gun. There's nothing to be frightened of."

"Ever had one shoved down your throat?" she asked, angry and quick, immediately regretting the impulsive question that revealed too much.

Dean took her face in both hands, forced her to look at

him. She was prepared to see revulsion in his eyes, but she was not prepared for anger and passion. "When?" he asked softly. "Who?"

She shook her head. "Just go home, Dean. Forget I said anything."

"How am I supposed to forget something like that?" He continued to hold her face gently, even when he lowered his head to kiss her...on the forehead.

If he didn't leave soon, she was going to ask him to stay. Goodness knows she didn't want to stay alone, not tonight, not with that memory she'd thought she'd buried well rising to the surface, so real it seemed as if that terrible night had happened yesterday, not seven years ago.

Reva shifted slightly against Dean. She knew he wanted her; if she'd had any doubts, tonight's reaction when he'd pressed her against the wall would have killed them all. He wanted her, and she didn't want to be alone.

"Fine," she whispered. "If you're not going to leave, then kiss me."

His mouth touched hers in a gentle first kiss. Hadn't she always known that Dean would kiss her before he left town? Of course she had. The unspoken promise of this kiss had been teasing her, dancing just out of reach, hiding from her. No, she'd been hiding from it. Running. Denying what she felt. Her lips parted as Dean kissed her.

The roar in her ears came back, gentler than before. This time it was the passion that made her blood rush, not fear, not memory of terrors long past.

She held on to Dean and let him kiss her; she kissed him back. Gently arousing, this was the kind of kiss that could help a woman forget. Tongues danced, tentatively, then more deeply and without restraint.

It wasn't just the kiss that swept her away, but the way Dean held her. His arms were so strong, so sheltering. She was safe here, warm and alive. She tingled, she quivered, her body responded to the kiss completely. And no matter how perfectly he kissed her, she wanted more.

As forgotten sensations came to life, Reva began to believe that Tewanda had made a valid point. They could have sex for the sake of sex, without love, without commitment, without the sharing of deep, dark secrets. She was a fully grown, modern woman living in the twenty-first century. She would be a fool to turn her back on something that felt so good, so right.

Besides, she didn't want to be alone, not tonight. She wanted Dean beside her, on top of her, between her and the world. Just for one night.

Dean took his mouth from hers, and she found herself unexpectedly breathless. Were they lying down? Apparently so. The sofa yielded unevenly against her back. Dean's weight was heavy and warm.

She wrapped her arms around his neck and held on. "Cooper's staying the night with Terrance."

"I know."

She raised her eyebrows.

"I saw Tewanda and the boys walk off this afternoon, then later on you headed that way with a duffel bag and came home alone and empty-handed."

"You're very observant."

"I'm a cop, remember? I'm paid to be observant."

She shivered. No, she had not remembered. She had forgotten, as she had forgotten so many things. "Retired, right?"

Dean sighed. "Not retired. On vacation."

If she had to lose her head over a man, why a cop? Cops asked too many questions. They insisted on having all the answers. They never gave up.

Lost too much in what she wanted, what she craved,

Reva decided it didn't matter that Dean was a cop, not where one night was concerned. She kissed him again. She'd made a fool of herself with the man, drooled over him, run from him, gotten tongue-tied and fumble-footed and tried to attack him. Twice. But the hard length she felt pressing against her thigh told her that he wanted her, anyway.

"You can stay here tonight," she said. Butterflies danced in her stomach. Something forgotten clenched, lower and harder. "I don't want to be alone."

"I'll stay if you want me to," he said.

They were stretched out on the couch, his warm weight on her, his hands in her hair and on her face. So close. They were so close to taking the next step, the step from which there was no retreat. A shift of his clothes and hers, a shift of her hips… Her body responded just thinking about how close they were.

"We can have sex," she said softly, deciding the words *make love* would promise much more than she was willing to give.

Dean kissed her again. His mouth delivered silent promises. He promised safety, pleasure, affection, a night she would always remember.

And then he took his mouth from hers and whispered, "Not tonight."

Chapter 7

Reva's entire body stiffened beneath his.

"I can't believe I just said that," Dean said.

He'd wanted her from the moment he'd seen her, before he'd known who she was. And even after he'd discovered her identity, desire he knew he couldn't act on had driven him half-crazy. None of that mattered. Not like this. Not while Reva was scared and looking for a place to hide.

"What's wrong?" she whispered.

"Are you on the pill?" Dean asked.

She shook her head.

"Got any other forms of birth control handy?"

Again she shook her head. This time, she added a sigh. "You should have something," she said, a hint of accusation in her voice. "I mean, you're a man. You're supposed to be prepared."

"I didn't expect this," he said honestly.

"Neither did I."

He didn't tell her that lack of birth control wasn't the

only reason he'd said not tonight. If she still wanted him when she was no longer scared, if she asked him again, he'd be ready. And willing. And definitely able.

"But I will stay," he said, kissing her again. "At least until I know you're okay." He sat up, brought her with him. If he was going to be a noble jackass tonight, he needed to get Reva out from under him. He might be a nice guy, but he wasn't a saint.

He sat back, and Reva's head immediately fell onto his shoulder. He raked one hand through her hair, trying not to look at her legs. They really were great legs. Having her here like this, so close and inviting, made him question everything that had led them to this point. Every decision, every move. Especially his insistence that they shouldn't go any further tonight.

And then he remembered her reaction to his pistol.

"You can tell me, you know," he said, "about the guy who did that to you."

Had it been Pinchon himself or one of his cronies who'd shoved a gun into her mouth? Didn't matter. Pinchon had dragged Reva into a world where things like that happened. He wanted to tell her that he understood, that he *knew*...but he couldn't. When he thought about what Pinchon had done to Reva, Dean didn't want to arrest the escaped con. He wanted to kill him. What a mess. What a tangled, messy state of affairs.

Something unwanted niggled at Dean's brain. If it had been Pinchon himself who'd hurt Reva, then why wasn't she terrified that the man might find her now that he'd broken out of prison? In the days following the escape, the news had been in all the major papers and they'd shown Pinchon's picture on CNN and the other news channels. Since then, coverage had been much more low-key, but still, she had to know.

Did Reva think she and her son were so well hidden here that Pinchon would never find her? If that was the case, she was more foolish than he'd ever imagined her to be. These days it was too easy to find a person, any person, no matter how small and isolated the town they chose to live in might be.

She certainly should have known better than to go walking into the restaurant on her own in the middle of the night when she'd heard a noise. Judging by that action, it wasn't Pinchon who scared her. What was she really afraid of?

"I've never told anyone even that much," she said. "I shouldn't have told you."

"Might help to talk about it."

She laughed harshly. "It happened a long time ago. How could it possibly help to talk about it now?"

Reva shifted one bare shoulder and rested her cheek against his chest. Damnation, she was not helping matters. It was bad enough that she was warm and soft and willing. Couldn't she at least be *still?*

"If you keep a secret buried long enough, it starts to fester," Dean said, ignoring Reva's small movements. "Sometimes it helps if you get it out. Let it loose. Set all your secrets free."

She considered his argument for a moment, and then she shook her head.

"You should've called me tonight when you heard the noise."

"I'm used to taking care of myself," she said. "I don't call on anyone else to handle my problems. Besides, I thought what I heard was just one of Mrs. Gibson's cats."

"It wasn't."

"I know. Who would want to break into the restaurant?" She shivered along the length of her body. Dean grabbed an afghan from the back of the couch and covered her with it. "Maybe it was just kids," she said as she snuggled beneath the afghan and into him. "Kids making mischief."

He could tell that was a convenient and easy explanation she wanted to believe. "If you hear any more noises, anything going bump in the night, you call me," he insisted.

"I can't—"

"You call me," he interrupted sharply.

She hesitated before replying. "I don't think I should get accustomed to calling someone else to handle my problems for me. Not even you. I have to be able to take care of my own difficulties."

"There's nothing wrong with asking for a little help now and then."

Reva relaxed and closed her eyes. "Yes, there is."

Five minutes later she was asleep with her head on his chest and her arm wrapped around him. She tried very hard not to trust anyone, not to depend on anyone for anything, but by sleeping this way Reva proved to Dean that she did trust him. And she needed him, like it or not. Dean looked at the woman in his arms, shook his head and wondered if he'd done the right thing.

Of course he had. But doing the right thing wasn't normally this physically painful.

Reva awoke with a crick in her neck and the sun on her face. It didn't take two full seconds for her to realize where she was and whom she slept on.

"Oh, no," she said softly as she sat up. Either her words or her movement woke Dean. He blinked twice and twisted his head to lay sleepy blue eyes on her.

"Oh, no, what?" he asked, his voice gravelly with sleep.

"Oh, no, you're here." She stood quickly, bringing the afghan with her since her pajamas were much too thin to keep the sun that poured through the window from revealing too much. "Oh, no, it's seven-thirty." *Oh, no, there's a gun in my kitchen, and did I really ask this man to have sex with me on the couch?* "Just a general oh, no," she said.

Dean Sinclair looked too good in the morning. Too much like a man, all long and hard and rough. Solid and warm. Untamed. His usually precise dark hair was ruffled, there was a dark shadow of stubble across his jaw, and his T-shirt was marred by a tiny wet spot. Drool, she realized in horror. Hers.

This was so unfair! He could at least have the decency to look sour and unpleasant on waking.

"You shouldn't be here," Reva said as she turned her back on him and walked toward the hallway.

"I fell asleep."

"You have to go now," Reva said in an even voice. "And take your gun with you." She shuddered as she walked down the hallway.

She listened. The couch squeaked slightly. Footsteps padded across the carpeted floor, then onto the kitchen tile floor. Those footsteps stopped, before the refrigerator, she imagined. That was where he'd said he'd put the gun. Behind the bread box.

Standing before the bedroom door, just a few feet from escape, Reva stopped. After a moment's thought she dropped the afghan and ran down the hallway. She reached Dean as he lifted a hand to open the front door, and grabbed the back of his T-shirt in a death grip. "Stop." When he did, she loosened her grip on his shirt and dropped the hand that had halted him.

"You told me to go," he said, not turning to look at her. Just as well.

"It's too late," she said. "Someone will see you leaving."

Dean shifted something in front of him, turned to face her and kept one hand behind his back. She never saw the gun she knew he carried. Would she panic this morning the way she had last night if he let her see the weapon? Last night the sight had surprised her, she told herself. If she had been prepared, stronger, more determined, she would not have fallen apart.

"What am I supposed to do?" he asked. "Stay here all day?"

Reva stared at the center of Dean's T-shirt. The tiny spot of drool was drying, thank goodness. Had she really slept with her head on his chest? She'd slept so well, had dreamed very nice dreams that were just now fading.

"You could stay here awhile, then sneak out," she said sensibly. "If anyone catches you, you could tell them you were working on the kitchen sink."

"If I was here to work on the sink, why would I be sneaking around?"

"Can't you sneak without it looking like you're sneaking?"

"I don't think so," Dean muttered.

Last night, asking him to sleep with her had seemed like a good idea. Primarily, she now realized, because she hadn't wanted to be alone. It was a poor excuse for taking a step she'd avoided for so long.

But there was something else she could not deny, something beyond a momentary fear of being alone. Dean Sinclair made her remember what it was like to love, to desire, to crave a kiss and more. She should hate him for that, for making her want what she couldn't have. If she slept with him once, there would most certainly be a second time and a third and a fourth, and the next thing you knew he'd be a part of her life and she'd have no choice but to tell him everything.

She didn't want to see the horror in Dean's eyes when she told him everything.

He lowered his head toward hers, just slightly, as if he intended to kiss her. Reva stepped back, and his descent stopped abruptly. "You can't walk out the front door. Mrs. Logan will see for sure. The kitchen door faces the Bodines' backyard, and they always sit out there in the morning drinking their coffee."

"What am I supposed to do?" Dean snapped. "Crawl out a window?"

"Perfect!" A rush of relief made her smile. "The window in Cooper's room is shielded by trees. No one would see you go out that way."

Dean's eyebrows rose. "I was joking."

"Please," Reva said softly.

Again Dean shifted his head toward hers. "Nothing happened last night. Why do you look so guilty?"

"It won't matter what we say. If anyone sees you…"

"What would the neighbors think?"

"Exactly."

Dean kept one hand behind his back. With the other, he cupped her neck and drew her nearer. Gently. Slowly. Reva stopped breathing a half second before he kissed her.

She adored the way he kissed, even though she knew she shouldn't. It was as if she drank him in through her lips, as if he drank her in, as well. Kissing Dean was warm and intimate; it robbed her mind of everything but sensation and forbidden possibilities.

When he'd first brought his mouth to hers, she'd been determined to make sure it was a short, passionless kiss. But it was Dean who broke away, much too late for short or passionless. "Next time I spend the night," he said in a low voice, "I won't sleep on the couch, and we will actually have something to hide come morning."

Reva shook her head. "You can't... We can't... Last night I made a mistake when I suggested... You were right when you said we shouldn't..."

"I said 'not tonight,'" Dean said calmly, ending her ridiculous and embarrassing stammering. "I didn't say never. I want you, Reva, but I want you unafraid. When the time comes, there won't be anything on your mind but me. No fear, no flashbacks." He traced a finger across her neck. "When you shake, it'll be for an entirely different reason than last night's unpleasant shivers. When you ask me to make love to you, it'll be because you want me, not because you don't want to be alone."

"I won't ask you for anything," Reva insisted. "Not ever again."

"Yes, you will," Dean said. He didn't give her a chance to argue, but stepped past her and toward the hallway. "Which room is Cooper's?"

"Second door on the left." She followed as he made his way down the hall into Cooper's bedroom and to the window. He paused there, glanced over his shoulder and grinned. He had a rare but startlingly beautiful smile. It touched her. She could certainly not get involved with a man who smiled like that.

He opened the window, looked around to make sure no one was near and then slipped out gracefully. His eyes met hers briefly, before he dropped to the ground.

The entire time, he'd made sure he kept his body between her and the gun. She never saw it, but she knew it was there.

Thoughtful and gorgeous; a deadly combination.

Dean took a roundabout way toward his rented room. Ancient trees shielded him. He kept his eyes open for morning walkers and joggers, kids on their way to school and Reva's employees. The only time he was exposed was when he ran across the street.

He concealed the gun, just in case he did run into anyone, by shoving it into his waistband and arranging his shirt to cover it. Not that anyone else would react the way Reva had, but still, it wouldn't do for people to see him running around town with a pistol tucked in his pants.

He let himself into Miss Evelyn's house, moving quietly. All he had to do was make it up the stairs and he'd be home free.

A couple of times he asked himself why he was cooperating in this ridiculous charade. He was thirty-five years old! Too damn old to be sneaking around, especially when he had nothing to hide.

The answer came too quick and too easy. He did this for Reva. She had to live in this town, and after he was gone he didn't want people to talk about her. And in a town like Somerset, they would talk.

He was halfway up the first flight of stairs when a wavering voice called, "Good morning," from the kitchen.

Dean turned on the stairs just as Miss Evelyn stepped into the foyer and tipped her face up. "Goodness gracious, you look a fright. Is the hot water on the fritz again?"

"No, ma'am," Dean said. "I just wanted to run down and grab a cup of coffee before I had my shower. Having a little trouble getting started this morning." He reversed himself and stepped quickly down the staircase. "The coffee smells so good I thought it might give me a boost."

His landlady followed him into the kitchen. "I'm planning to make more sugar cookies this afternoon. I'll set aside a big plateful of them for you."

Dean poured his coffee and racked his brain. They'd already mailed three boxes of cookies to Troy. "I really don't have much of a sweet tooth. Besides—" he turned with the coffee cup in hand and patted his stomach lightly "—I need to watch my weight."

Miss Evelyn nodded. "It was Alan who liked my cookies so much, wasn't it?"

Dean nodded. "Yes, ma'am."

"I thought so." She patted her own nonexistent belly. The woman was thin as a rail. "He carried a bit of a paunch."

"A bit," Dean said, hiding his smile by raising the coffee cup and taking a long sip.

"He's married, isn't he?"

"Yes, he is."

"I thought so. He has a married look about him, a content and settled look. And then there was the wedding ring of course," she added. "Why aren't you married?"

Dean hadn't been prepared for the question. He almost spilled his coffee. "Just never met the right woman, I guess." He gave the standard answer, leaving out a large part of the truth. He'd raised his family when he'd taken on the care of his brothers and his sister, since he was the eldest and their parents had little time for their children. The last thing he needed or wanted was someone else to take care of. A clinging woman, kids, more responsibilities than he already had.

Then there was the job. He loved his work as a deputy U.S. marshal, and he was good at it. But the job meant traveling, odd hours and danger many women could not accept.

"Hogwash." Miss Evelyn pulled out a chair from the kitchen table and sat.

"Excuse me?"

"You heard me. I said hogwash. Sit down." She indicated the chair to her left, and Dean headed that way with his coffee.

"I really need to get…"

"I said sit down. I'm old enough to be your grandmother, and I don't have many years left." She coughed and fluttered a hand over her chest, feigning weakness. "Humor me."

Dean sat.

"You're one of those fellas that thinks too much," Miss Evelyn said succinctly, no more hint of weakness in her voice. "I knew that the first time I saw you. You probably sit around worrying about all the problems you might find around the bend, and while you're creating troubles that haven't had a chance to happen yet, life passes you by."

"I'm not—"

"Don't interrupt. It's rude."

Dean sat back in his chair. "Yes, ma'am."

"Sometimes you just have to reach for the brass ring without worrying that you might slip off the saddle. It's true, you might fall off the merry-go-round and eat a little dust, but if you're smart and resilient, you just hop right back on up there and start reaching for the brass ring again."

His love life as a merry-go-round. Great.

"That's interesting, but—"

"You're interrupting again."

"Sorry. I thought you were finished."

"Nope." The old lady took a sip of her coffee, which looked to be more milk than coffee. "I don't believe I am finished."

"Can I ask a question?"

"Of course, young man."

Dean leaned into the table. "What if when you fall off

the merry-go-round, you get more than a mouthful of dust? What if you end up mangled in the mechanism beneath the ride?''

Miss Evelyn grinned wickedly. Like him, she leaned forward. ''What if when you finally grab that brass ring and come away with it in your hand, you discover it's not brass, but gold. A priceless treasure. Something worth holding on to for a lifetime?''

Dean stood. ''Miss Evelyn, you're a romantic.''

''That I am,'' she said with a sigh.

''And I need to have a shower and get to work.'' He took his coffee cup with him, escaping the kitchen before his landlady could come up with more sage advice. He ran up the stairs, entered the upstairs parlor and sighed deeply. The morning had been just a little bit too exciting so far.

He grabbed his cell phone and dialed quickly. He had one thing to do before he took that shower.

Clint answered on the second ring. ''Dean!'' he said. Ah, the joys of caller-ID. ''It's a little early for you. Is everything okay?''

''Everything's fine.'' *If you discount the fact that the merry-go-round that's my love life is spinning out of control.* ''Could you do me a favor?''

Chapter 8

Reva managed to get to the kitchen before anyone else, barely, and she soon discovered the source of the noise that had called her into the restaurant last night. Bits of broken glass were scattered across the tile floor. She cleaned up the mess quickly.

It didn't look as if anything had been taken, but she was pretty sure a few items were not where she'd seen them last. A vase had been moved aside, an old pitcher was not where it should be. One drawer had been left open an inch or two, but it could have been left that way yesterday.

The cookbooks on the bookshelf just inside the kitchen door were not in the proper order, Reva realized as she passed. Tewanda had probably rearranged the books unintentionally. Maybe Miss Frances was the culprit. She was always looking for new recipes to try at home and had been known to spend her time browsing through the cookbooks.

There really wasn't any reason to tell Tewanda or the

sheriff or anyone else what had happened last night. If she reported the break-in, Dean's involvement might come out. That would never do. It was probably just kids, anyway. There were a few from just outside town who had been known to cause a little trouble now and then.

That's all this was—a little trouble.

As soon as the ladies arrived and got busy in the kitchen, Reva closeted herself in her office.

Her mind wouldn't stay settled long enough to get any work accomplished. She puttered, organized paperwork that didn't need to be organized. Her mind was most definitely elsewhere.

She had never lacked for troubles. These days Cooper and the restaurant provided more than enough anxiety for any one woman. Reva had managed to completely lock away worries about her own life, especially where men were concerned. She had no time for those complications, no desire to muck up her life when she'd finally found serenity. She'd worked hard to make a new life. She couldn't risk allowing a man to tear down everything she'd built.

This morning it wasn't her son or her business that caused her distress. It wasn't even the fact that she'd told Dean too much last night or that he carried a gun, though those tidbits offered plenty of concern.

No, what she worried about this morning was the way he had so confidently told her she would ask him to sleep with her again.

Dean hadn't used the words *sleep with* or *have sex,* as she had last night. He'd said *make love.* Reva shuddered. She knew it was an expression often used when there was no love involved, but the way Dean had said the words stayed with her, as if she could never shake them off. As if those words meant something grand and promising and new. Love was the last thing she wanted in her life. Talk about anxiety!

Reva leaned back in her chair and closed her eyes. No more daydreaming, no more thinking about what she could not have. She had Cooper and she had the restaurant; she did not need to add Dean to the mix. A man would bring more trouble than she could handle at the moment. Yes, it would be nice to let him kiss her again, to experience the weight of his body on hers and feel the evidence of his arousal pressing against her, promising more. Dean said he'd make her shake, and she had no doubt that he could. Easily. Too easily. She shook just thinking about him!

But she didn't need him, and a night or two of fun wouldn't be worth all the pain and heartache that were sure to follow. She knew that deep down, with a hard-won conviction. Now all she had to do was convince herself.

Dean waited until the lunch crowd had dispersed before he tackled the chore of putting new locks on all the restaurant doors. He kept waiting for the sheriff to show up to examine the crime scene. All day he'd watched. Nothing. At first he'd thought Reva might've asked the lawman to stay away until after her customers and employees had left for the day, but three o'clock had come and gone. The last of the customers had departed long ago, and only a couple of employees remained.

He hadn't seen Reva all afternoon. Had she taken to hiding from him again?

When Miss Edna brought him a glass of tea and said absolutely nothing about last night's break-in, Dean put two and two together. He asked if Reva was in, and the old woman directed him to the second-floor office. He drained his glass of tea and left it on the kitchen counter, then made his way through the old house that was becoming so familiar to him. He didn't try to soften his step on the stair. Reva would know he was coming.

The door was closed, so he knocked. After a moment he was answered with a much too soft "Come in."

He stepped into the office and closed the door behind him. "You didn't call the sheriff."

"Well." Reva leaned back in her chair. "Hello to you, too."

"Hello. You didn't call the sheriff."

The composed businesswoman sitting behind the desk didn't look like the frightened woman who'd asked him to have sex with her just a few hours earlier. She was serene, pulled together. Incredibly cool. "I decided there was no need."

"Someone broke into the restaurant," Dean snapped.

"Nothing's missing," she said calmly. "It was probably kids out to make mischief, which is hardly worth the trouble of filing a report with the sheriff."

Dean leaned against the closed door. "I understand Sheriff Andrews is sweet on you."

Aha. That put a chink in her icy armor. She didn't react strongly, but her deep-brown eyes were no longer quite so still. A hint of a blush bloomed on her cheeks. "Where did you hear such a thing?"

"As you have so often told me, rumors spread quickly in a small town."

Reva pursed her lips. "There's nothing between me and the sheriff, I assure you."

"I didn't say there was. I said I heard he was sweet on you." Dean stepped away from the door. "Carries a gun, doesn't he," he said in a lowered voice.

Reva went pale.

"I don't want to scare you," Dean said quickly. "I'm just trying to understand."

When he'd come here, his business had been official. There was no way he could sleep with a woman who was under surveillance. Not if he wanted to keep his job. And he loved his job. But he wasn't official anymore. He was on vacation. If he just happened to be keeping an eye on Reva at the same time, it was purely on his own. His own time. His own risks.

He reached Reva's desk and leaned forward, placing his hands on the edge and holding himself there. "Has Miss Evelyn ever talked to you about merry-go-rounds?"

"What?"

"Merry-go-rounds. Brass rings. Slippery saddles."

"No," she said softly.

"You should ask her about it sometime. Have dinner with me?"

The abrupt dinner invitation caught her off guard. She almost jumped out of her skin. "No! I mean, I have other plans."

"What plans?"

"None of your business," she said.

"How about dessert?"

Reva shook her head. "Mr. Sinclair, I—"

"Mr. Sinclair?" he asked. "When the hell did I become *Mr. Sinclair?*"

She didn't answer. At least she had the decency to look him in the eye. "When are you going home?"

"I haven't decided."

"But you are leaving Somerset."

"Eventually."

She looked relieved.

"Anxious to get rid of me?"

Before she could answer, the rumble of a souped-up vehicle on the street below grabbed his attention. Reva's, too, since she rose from her chair and walked to the window. Dean was right behind her, staring over her shoulder as a white pickup pulled to the curb across the street, directly in front of the Fister house. The loud engine died abruptly and the driver's-side door opened.

Limbs and leaves were in his way, so Dean's vision was less than perfect. But he saw enough.

"Crap," he mumbled beneath his breath.

"Who is that?" Reva asked.

Dean hurried from the room. "My brother."

He ran across the street just as Clint lifted the second twin from an infant car seat. Dean's youngest brother juggled two babies and a huge diaper bag without a hitch.

"What are you doing here?" Dean asked as he stepped up on the curb.

Clint grinned. "You've never called and asked for a favor before. I wanted to make sure you got what you wanted ASAP."

"I said Fed-Ex," Dean said softly.

"The ranch is less than two hours away," Clint explained. "It was no trouble. Besides, when my straight-arrow brother asks me to overnight him a box of condoms, I get curious."

"Curiosity is a very dangerous personality trait," Dean said darkly.

"That's not the only reason I'm here. Zane and Riley wanted to see their Uncle Dean. Isn't that right, boys?"

Zane and Riley, Clint and Mary's twin boys, were both fast asleep in their father's arms.

"Where's Mary?" Dean asked.

"Someone had the poor sense to get murdered in Jackson County. Mary's working."

"And you're baby-sitting."

"Yep."

Clint's eyes focused on something over Dean's shoulder. It was the smile, though, that gave away Reva's approach. "Well, well," Clint said softly.

Dean turned around to face Reva. Why couldn't she hide from him now? If ever there was a time he'd be happy for her to ensconce herself in her office with the door closed, this was it. The expression on her face as she looked at the babies told Dean why she'd followed him to the street.

"Hello," Clint said as Reva stepped up onto the sidewalk.

"Hi." Her eyes stayed on the babies.

Reluctantly Dean introduced Reva and Clint. No good would come of this, he knew it.

"How old are they?" Reva asked when the introductions and polite hellos were done.

"Two months," Clint said, shifting the sleeping babies so that their little faces were revealed.

"Twins," Reva said unnecessarily. "Identical?"

Clint nodded.

Reva lifted her arms. "May I?"

Clint transferred one of the babies to Reva with care. "This is Zane," he said. "He's the oldest, by five and a half minutes."

"He's so beautiful," Reva said softly. She glanced at Dean. "Aren't they just beautiful?"

"Sure," Dean said uncomfortably. "I guess."

"You *guess?*" Reva smiled too widely. "There's nothing in the world more adorable than a baby."

"Here." Clint dropped his diaper bag to the sidewalk and dumped the other kid, Riley, into Dean's arms. Before Dean could give the kid back, Clint walked away. He let down the tail end of the truck and reached into the bed. "I brought that, uh, stuff you asked for," he said.

"Stuff?" Reva asked, looking up at Dean.

"It can wait until later," Dean said while the kid he held decided to wake up. It squirmed, wrinkled its nose and began to squall.

Clint pulled a huge box out of the bed of his truck. Dean had a flash of a nightmare: Clint tripping, the box coming open, thousands of condoms—his youngest brother's idea of a joke—spilling onto the sidewalk.

Fortunately for Dean, Clint Sinclair never tripped.

"Where should I stash this?"

"Third floor." Dean nodded toward the front door of Miss Evelyn's house.

Dean breathed a sigh of relief as Clint disappeared inside.

He watched Reva continue to smile at the baby she held. Zane. The eldest. If Clint's boys were anything like their daddy, the coming years would be interesting, to say the least. Clint had always been into something. Not maliciously, but that curiosity of his had sometimes gotten the better of him.

Reva stared down at Zane as if she was reaching back in her memory, seeing Cooper when he was small. Then again, maybe she was looking into the future, not the past.

"Shouldn't Cooper be home soon?" Dean asked, bouncing Riley lightly. When he bounced, the kid didn't cry. He hated the crying. Hated it. Wailing of any kind, from woman or child, made him feel helpless.

"Cooper had T-ball practice after school," Reva said. "He won't be home for another hour at least."

So he couldn't get rid of her that way.

Why did it bother him to watch Reva cuddle and bounce a baby? It was the expression on her face, an expression that said very clearly, *I want one,* that troubled him. Reva was the kind of woman who should have a houseful of kids, and she was certainly young enough to have a few more babies. Dean knew he wasn't going to be the man to give them to her. Was that what bothered him? The thought of another man fulfilling the maternal dreams that made Reva's face more beautiful than ever?

Clint came bursting through the front door too soon, Miss Evelyn in his wake and the enormous box of condoms properly secured somewhere out of sight.

"Babies!" Miss Evelyn said with glee. "Tiny ones!"

"Do you have a place I can heat up their bottles?" Clint asked.

"Of course I do," Miss Evelyn said. "And there are sugar cookies for the rest of you."

"Yeah, Clint," Dean said as he handed over Riley and then scooped up the diaper bag and draped the strap over his little brother's shoulder. "Have some cookies."

Payback time.

As they all walked toward the front door, Miss Evelyn dropped back and leaned in close to Dean. "Sonny, *that* is the golden ring." She pointed to Clint and the baby he carried. "Breathtaking, isn't it?"

Reva held on to Zane and followed the Sinclair men and Miss Evelyn into the house. She really should return the baby to Clint and go back to work, but no. She wanted to hang on to this sweet-smelling, beautiful baby a while longer.

She would love to have another child one day. Maybe two. But she knew that would never happen. She couldn't allow herself to get that close to a man. Physically, maybe. Emotionally, to build a family and everything that came with it, no.

But she would gladly hold on to someone else's baby for a while.

The sight of a very uncomfortable Dean holding a baby

had warmed her heart, more than it should. He'd been so obviously uncomfortable! Always cool, never at a loss, Dean Sinclair had been momentarily as helpless as the baby he cradled. She had a feeling babies were not in his immediate plans. Too much trouble for a man like him, she imagined.

In the kitchen of the Fister house, Clint once again handed a baby to an unprepared and unwilling Dean. Miss Evelyn and Clint warmed the bottles, while Dean and Reva bounced the hungry babies. Zane, the more patient of the two, only squirmed. Riley, the child Dean held, whimpered, wriggled and then started to scream.

"Take this kid," Dean said, stalking toward his brother.

"Oh, come here, you big baby," Reva said, following Dean to the sink. "You take Zane and I'll calm Riley down."

He turned and glared at her, but seemed agreeable. They swapped babies, which wasn't all that easy a task. She and Dean stood close together, too close, while they shuffled and readjusted the children they held. The moment was as intimate as anything that had passed last night. As soon as each baby had been securely transferred, Reva and Dean each took a quick step back.

She'd always cared for Cooper on her own, and she'd never regretted her decision to keep her child. But she often wondered what it would be like to have a man around to share the responsibilities. To warm bottles and walk a baby at night and… But it was only wondering. No matter how nice that false picture might be, it was just that. False.

Her life was good now. She was happy. Painting a picture of another life she would never have wouldn't do her any good at all.

When the bottles were warm, Clint carried them to the

table. "Would you mind?" he said, handing one bottle to Reva.

"Not at all." Riley, who had calmed down considerably since being handed to her, clamped on to the nipple and began to suck greedily.

It looked as though Dean was going to return Zane to Clint, but Miss Evelyn snatched the bottle from Clint's hand and pushed it at Dean. "Here. You give it a try. This young man looks like he could use some cookies and milk."

She expected Dean to protest, but he took the bottle and grinned crookedly. "Sure. Have some cookies and milk, Clint."

While the babies ate, Miss Evelyn assembled a plate of sugar cookies for Clint and poured him a big glass of milk. Undaunted, Clint sat at the table close to the babies. It was obvious from the look on his face that he adored these baby boys.

Clint took a drink of milk, then grabbed a sugar cookie and bit into it. He chewed for a moment, then took another long drink of milk.

"How do you like my sugar cookies?" Miss Evelyn asked with a smile.

Dean's grin stayed in place.

"Well," Clint began with a shake of his head, "they could use a bit more sugar."

Miss Evelyn appeared undaunted. "Do you really think so?"

Clint nodded, then took another small bite. "And is that almond flavoring I taste?"

"Yes it is," Miss Evelyn said.

"Too much," Clint said. "Cut it by half or try vanilla."

Dean's smile was gone, and he glared at his brother.

"Don't look at me that way. I'm just being honest."

Clint gave Miss Evelyn a charming smile. "I hope you don't mind me being honest, ma'am. My wife is learning how to cook and having quite a time of it. I have discovered that honesty is the best policy in this as in all things." He cut his eyes to Dean. "My big brother has been trying to teach me that for years."

"You know, I think you might be right. My late husband always said he loved my sugar cookies, but personally I never cared for this recipe much."

Dean did not appear to be particularly happy at the moment, even though he'd been smiling a few moments ago and the baby in his arms was finally content.

He'd preached honesty to his little brother. Reva's stomach did a sick flip. What would he say if he knew how many secrets she'd kept, from him and everyone else?

Dean threw open the door to his room and led Clint inside. Downstairs, Reva and Miss Evelyn were burping and changing the babies. They seemed delighted to take over the chores, and Dean wasn't about to fight for the opportunity to get peed on by one of Clint's kids.

Besides, he needed a moment alone with his little brother.

The box, which was slightly more than two feet square, sat in the middle of the floor. Dean stood there for a moment and stared down. "I ask you for a simple favor…"

Clint took a knife from his pocket, dropped down and cut open the cardboard box. "When you called, you didn't specify how big a box or what brand or if you prefer plain or fancy."

"Fancy?"

Clint reached into the carton and grabbed a handful. Dean glanced down. Holy crap, the box really was full of condoms. Some packaged, some foil-wrapped and floating loose. "Flavored, colored, some with doodads—"

"Doodads?"

"And these glow in the dark." Clint waggled his eyebrows, then opened the box and took one foil wrapper out. "I think I might just keep one of these," he said, slipping the glow-in-the-dark condom into the pocket of his jeans.

"I said Fed-Ex," Dean told him again.

Clint stood and studied Dean cautiously. "Want to explain to me why you need someone to deliver your birth control to the door, these days?"

Dean took a step closer and lowered his voice, just in case someone might be listening. Sound did carry in these old houses. "This is a small town. If I walk to the drugstore and buy so much as one condom, word will be all over Somerset before sundown."

"So? What do you care? It's no one's business but your own. You are an adult. Besides, you're not going to be here forever, are you?"

"No."

"So who cares?"

"It's not *my* reputation I'm worried about," Dean said in an even lower voice.

"Oh," Clint said, realization dawning. "I get it. Very considerate of you." He shifted his booted feet. "But why not drive to another town and make your purchases there?"

"No car," Dean said. "Long story."

"No car?" Clint looked horrified. "You're stranded here. Stuck. Oh, man, that just won't do. Are there cornfields? Kids with strange, eerie eyes?"

"No," Dean said, in no mood for his brother's warped sense of humor at the moment.

"This trip of yours is business, right?" Clint asked.

"Not anymore," Dean said. "Started out that way, but right now I'm officially on vacation." The lines between official and unofficial had become blurred. The lines were never blurred, not for Dean. Not until he'd come to Somerset.

Clint nodded his head. "I tell you what. I'll leave you my truck. Mary can drive up tonight and collect me and the kids."

"Thanks, but that would be way too much trouble."

"After everything you've done for me? It's nothing. Really." Again he waggled his eyebrows. "Besides, the boys always sleep well after a long ride in the car." He glanced into the box again. "Ooh, doodads. May I?" he gestured toward the box.

"Be my guest," Dean said, shaking his head. "There's more than enough."

He wasn't even sure that he'd need *one*.

Chapter 9

The five- and six-year-olds T-ball team was small, and when the team from nearby Cross City came in for a game, they always got pummeled.

But the Somerset Tigers did have fun.

Reva was lost in the game, watching Cooper play. Badly. He tried and he had a good time, but her son was not a natural athlete. She didn't care. She liked watching him have fun. He was so openly and exuberantly joyous at times it was as if the joy traveled from him to her and lifted her spirits. Cooper looked toward the stands and grinned, waving almost frantically. Reva waved back—and then realized that her son was not signaling her but Dean, who had just arrived and was making his way toward her.

She'd managed to avoid Dean all day, after the previous night's visit with his brother and family. She'd only gotten to spend a few minutes with Mary, but she'd liked the woman immediately. Clint's face had lit up when his wife stepped out of the car.

Like Tewanda and her husband, it seemed they had everything.

Dean sat next to her on the metal bleachers. She wanted to shoo him away, but that would cause more talk than allowing him to sit beside her.

"What are you doing here?" she asked in a soft voice.

"Cooper asked me to come to the game," Dean explained.

Dean turned his attention to the ball game. Reva wished she could do the same. Having him right beside her, so close his arm almost brushed hers, distressed her. Darn his hide, she didn't even have to look at him to be distracted. Just knowing he was there ruined her moment of peace.

Not that Dean did anything to call attention to himself. He didn't ask her to dinner, didn't try to make idle chitchat or mention the break-in or anything else that had happened that night. He shouted encouragement at all the right places, watching Cooper the way Reva usually did.

She could not ignore him; that kind of strength wasn't in her. "You have a nice family," she said, searching for something safe to say.

He snorted.

Even though she was nervous and stirred up and just a little bit inside out, she laughed. "Not a very flattering response."

"You don't know my family all that well. Yeah, they can look normal on first meeting, but trust me, nothing about my family is normal."

"It's nice, though," she said. She'd listened closely to Dean and Clint last night, eavesdropping shamelessly. "To have brothers and a sister and all the family that comes with them, that's really nice. They're all married?"

"Yep. I'm the only holdout."

Reva relaxed a little and leaned back on the metal

bleachers. "Don't ever take them for granted. I wish I had a family."

He turned to her. "No brothers or sisters or parents?"

She shook her head. "It's always been just me and Cooper. And we've done just fine," she added quickly. "Not all families are as nice as yours." Her own had certainly never been.

Dean turned his eyes to the field again. "Cooper's lucky. You're a great mother."

Was he saying that just to get on her good side? "I wonder some days."

"I can see it. So can everyone else, I'm sure." He glanced at her, his blue eyes unreadable. "Has it been hard raising him alone?"

"It's all I know," she said. "I do feel guilty on occasion because I haven't given Cooper the ideal, two-parent, two-and-a-half-child life."

Dean nodded absently. "Having two parents around doesn't necessarily mean they're going to be any good at the job. I had a mother and father at home, growing up. My father worked all the time. I don't think he saw me or my brothers play a single baseball game." His eyes crinkled. "My mother was so busy with her clubs and meetings and social events she wasn't around any more than my father." Again Dean looked at her. "Do you know, they haven't even seen Clint's twins yet? The kids are two months old, and the folks just haven't been able to find the time to make the trip. Eventually Clint and Mary will take the twins to meet their grandparents, but they won't stay long. Apparently having little kids around again disrupts the house." He shook his head.

Reva tried to find a way to explain away the elder Sinclairs' indifference—and couldn't. "That sucks."

Dean smiled at her succinct observation. "Yeah."

Reva's own mother, Vicky Lynn Macklin, had been in-attentive at best. She'd directed her energies not to caring for her child, but to searching for a man to replace the one who'd left her pregnant. The stepfather who had come into Reva's life when she'd been twelve had been stable, but not exactly loving. As soon as he'd died, Vicky Lynn had taken off. Reva hadn't seen her since.

She couldn't go back and change her childhood, choose another mother or a father who would stick around. But she would have loved to have a brother like Dean or Clint, or a sister like Tewanda. She suspected those bonds went so deep nothing could ever sever them. "So your parents weren't Ozzie and Harriet. You have your brothers and a sister. That's a good thing."

"Yeah."

"And they're all married with kids."

Dean nodded. "The family is growing. Everyone's re-producing."

"Everyone but you," she said, immediately regretting her words. She tried to turn her attention to the ball field again. It had been a very personal conversation up to this point, but she'd just crossed a line she should not have crossed. "Sorry. None of my business."

Dean let her blunder go for a moment, and then he asked, "What if I did have kids one day, and it turned out I was no better a father than my own?"

He sounded so uncertain she couldn't help but reach out to take his hand. Dean Sinclair was always sure of what he wanted, of who he was. It touched her, deeply, to realize that he had fears of his own. The moment their palms met, she released him. Somehow the brief touch had been more intimate than having the man lying on top of her!

There was an awkward moment, a strained silence, and then Cooper saved them. Dean pointed to the outfield.

"Your son is wearing his glove on his head." A moment later Dean laughed, and everything was all right again.

Standing before the dugout, Coach Charles Hardy waved frantically at the outfield. Tewanda stood not too far from her husband, watching the game. But as Reva's eyes scanned the sidelines, Tewanda glanced toward the stands. And grinned widely, as if she knew an enticing secret.

Reva sighed and tried to return her attention to the game. How had things gotten so out of hand? She was much too attracted to Dean Sinclair. Worse, she *liked* him. Physical attraction she could explain away if she tried hard enough. But to like the man? Impossible. Then there was the prowler dilemma. Dean had put new locks on all the doors and said he'd take a walk around the place at least once a night before going to bed, but she couldn't help but wonder who would do such a thing. Was it troublemaking kids, as she'd suspected all along? And would they try to break in again?

Tewanda had been counseling Reva to sleep with Dean and get the itch scratched, consequences be damned. If anyone had seen him sneaking out of her house yesterday morning, the rumors would already be circulating. But rumors were the least of her problems at the moment. Dean had a gun, and like it or not, rational or not, guns were her greatest fear. She hated them.

Nothing could come of her attraction to Dean, and yet she couldn't manage to ignore it. Things couldn't possibly get any worse!

She was wrong. Sheriff Ben Andrews climbed onto the stands and sat beside her. Now she had Dean on one side and an armed sheriff on the other.

The sheriff was sweet on Reva, according to Miss Evelyn. Dean hadn't had any feelings one way or the other about the man when they'd first met, but at the moment he didn't much care for the young lawman who looked more like a football player than a sheriff.

Ben Andrews knew exactly why Dean was in Somerset, but he was not at liberty to share that information.

"Sheriff, this is Dean Sinclair," Reva said crisply. "Dean, this is Sheriff Andrews."

"Pleased to meet you," the sheriff said, looking and sounding not at all pleased. "I've heard a lot about you."

No doubt. Dean nodded in response, noting the location of the lawman's weapon. It was holstered on the opposite hip from the one that rested too close to Reva. That was a good thing, Dean decided as he raised his eyes to find the sheriff glaring at him again.

Sheriff Andrews's primary office was located in Cross City, but he had an auxiliary office here in Somerset. There was usually a deputy or two on duty, but the sheriff limited his days in the Somerset office, or so Dean had heard.

"What brings you to the ballpark, Sheriff?" Dean asked, his eyes on Cooper.

"Call me Ben," the lawman said. "Shoot, I feel like I already know you. Dean, isn't it?"

Dean turned his head slowly to give the sheriff a warning glare. "That's right."

"Well, Dean, I came out to watch the ball game." The sheriff's drawl was just a little bit too deep, as if he was putting it on for show. "And to see Reva and Cooper. It's been too long since I called on the best cook and the prettiest woman in the county."

It wasn't Dean's imagination that Reva's body stiffened slightly.

"Really, Ben," she said softly, blushing.

"Just the truth, Reva," Andrews said. He leaned back

and pretended to watch the game. "Besides, I've been trying to call you all week. Did Tewanda pass on the messages?"

"Yes, she did," Reva said quickly. "Sorry I haven't returned your calls. I've just been very busy this week."

Andrews glanced sharply at Dean. "Do tell."

After a few minutes the sheriff sat up straighter. He adjusted the tie of his khaki shirt and shifted about on the metal bleacher seat as if he was sitting on a small rock. Yeah, the man was definitely uncomfortable.

Finally the sheriff said, "There's a dance Saturday night at the Cross City VFW. I have to go, you know how it is, and I thought maybe you'd like to join me."

"I can't," Reva answered with a shake of her head. "I, uh, have plans."

"Plans," the sheriff repeated in a low voice.

"Yes, I'm afraid so."

"What plans?"

Dean had been here long enough to know that Reva's life was regimented. Dull. She worked, she took care of Cooper, she was a good mother and a savvy businesswoman. She did not have plans for Saturday night. Surely everyone knew that, including the persistent sheriff.

Dean glared at Andrews. He could understand the lawman's infatuation with Reva, but she'd made her feelings on the matter clear. More than clear. "She has a date with me," he said quietly.

Reva's head snapped around and she looked up at him with wide, dark eyes.

"A date," Andrews repeated. Poor guy, he sounded like someone had let the wind out of his sails.

Reva took a deep breath and turned to face the sheriff. "Yes, I guess you could call it a date. Dean is coming over to have dinner with Cooper and me."

Smooth. Very smooth. She included Cooper in the mix to keep things safe and still managed to maintain her excuse for not accepting the sheriff's invitation.

"I see," Andrews said, standing cautiously. "Sinclair." He turned his full, angry attention to Dean. "One of these days you and I need to have ourselves a long talk."

"Any time, Sheriff," Dean answered. "Any time."

Reva kept her eyes straight ahead as the three of them walked toward home. *The three of them.* Oh, that sounded so natural, so right. There wasn't much light left in the sky, just a hint. The shadows along the sidewalk were already deep.

Cooper and Dean walked behind her, talking about T-ball and batting stances and the differences between a cap and a glove. A cap went on the head, Dean explained with an abundance of patience, the glove did not. Yes, testosterone was heavy in the air; but not as heavy as it had been when the sheriff and Dean had been talking to each other.

Reva's stomach did a sick little flip. Surely Dean understood that they weren't really going to have dinner together on Saturday night. She was grateful for his improvisational excuse, but the "date" was a ruse, nothing more.

Ben Andrews was a nice enough guy, but he was doggedly tenacious. Maybe if he believed she was willing to date other men, just not him, he'd back off. She hated to hurt Ben's feelings, but she didn't want to spend another three years telling him no on a regular basis.

"Mom," Cooper said brightly as he skipped forward to walk beside her. "This weekend Mr. Sinclair is going to teach me how to catch a fly ball!"

"You know how to catch a fly ball," she said.

"He's going to teach me how to catch *good.* He played

left field. He knows how to catch a fly ball.'' Cooper's words were fast, as usual, his sentences running together.

"I'm sure Mr. Sinclair has other things to do with his weekend.''

Dean stepped up beside her. Again she was bracketed by two males. One little, one not so little. "Not really,'' he said.

Reva sighed. The last thing she wanted to see was Dean and Cooper playing catch in the yard as a father and son might. She was already in too deep, and to watch such a simple activity would probably hurt like hell. It would remind her too clearly of what she could not give her son. But how could she forbid something so harmless?

As they neared home, Cooper took off running. They had almost reached Miss Evelyn's house. Surely Dean would say good-night and cross the street now. Heavens, she could barely breathe when he was this close to her!

But Dean didn't say good-night. He watched Cooper cut through the yard and head for home.

"Does Cooper have his own key?'' Dean asked.

"The kitchen door is unlocked,'' Reva answered.

Dean's response was to take her arm in a firm grasp and come to a dead stop on the sidewalk. "What?''

Reva turned to face him. She had to look up to see the stormy blue eyes and firmly set jaw. "I told you, people don't lock their doors in Somerset.''

"That's ridiculous. How can you be sure your home is secure if you don't lock your doors?''

Reva glanced at the hand on her arm, and Dean reluctantly dropped it. "I always lock the restaurant doors, and that didn't stop the person who broke in the other night.''

A muscle in Dean's jaw jumped. "You should be more careful.''

"This isn't Atlanta, Dean. It's Somerset. All the neighbors know there's a key under the mat if the door is locked and they need to get in.''

"You keep a key under the mat?'' he asked, obviously appalled.

"Sure. Look,'' she resumed her easy trek toward home, and Dean stayed beside her. "If someone really wants to get into my house, into *any* house, they'll manage somehow. Break a window, bust a lock—I don't exactly live in a fortress.''

He didn't head for his rented room, but remained with her as she stepped onto the grass and turned toward home. "I know that's true, but you could have an alarm system put in.''

She laughed. "An alarm system? In Somerset?''

He shook his head.

"Why are you following me home?'' she asked as they passed beneath the tree where she'd caught him lurking that first night.

"I just want to take a look around, make sure everything's all right before I go back to my room.''

She didn't say anything for a few minutes. Home grew closer. Her heart, what was left of it, grew a little heavier. "You're not going to quit your job and become a small-town handyman, are you.''

"We had this discussion yesterday.''

Yes, but it couldn't hurt to drive the point home once again. "You're too much a cop for anything else. You might enjoy your vacation, but you were made to take care of other people. I can't see another career making you happy.''

"I'm enjoying my time here, I really am.''

"I don't doubt that,'' she said. "But you're not going to stay.''

"No,'' he answered softly.

Just as well. More than that, exactly what she'd wanted all along! If she ever did decide to let her guard down and love again, it couldn't be a cop. A man who carried a gun, who dealt with criminals and danger every day, who would have access to information best kept buried.

"It's nice of you to spend time with Cooper," she said as she stepped onto the porch of her cottage. "It is, truly. But please don't make him think you're going to stay. Don't make him think you're…someone you're not, then walk away and break his heart."

Dean stopped on the bottom step. She wasn't going to invite him in, not tonight.

"What about your heart?" he asked.

"My heart is not in danger," she said coolly. It was the truth. She didn't have enough left to break.

Dean climbed the stairs, trying to be quiet. The last thing he needed tonight was more advice from his landlady.

He knew the moment he opened the door to the upstairs parlor that he was not alone. Miss Evelyn never locked her doors, either.

When Dean saw the flash of khaki in the corner chair, he was grateful he'd moved the huge box of condoms to his bedroom.

"I didn't see your car in the driveway," Dean said as he closed the door.

"I parked on the next street over and walked," Andrews said, his Tennessee accent thick. "Thought maybe you and I should have a little talk, private like."

Dean switched on the antique table lamp by the door. "Talk away, Sheriff."

"Does Reva know who you are and why you're here?"

Right to the point. "No."

"Then by all rights I should kick your ass, no matter who the hell you work for."

"You can try."

Sheriff Andrews remained seated and relaxed. "Is this really her?" He reached out to the table beside him and lifted the old, grainy photo of Reva.

Dean's heart thudded hard. No matter what, that photo could not make the rounds here in Somerset. "That photograph is property of the U.S. Marshals Service, Sheriff. It is as confidential as the reason for my presence here."

"I didn't plan to give it to the newspaper," Andrews said gruffly. He returned the photo to the table facedown. "And I'm not going to tell anyone who you are or why you're here. That kind of information would be hurtful to Reva, and I won't stand for that." The big man rose to his feet. "But I also won't stand for you coming in here and taking advantage of her."

"I haven't taken advantage of anyone."

"See that you don't." Andrews passed close to Dean on his way to the door. As he stood there, with his hand on the doorknob, he added in a lowered voice, "If you're going to look at a woman the way you look at Reva Macklin, you shouldn't lie to her."

"I don't have any choice in the matter."

"Of course you do. There's always a choice, Sinclair. Always. I have a choice myself." He glanced over his shoulder. "I could tell her the truth. I could tell her who you are, why you're here, and that you came here believing she was somehow in cahoots with this old boyfriend of hers."

"Everything you were told about this assignment was confidential."

"Like I said, there's always a choice." The sheriff nodded his head and opened the door. "You tell her, Sinclair, or I will."

Chapter 10

"So," Miss Edna purred as she swept through the front door at eight-fifteen on Friday morning. "What are you cooking for that nice young man tomorrow night?"

For a moment Reva stood in the entryway in stunned silence. "Excuse me?"

"That nice-looking fella who's been fixing up the place. Dean of course. I hear you're cooking dinner for him tomorrow night." She lifted her eyebrows and smiled. "A date! How exciting."

Gossip apparently now traveled through Somerset at the speed of sound.

"Where did you hear that?"

"Well," Miss Edna confided. "Lisa Carlton was at the ball game last night, and of course she couldn't help but notice that you were being paid court to by two handsome young men. She heard you mention a date for Saturday night, and she just happened to have mentioned it to her sister Constance on the phone after she got home, as they were planning their menus for Sunday's picnic raffle, and of course Constance told—''

''That's all I need to know,'' Reva interrupted, palm up. If she told Edna there was no date, word would get to the sheriff. Probably long before noon.

''So what are you going to prepare?'' Edna continued. ''Surely you've decided on a menu.''

''Not yet.''

''Not yet!'' Miss Edna was properly horrified. ''Dean has eaten here many times, but while they were your recipes, you did not actually prepare the meals. The first meal you prepare for a man with your own hands is special, you know. You must give the menu proper consideration.''

''I will.'' Maybe she'd make grilled cheese sandwiches and tomato soup from a can. She certainly wasn't out to impress Dean Sinclair with her culinary skills.

At least she'd been smart enough to include Cooper in the invitation. With her son there, no one could possibly call the dinner romantic. It was a date only in the broadest sense of the word.

Tewanda breezed in, an impossibly wicked smile spreading across her face. ''I hear I'm going to be babysitting tomorrow night.''

''You are not!'' Reva declared.

''Of course I am,'' Tewanda said as she and Edna headed for the kitchen. ''I already told Cooper he could spend the night. Charles is making pizza for the boys, and we'll rent a few videos.''

''That's not necessary,'' Reva said as she followed her employees to the kitchen.

''Of course it's necessary. This will be your first date in…well, in as long as I've known you, and that's going on three years. You do not need Cooper there to chaperon.''

"It's not a date," Reva insisted. "I'm just cooking dinner for a friend." Maybe grilled cheese sandwiches *without* the soup.

"So now he's a *friend,*" Tewanda said suggestively. "What are you going to wear for your date?"

"It's not a date!"

Edna and Tewanda ignored Reva and started discussing the plans for today's lunch menu. Reva turned around and stalked away, muttering as she headed for the peace and quiet of her office, "It is *not* a date!"

Her office was quiet, but there was no peace to be found. She paced and chewed on one fingernail. When she was finally able to quit pacing and sit, she fingered the papers on her desk without being truly aware of what she saw.

Eventually her heart rate slowed and she took a deep breath. She had a date. Like it or not, she had a *date* with Dean Sinclair. If she'd found herself cornered and sharing a meal with the sheriff or anyone else, she wouldn't be so tied in knots. With anyone but Dean, she could be assured that the date would be safe. Meaningless. Uneventful.

Dean offered none of those things. Time with him was definitely not meaningless. Why did that scare her so? He was a good man, she didn't have any doubt of that. That was not her problem. The problem was, she liked him too much. She liked him and she wanted more, even though she knew she could never have more.

Movement outside caught her attention. It was Dean, walking across the street, dressed for work. Everything about him—the way he moved, the shape of his body in jeans and snug T-shirt, the curve of his shoulder and his neck, the face she could not see clearly from this distance—wakened something inside her that had been sleeping for too long. He wakened the woman within, the part of herself she had denied for Cooper's sake and for her own sake. For the sake of her battered heart.

She wanted to touch Dean again, kiss him again, and like it or not, she wanted the *more* she could not, should not, have.

Dean cursed as he never had before, borrowing a few of Boone's favorite words. Fortunately Reva's employees were gone for the day. He definitely wasn't fit company for blue-haired old ladies, not as he struggled with this afternoon's chore.

Wallpaper. To the untrained eye the task appeared simple enough. He had followed the directions, but the damn paper stuck where it wasn't supposed to and didn't stick where it was supposed to.

At the moment the wet, uncooperative paper stuck to him and to itself, folding in where it shouldn't, falling in the most bothersome way.

Dean was transforming the bedchamber where he'd had an abbreviated lunch with Reva into a sitting parlor. That was the plan at least. The old dresser would have to be moved to another room, but the fainting couch, that faded burgundy contraption with the serpentine back and the carved legs, would probably stay.

Working in Reva's yard was hard work, but he could actually see something happening as the days passed. He'd never be a true handyman, he knew that, but the lush grounds surrounding Miss Reva's were starting to look good. This morning, as he'd hauled away more dead limbs, it had actually crossed Dean's mind that he should think about buying a house of his own.

How much of the allure of his bogus job was Reva herself? There was something about turning around in the middle of a chore to find her standing on the porch or under a tree or in a window, watching him. Those too-brief moments were stimulating and heartwarming. Dean snorted at his own foolishness. He didn't do heartwarming. It was too damn much trouble.

Maybe he would give up apartment life and buy a house one day, though, as long as he never had to mess with wallpaper.

He stopped cursing when he heard footsteps on the stairs. Quick and light—he recognized that step.

"Dean?" Reva called as she reached the top of the stairs.

"In here," he called as he removed a length of the wallpaper's sticky side from his shirt.

"What's wrong?" Reva stopped in the doorway of the room that would soon be an upstairs parlor—if he ever got the damned wallpaper on the wall where it belonged. "I heard you…" She stopped speaking and smiled as she leaned against the doorjamb and looked him up and down.

She always had an old-fashioned look about her, as if she'd just stepped out of another time. A gentler time. It was the clothes, he imagined. Today's dress was calf-length, pale lavender dotted with small flowers, and it was fastened along the front from top to bottom with tiny, pearl-like buttons that begged to be undone. No, it wasn't the dress. It was the fresh curve of her cheek and the wave in her honey-blond hair that made her look as if she belonged in the 1940s.

Her smile was gentle.

"It isn't funny," Dean said in a low voice.

"Yes, it is," she responded.

Dean's frustration faded. Reva should smile this way more often. There wasn't any fear on her face at the moment, no worry, no icy resolve. She was just Reva, content and amused.

"You could get in here and help me out," he suggested gruffly.

Reva stepped into the room and was soon bathed in the sunlight that poured through the window. The material of her lavender dress was thin, and for a moment he caught sight of the outline of her fabulous legs.

"What do you want me to do?"

That was a loaded question. Dean tried to dismiss the turn his thoughts took. "Hold the paper straight at the bottom while I get the top section where it's supposed to be. With any luck maybe I can get it in place before the glue dries."

She had to kneel beside him to do as he asked. Dean didn't look down at her hair or take a moment to enjoy the way the scooped neckline of her dress fell slightly away from her body. He kept his eyes on the wallpaper, lining up the damned stuff so that it matched the strip he'd already managed to get into place.

No, he couldn't see Reva, but he could certainly feel her. She was right there, brushing against his leg in that soft, feathery way only a woman can. At one point she apparently decided she wasn't holding the paper correctly, because she moved her body to the side so that she was actually *between* Dean and the wall. When she shifted her body, her breath landed warm and arousing on his leg, penetrating the thick denim and making him shudder.

Dean concentrated on the task of lining up the wallpaper so Reva could move aside. Asking for her help hadn't been such a bright idea, after all.

No matter how anxious he was to finish, this wasn't a chore that could be rushed. He moved one way, Reva turned another. Soon she wasn't kneeling at all, but sitting on the floor between his legs, both hands on the wallpaper, her gauzy skirt pooled around her legs. Every time he moved so that one of his legs brushed against her, sparks shot through his body. By the time he had the top half of the wallpaper where it should be, he had an erection that strained against his jeans, and no matter how diligently he tried, he could not concentrate on the simple task that had had him cussing a blue streak a few minutes earlier.

He worked his hands down the wall, smoothing the wallpaper as he went. Eventually Reva scooted aside and rose to her feet, allowing him to finish on his own. He brushed out a couple of rough spots and trimmed a strip off the bottom. Reva had plenty of time to step away, leave the room, make a safe and smart escape. She didn't.

When Dean finished with the strip of wallpaper and turned his attention to Reva again, there was no longer an easy smile on her face. Pale cheeks were flushed, eyes bright, lips taunting and tantalizing. The ultrafeminine dress she wore was slightly twisted from moving about on the floor. Her hair, usually so sleek and controlled, looked as if he'd already run his fingers through the strands. A lock fell across one cheek.

"You should go now," he said, turning his head to search for nonexistent flaws in the wallpaper.

"You're probably right," she said in a soft, stirring voice. But she didn't make a move for the door.

Dean cursed again as he reached out, took Reva's arm and gently pulled her to him. She wasn't surprised, and she didn't hold back or mutter a demur protest. She fell into him, lifted her face to look him in the eye and placed her hand on his waist.

When her lips parted, he expected a belated *We shouldn't do this* or a horrified *What was I thinking?*

And still, he wasn't surprised when she whispered, "Maybe you'd better kiss me now."

* * *

Reva didn't allow herself to be swept away. It was a dangerous thing to lose control, to let reason go and simply feel, to crave and ache and yearn.

When Dean's mouth touched hers, she quit torturing herself with questions she couldn't possibility answer. Why him? Why now? She had been content to live without a man for the past seven years, hadn't she? Yes, she had, until Dean Sinclair had come storming into her life.

No, Dean hadn't stormed. He'd crept into her life, crawling under her skin an inch at a time until there was no shaking him loose. He was relentless, gently demanding and ever present. And every time he looked at her, she wanted him more.

He wouldn't stay here in Somerset, and that was a good thing. That was, in fact, the only reason she could allow herself to fulfill this fantasy. She didn't have forever to offer anyone. But she did have today.

She loved the way Dean kissed her, as if he wanted to devour her mouth, as if he could never get enough. His lips were firm and yet soft, demanding but not hurtful. There was no doubt in her mind that he wanted her. She had worked very hard to hide her attraction to him; he didn't have that luxury. At one point when she'd been holding wallpaper, she'd shifted and turned her head and found herself staring at the proof.

Dean caught her body against his and deepened the kiss for a long moment before pulling his mouth away. "Is anyone else here?" he whispered.

"No," Reva answered, her voice as soft as his. "Just us."

"Cooper?"

"T-ball practice."

Dean captured her mouth again and parted her lips with his tongue for a soul-searing kiss she felt to her bones. His hands were steady and warm as they held her against his solid body. Together they moved across the floor as they kissed, until Reva's back met the wall.

Sandwiched between the wall and this tall, solidly built man, Reva felt not trapped, but caught up in something powerful and beautiful. Her body and Dean's...they had been dancing toward this moment since the night they'd met. She'd fought every step of the way, but she was tired of fighting.

Reva touched Dean's neck with curious fingers, brushed her thumb against the beat of his pulse. He was warm and hard, soft and rough, all at the same time. Touching him was addictive, she was certain. The kiss went on, and she soon wanted more. She wanted everything. She wrapped her arms around him and held on tight, telling Dean with her kiss what she wanted.

He unfastened the tiny buttons down the front of her dress, and all the while he continued to kiss her. Lips, tongue, a gentle nip of her lower lip. His hands and his mouth were more skilled at undressing and arousing her than they were with a hammer. Each move was smooth, easy, practically mindless.

Reva closed her eyes and wallowed in sensation. Dean's mouth, his tongue, his hands. Nothing else mattered at this moment. Nothing. When her dress was unfastened to the waist, he very gently pushed the garment off her shoulders. A quick twist of his fingers, and her bra came undone and was tossed aside. One hand gently cupped a breast, and the sensation was so intense she moaned and deepened the kiss, inviting more, demanding more.

When Dean bent down to take a sensitive nipple into his mouth, she arched against him. Pleasure, tangible and extreme, shot through her at the touch of his mouth, grew as he continued to lavish attentions on her. Her heart thundered. She grew damp, she clenched and unclenched in anticipation. With a gentle undulation and a telling quiver, her body responded. She held Dean's head to her breast while he suckled and laved and drove her beyond desire and into burning need.

A new thought shook her, gently roused unwelcomed reason. "Do you have a—"

"Yes," he answered before she finished the question.

Reva relaxed, smiled, leaned her head back as Dean moved his attention to her other breast.

One of Dean's capable hands slipped up her leg and under her skirt to snag her panties. He drew them down; she kicked them away.

"I love your legs," he said, running his hands over her thighs. "Smooth, strong, long. I dream about them wrapped around me."

His mouth returned to hers, and he kissed her so deeply she felt that meeting of their mouths everywhere. When he touched her intimately, adding an arousing caress to the kiss, her knees almost buckled.

Dean lifted her, took her more securely in his arms and carried her away from the wall. She wrapped her legs around his waist so that his arousal pressed against her, where she wanted him. Where she needed him. She didn't know where he was taking her, and she didn't care.

He laid her down on the fainting couch, which had been pushed against one wall. The bed was narrow but soft. Before he could pull away, she tugged on his T-shirt. She was more exposed than not; it was only fair that she be able to see him, touch him, hold his bare body close to hers. She wanted it all, flesh to flesh and heart to heart.

Dean helped her tug the shirt off and toss it aside, and then she reached for the buckle and zipper of his jeans.

Her mouth went dry, her heart caught in her throat as

she freed his erection. Hot and hard, silky as night, he filled her hand. She stroked him, learning his length, making him moan as he had made her moan.

Dean reached into his back pocket for his wallet, withdrew it, threw it open and snagged a single foil-wrapped condom before dropping the wallet to the floor. He sheathed himself; she helped him.

With his gentle hands on her inner thighs, he spread her legs wider. Her dress was bunched around her waist, the top pushed down, the skirt pushed up. She was bare, exposed.

But she didn't feel at all vulnerable. She wanted this moment with every fiber of her being. Reva looked boldly into Dean's face. He stared down at her with passion and fire and an unexpected fierceness in his eyes. Dean Sinclair was usually so much in control, so steady, that the ferocity of that stare surprised her, and a new shudder worked through her body.

She raked her fingers through his hair, brushed the fingers of one hand across his cheek. How could a man be fierce and tender at the same time? Dean was an extraordinary man, and at the moment, at this very moment, he was hers.

After all these years, after all the fears she'd faced and denied and conquered, she was not afraid of this. Not anymore.

He guided himself to her, and gently, slowly entered her anxious body. Reva closed her eyes and savored the sensation. She wrapped her legs around his and urged him deeper, snaked her arms around his neck and held him tightly. Her bare breasts pressed against his chest, her legs and his were entwined. When their mouths fused together once again, they were joined tightly from mouth to thigh.

Dean's tongue danced with hers as his hips rocked. He

made love to her. And there *was* love, not just sex. There was a gentleness and a beauty here that made this coming together intimate in a way that went beyond the physical. At this moment, in this time, in this room, he loved her. And she loved him.

Each thrust was quicker than the last, deeper, more intense, until Reva was breathless and her body soared toward completion. She climaxed with a cry, the pleasure so intense it took her by surprise. Wave after wave of release rippled through her. Her body shuddered around Dean's, and he drove deeply once, then again. He shuddered just as she did. Their bodies shook together, breathless and sated and sweating.

Dean lifted himself slowly, but did not leave her. He was so beautiful he made her heart lurch. The man above and inside her was hard and muscled, sweating and heavy-lidded. He was everything a man was supposed to be, inside and out.

"I didn't plan for it to be this way," he said.

She flicked her fingers through his hair and smiled. "Neither did I."

"Tell me you're not sorry."

"I'm not sorry."

He kissed her gently. "I never lose control, Reva. Never. But I swear, one kiss from you and I stop thinking straight."

Reva kissed Dean's sweaty neck and laid an easy hand on his side. With that hand she could feel his heartbeat, hard and fast, monitor his breathing, also hard and fast. If she thought she was the only one swept away by this attraction between them, she might be afraid.

But she was not the only one.

"Tell me you're not sorry," she whispered.

Dean laid a hand on her bare breast, twisted his head so he could look her in the eye. He gave her one of those half smiles that drove her wild. "Honey, I am definitely not sorry."

Chapter 11

Dean sat in a dark room watching the quiet street below.

His stomach knotted, his head pounded. He should be at Reva's right now, shouldn't he? It wouldn't be like this afternoon. Cooper would be around to make sure they were on their best behavior. But he should be there, anyway. Dean knew it in his twisted gut.

He had screwed up before, but not like this. This was likely the biggest screwup of his life. Unfixable. Unforgivable. He should've told Reva why he was here before he'd slept with her. Before, not after. But one thing had led to another, and before he knew what was happening, he wanted to be inside her more than he wanted to tell the truth, more than he wanted anything. He hadn't even thought of the lies between them when she'd asked him to kiss her. Now, she'd said. Kiss me now. He had. And a few minutes later she'd been lying beneath him with her hands exploring and her body opened to him and her breath catching in her throat as she waited for him to fill her. Like a man starving for a woman, he'd made love to her.

What was he going to do now? Walk in like nothing had happened and say, "Oh, by the way…"

No. There would be no talking his way out of this one.

When the phone rang, he was glad of the distraction.

"Sinclair."

"You don't sound happy," Alan said.

"I'm not. What have you got?"

"Nothing, really. Pinchon is still on the loose and from everything we've been able to gather, staying in this general area. He's a slippery SOB. How's the vacation, Don Juan?"

The first response that came to mind was horribly obscene. Dean decided to keep it to himself. "Fine."

Alan laughed. "That was the most disgusted-sounding 'fine' I've ever heard in my life."

"Well, there you go," Dean said.

"Has Reva said anything to you about her ex-boyfriend breaking out of prison?"

Dean's heart got heavy. His gut suffered another ugly twist. "Not a word." And that was the stickler, wasn't it? Reva should be scared. At the very least, she should be *concerned*. For Cooper's sake, if not her own. She wasn't worried. She didn't even lock her doors most of the time.

Tomorrow night he would confront her with everything, and he'd tell her the truth. The whole ugly truth. She was making him dinner. Cooper would be spending the night with Tewanda. Reva had told him all about the plans for Saturday night while they'd sat on the monstrous piece of furniture she called a fainting couch and straightened their clothes.

Reva expected a romantic evening, and he wanted to give her that more than anything.

Instead, there were going to be fireworks.

* * *

"Well, well," Tewanda said. "A real day off?"

"You don't need me," Reva answered. "And if you do, I'm close by."

"The last time you took a day off, Cooper had a fever of 102."

"I know," Reva said.

The two of them stood in the foyer of Miss Reva's. Edna, Nicole and Judith were already busy in the kitchen.

"Does this day off have anything to do with your date that's not a date?"

Reva smiled. Was Tewanda able to see the change in her? Did she glow outside, as well as in? Her relationship with Dean was temporary, she knew that. It was impulsive and unwise. But it was also extraordinary. "It's a date. What on earth am I going to wear?"

"Something sexy," Tewanda suggested.

"I don't own anything sexy," Reva said with a short laugh.

Tewanda didn't argue with her. "I can loan you my red silk dress. You'll have to scrape his tongue off the floor."

Reva shook her head. "Thanks, but no thanks. That red dress looks great on you, but it's not my style."

"You could always meet him at the door naked."

"I don't think so!"

Tewanda's smile softened. "I don't think it matters what you wear. Studly is crazy about you."

Reva's heart did a quick flip in her chest. She didn't want Dean to be crazy about her. They had a strictly physical relationship, and it had to stay that way.

"What are you cooking?"

Reva gladly told Tewanda about her menu for the evening. No grilled cheese sandwiches, no tomato soup. She wanted to knock Dean's socks off when they sat down to dinner.

She wanted to knock his socks off after dinner, too.

"Way to go, sweetie," Tewanda said. "If the way to a man's heart is through his stomach, studly won't have a chance."

It wasn't Dean's heart she was interested in. There was no room in her life for any man's heart. "The menu is fine," Reva said. "I'm not worried about the food. But what am I going to *wear?*"

Dean threw a baseball high in the air. It took a gentle arc toward Cooper, who ran back and forth in the yard beyond the cottage. The kid zigged and zagged.

"Keep your eye on the ball," Dean shouted.

Cooper finally planted his feet and set his glove. The ball landed in the grass about three feet behind him. The kid picked up the baseball and threw it to Dean so they could try again. His aim was off and the ball went about six feet to Dean's right.

And so the afternoon had gone.

"How about we take a break?" Dean asked as he retrieved the ball.

"I'm not tired," Cooper said as he ran forward. "I need to practice."

"Just a break, kid. We'll get back to work after we have something to drink."

"I want lemonade," Cooper said as they walked toward the house.

"I could use a cup of coffee."

Cooper climbed the cottage steps and stopped, turning to look Dean squarely in the eye. Blond hair had been mussed by the afternoon's activities, and his cheeks were pink from exertion. Cooper's expression was serious as he said, "Caffeine is a drug."

"Oh, it is?"

"That's what Sheriff Andrews said when he came to school to talk about drugs. Are you 'dicted?"

"Addicted," Dean said, correcting the child almost automatically. "Probably."

"My mama won't let me have caffeine," Cooper said in that bright voice of his.

"Your mama's a smart woman," Dean replied, horrified by the very thought of Cooper on caffeine.

"I know. She won't let me have candy, either. Except sometimes a little bit on a special occasion, like Halloween. But I can't have too much candy because Mama says it make me riper."

"I'm thinking you mean hyper."

"Yeah, that's it." Cooper spun around and ran to the front door, throwing the door open with more energy than anyone should have after an hour of chasing a baseball. Even a six-year-old. "Mom!" he shouted. "Can Mr. Dean come in?"

Dean stepped onto the porch just in time to hear Reva say, "No!" in a surprised voice.

"But he needs coffee," Cooper said as he walked into the living room, leaving the door open. "He's 'dicted."

From another part of the house, the kitchen perhaps, Reva laughed. "I'll make Mr. Dean some coffee."

"And I want lemonade," Cooper added.

Dean sat in one of the rockers on the front porch, took a deep breath and enjoyed the quiet. Cooper was a great kid, but he could be absolutely exhausting.

And why wouldn't Reva let him into the house?

One part of him, the same misbehaving part that had gotten him into trouble yesterday, imagined that Reva didn't want him in the house because she was preparing all sorts of surprises for their date. A more deeply ingrained and naturally suspicious part of him wondered what she was hiding.

She was definitely hiding something. The question was, how much? Was she still involved with Eddie Pinchon in any way? He couldn't see any deception when he looked at Reva, but he was blinded where she was concerned.

In a few minutes Cooper came bouncing onto the front porch. Reva walked right behind him, carrying a large white coffee cup. "Here you go," she said with a gentle smile.

"Thanks." He took the hot mug and studied the woman who had carried it to him. Slowly. Her hair was pulled up and away from her face. Her snugly fitting T-shirt was royal-blue and dusted with flour. The cutoffs she wore revealed those legs he admired.

"No problem." She stared at him for a moment, her smile grew a little bit wider, and then she sashayed back into the house and to whatever secrets she kept there.

Cooper leaned back in the rocking chair that matched Dean's and took a deep drink of lemonade. "Next year instead of T-ball, we play coach pitch. If you're still around, maybe you can help me learn how to bat."

"I won't be around next year," Dean said. He wouldn't lie to the kid and tell him otherwise, not even for a few days.

"Oh. Maybe Coach Charles will be our coach again and he can help me. Some of the dads usually help the coach, even though most of the time he doesn't want help. But next year he'll want help for sure because we all have to learn how to bat." He took another long drink of lemonade and then said, "My dad is dead. He died before I was born."

The statement came out of nowhere. Dean took a sip of hot coffee while he tried to decide what to say. So Reva had told the kid his father was dead. Not the work of a woman who planned to take up with the bastard again. "I'm sorry to hear that."

"Me, too. Sometimes I think I should try to find another one, you know, a stepfather like Jimmy Lee got last year when his mama got married. But Mama says we don't need a dad."

Dean didn't know what to say. He finally decided on a safe "You have a great mother."

Cooper laid wide blue eyes on Dean and gave him his full attention. "Do you really think she's *great?*"

"Sure I do." Dean drained his coffee and set the cup on the porch beside the rocking chair. Before Cooper could say more, before the kid could suggest the possibility that Dean might become his new dad, Dean grabbed up the baseball and headed for the yard.

"Come on, we don't have all day. Before I'm done with you, you'll be the best T-ball center fielder in the state of Tennessee."

Cooper drained his lemonade and followed Dean, skipping past him and tossing his glove into the air.

Reva vacillated between being excited about the evening to come and being absolutely terrified. While the Cornish hens were in the oven, she went through her closet almost frantically, hoping to find something she'd forgotten she owned. Something sexy, something eye-popping. She wanted to open the door when Dean arrived and have him take one look at her and say, "Wow." What would make Dean Sinclair go "Wow?" Maybe she should have borrowed Tewanda's red silk dress.

There had been a time when everything she'd owned

had been too tight, too short and low-cut. Eddie had insisted. That had been Eddie's idea of sexy. And her mother's, too, Reva admitted, which was why she'd bought into the concept for as long as she had. And the concept was, *If you've got it, flaunt it.*

Her hand stopped, midsearch. What on earth was she doing? Dean liked her just the way she was. She didn't have to dress up like someone else to impress him. An unexpected calm settled over her. Yes, she wanted to look nice tonight. That didn't mean she had to pretend to be someone she wasn't. Those days were behind her.

She finally settled on a simple black sheath. Shoes that had a little heel, but not too much. Pearls—fake, but elegant. Pearl studs, also fake, for her ears. She wouldn't dress until she was finished in the kitchen, but she wanted everything laid out so she wouldn't be running around the house at the last minute searching for something she'd forgotten.

Through the window, she saw Dean toss another ball high in the air. Cooper ran one way, then another, then back. Finally he stopped, positioned himself and caught the ball in his glove. It wasn't the first he'd caught this afternoon; he now caught more than he missed.

The latest catch was followed by her son's happy dance of triumph, which made Dean laugh. She couldn't hear the laugh, but she could see his face clearly enough. Why did she have a feeling Dean Sinclair didn't laugh this way very often?

If she could afford the luxury, she'd try to convince Dean to stay here in Somerset. If she ever took a man into her life again, it would have to be someone like him. Dean was so solid and real, and he was wonderful with Cooper. The way he made her feel when he looked at her, when he touched her, that was nice. But it wasn't everything. Sex wasn't everything.

But it was all she could have. If Dean hadn't promised her that he wouldn't stay, tonight could never happen.

It was almost dark as Dean walked across the yard toward Reva's front door. He had showered, shaved and dressed in khakis and a golf shirt, the only casual outfit he'd packed when he'd come to Somerset. He felt like there were a hundred eyes on him—and he was probably right. Miss Evelyn had seemed much too interested in his date, going so far as to hand him a bouquet of yellow roses from her own garden as he left the house. The flowers were wrapped in tissue paper, and there were no thorns. His landlady had removed them all.

As he'd walked from the house, he'd heard her say something about the brass ring again.

Dean's step slowed. There would be no brass ring for him, not tonight, not ever. Before things went any further, he had to tell Reva why he had come to Somerset in the first place. Maybe when he told her that he was no longer here on official business but of his own volition, maybe she wouldn't kill him. Maybe.

He would not apologize for doing his job. His decisions hadn't been flawless since coming to Somerset, but that didn't change the fact that in the end he was right. Eddie had to be found and stopped, and if that meant surveilling his acquaintances, old and new, then there was nothing to be done for it.

Maybe she'd understand.

Fat chance.

Dean climbed the steps and knocked on the front door. How best to start? *There's something I have to tell you. Something I should have told you days ago. I'm not just a cop. I'm a federal agent and I came here to watch you. By the way, do you know where Eddie Pinchon is hiding out?*

Yeah, she was going to kill him.

She opened the door and his mind went blank. "Wow." It was all he could manage.

Reva smiled and her dark eyes positively twinkled. "You're right on time."

Dean stepped inside, handing her the roses and checking her out without shame. From head to toe, she was perfect. Hair silky, dress simple and showing off her shape, just a little bit of leg revealed. Perfect.

And he was going to ruin the evening before it got started.

"Reva," he began. "I really have to—"

He didn't get far. She held the roses to the side, leaned in and up, and kissed him. It was a gentle, sweet, welcoming kiss and it stopped him cold.

"I'll put these in water," she said as she walked away. He followed. "Dinner's almost ready."

"Smells good," he said gruffly.

He peered through the kitchen door to the dining room. The dark, antique furniture in that room suited the cottage, but the elegant table and chairs were rarely used. It was the kitchen where Reva and Cooper took their meals; Reva had told him that a few days ago when he'd been fixing the drip in the kitchen sink.

Tonight she had gone all out. The dining room was decorated with a dozen candles and an assortment of flowers from her garden. Two places were set with china, silver and crystal. She had managed to make the room cozy and elegantly romantic at the same time. A couple of dishes had already been placed on the table, and a very fancy chocolate cake had been placed atop the buffet.

He couldn't tell her now, not when she'd gone to so much trouble.

After dinner.

Chapter 12

Reva took Dean's hand and led him from the dining room, shaking her head when he offered to help her clear the dishes from the table and clean up the mess she'd made in the kitchen. That could wait.

Dean had eaten well enough. He'd claimed to love the oysters Rockefeller and the Cornish hens with cherry sauce, the steamed asparagus and the homemade rolls. But he'd seemed distracted all through dinner. Perhaps he was thinking ahead, as she was. She wanted it all. The dinner, the conversation, the kissing. This had to be a night that would provide her with memories to last a lifetime.

"We'll have cake and coffee later," she said as they walked into the main room. Should she put on the Norah Jones CD? Or take her chances with the quiet?

No music, Reva decided. She didn't want anything to distract her. She sat on the sofa and tugged on Dean's hand to invite him to sit beside her. He sat, much too reluctantly.

"Everything was really great," he said. No smile. No twinkle in his eye.

"Thank you." She brushed his hair with her fingertips. Maybe he was just nervous. She was, though she tried to hide it. She was nervous about what was to come. But she was also excited, especially when she remembered yesterday afternoon. She'd forgotten passion, she'd buried it so deeply. Dean awakened a part of herself she'd left sleeping for too long. Only Dean.

"Reva, there's something I have to tell you."

She didn't like the way he said those simple words. The tone told of unwanted information to come. So did the indecision in his blue eyes and the set of his mouth. He should be kissing her already, not delivering bad news. And he did look like a man who was about to deliver bad news.

He didn't want her and wasn't sure how to tell her. That thought gave Reva a chill. She'd been so sure that he felt the same way she did, that even if they didn't have anything else, they had passion. His *and* hers.

"When I came here—"

Reva very quickly leaned up and in and pressed her mouth to Dean's, surprising him, silencing him, kissing him. It was the only way to know how he felt. Words wouldn't tell her how he felt, but his reaction to her kiss would. After a very brief moment one arm circled her, and Dean began to kiss her back. Yes, he wanted her. He craved her; she tasted that craving in his kiss. But he did, eventually, draw his mouth from hers and back away.

"Listen—"

"No." She placed a hand on his cheek, staring at his mouth, not his eyes. It was safer that way. His mouth looked well kissed and promised more. "No secrets, Dean, no confessions. You don't tell me yours, and I won't tell you mine.''

"But—"

"Have you changed your mind? Are you going to stay in Somerset?"

"No."

"Of course you're not," she whispered. "You're not cut out for a place like this. It might make for a nice break from your reality, but living in a small town would eventually drive you crazy. Tonight isn't the start of a relationship that requires full disclosure. It's just about tonight.''

"I don't want to hurt you."

"You won't," she said. "You can't." No one had the power to hurt her anymore. She didn't allow anyone that opportunity.

Her hand swept down to his neck and lingered there. She held on, keeping him close, brushing her fingers against his skin. "Make me feel like a woman, Dean," she whispered. "That's all I'm asking for. I haven't felt this way in so long...and I need it. I need you. Don't ruin tonight with some long-drawn-out confession about why you can't stay or why we're not right for each other. I know this isn't permanent, and I know you're not looking for anything more than a vacation fling. If you were, you wouldn't be here. I wouldn't be here. I don't have that much to give. But I do have tonight and maybe tomorrow and maybe the day after that. Make this a night I won't ever forget. Don't ruin it with—''

This time he silenced her with a kiss. His tongue parted her lips, and the gentle, relentless throb began at the center of her body. The awkward conversation was over, thank goodness, and there was just this...this touch she had been thinking of and craving all day. Dean's body hovered over hers, and he held her close. Close, but not too tightly. She fit against him perfectly, curve for curve, hill to valley. He was so large and she felt so small against him. How was it possible that they fit together, like two pieces of a puzzle?

For a little while, she was sure she could kiss Dean all night. She floated, her head spun, her mouth devoured, as his did. He touched her, raking the palm of his hand over her breasts, caressing her thigh, and soon the kiss was not enough. She knew what she wanted and so did Dean.

He stood slowly, took her hand and assisted her to her feet. "No couches this time," he said.

The idea of taking Dean into her bed made her shiver. She'd been thinking about it all day. Dean naked beneath the sheets. Her sheets. Her body against his from head to toe. She led him to the hallway, her hand still in his, and walked toward her bedroom. They didn't run, they didn't hurry. They had all night, and no matter how anxious she was to lie beneath Dean, there was no need to rush.

Before they'd gone far, he began to unzip her dress. He moved slowly, the zipper descending an inch or so with each step they took. Again Reva shivered.

She didn't turn on the overhead fixture in her bedroom, but the lamp in the hallway shed enough light into the room to gently illuminate her elaborately fashioned iron-post bed and, as she turned, Dean. Like everything else tonight, the light was perfect. She deserved a few perfect nights, and she'd had so few.

Her back to Dean, she drew down the quilt she slept beneath every night to expose plain white sheets.

When she turned to face Dean again, he slipped her unzipped dress over her shoulders and down. It fell to the floor and she kicked it away. She stood before him in black panties and bra and her high-heeled shoes. He took a moment to study her thoroughly, and finally he smiled.

"You have turned my world upside down, Reva Macklin."

"Is that a good thing?" she whispered.

"I haven't decided yet." He took her in his arms and kissed her again, as if he was hungry for her after being away for a long time. She knew how he felt. How could she need him so much when she'd lived without him all her life?

He unfastened the bra and gently removed it. It dropped to the floor to land silently beside her dress. Dean lowered her to the bed, moving slowly, deliberately, hovering above her as he moved his mouth to her breasts to lick and suckle and arouse.

Reva closed her eyes and allowed herself to simply feel. Dean's warm mouth, the cool sheet at her back, Dean's hands, his body above hers. It all worked together, like a well-choreographed dance. Every shift of his mouth, every flicker of his tongue, made the relentless beat in her gut increase. Thrum. Thrum. *Thrum.*

Dean was still completely dressed, and if he touched her, she was going to come.

She began to tug gently on his shirt, silently telling him to take it off. He did, sitting up and yanking the shirt off and tossing it aside, then removing her shoes and hooking one finger through the waistband of her panties. Those he removed slowly, an inch at a time, kissing her as the last of her clothing shifted down. He kissed her mouth, her breasts, her stomach, as he inched the underwear down with attentive fingers.

When the underwear was finally tossed aside, Dean ran his hands up the inside of her legs, parting them tenderly. Reva's heart thundered, and the thrum at her core grew more insistent.

Dean kissed her inner thigh, and Reva closed her eyes

and sighed. Everything he did to her aroused her more, every touch was gentle and yet powerful. She wanted it to end, and yet she didn't. If she could grab on to this feeling and keep it all night, she would. He kept her on the brink, shivering with anticipation. Ripples of pleasure fluttered through her body from head to toe.

When he brought his mouth to her most intimate place, she arched in surprise, then moaned in pleasure. The little sound escaped from deep in her throat, and she could not stop it. His tongue flickered and she shattered, grasping the sheet in her hands and crying out hoarsely as he continued to make love to her with his tongue.

Sated and drained, she could barely breathe. Her knees shook. Her heart pounded so hard she was sure Dean could hear it.

He crept up slowly, strangely graceful for such a large man.

"You're not even undressed," she said with a lazy smile. She reached for his belt buckle. "Yet."

Dean grabbed a condom from his wallet as Reva finished undressing him. With her hands on his body, her mouth kissing his, it had been easy to allow himself to believe that nothing else mattered beyond what was happening right now.

She was so beautiful—warm skin on white sheets, silky hair spread across the bed, smile sexy and shy. Yes, shy, even now.

Her hands were not shy. She touched him, exploring with curious, arousing fingers. She wasn't satisfied until he was as naked as she was, until there was nothing between them. Flesh on flesh, heartbeats racing, outside world forgotten for the night.

His cell phone, a few feet away with his pants, began to ring.

"Don't answer it," Reva whispered, as if the person on the other end of the phone might hear.

"Don't worry."

He kissed her, and she answered with passion. No more shyness as her tongue danced with his, as her hand rested on his hip. After a few rings, the phone went silent.

Reva playfully snatched the condom from his hand and opened the foil package. When she removed the condom itself from the package, she pursed her lips and lifted the thing to catch the light. "I think there's something wrong with this."

Dean groaned. "It's blue." He'd grabbed a couple of condoms from the box Clint had delivered to Somerset, not paying any attention at all to details. His mind had been elsewhere at the time. He hadn't been at all certain he'd need one. There was another condom in his wallet. It probably glowed in the dark. "But it'll have to do." He'd waited as long as he could.

Reva smiled as she helped him sheath himself, her hands driving him beyond the point of no return. He needed to be inside her this time, to make her scream again, to feel her contract around him. She wanted to feel like a woman, she wanted a night to remember. He was damn well going to do his best to give that night to her.

Reva's smile faded as he caressed her. Her eyes closed and she sighed. When he guided himself to her, she lifted her hips and urged him deeper, faster. Her legs wrapped around his hips, and she arched up and into him. Tight and hot, she took him in.

They found a rhythm, their own rhythm, and danced on the edge of perfection. They danced gently until their bodies took over and demanded more. They mated, mindless and fierce, until together they reached the end. Reva cried out beneath him, held on tight while her body quivered and her inner muscles milked him. He went over the edge with her, lost in the pleasure of release.

She continued to hold him as their heartbeats and breathing slowed. Drained and boneless, they clung to one another.

Reva moved first, raking her fingertips through his hair.

"You're blue," she whispered, a smile in her voice.

Dean lifted his head and looked at the woman beneath him, the woman he remained joined to. And he wished with all his heart that things were different. If she didn't have a past with Eddie Pinchon, if he hadn't promised her he wouldn't stay, if he hadn't lied by not telling her why he was here, everything would be different. A week ago he'd have sworn to anyone who'd listen that he didn't want a woman in his life. He'd tried a couple of times, and it hadn't worked. There had never been a woman as important as the job. Besides, he'd been tied down much of his life by the brothers and sister he'd practically raised, and to be shackled forever…well, it wasn't for him.

So why did Reva make him wish for the brass ring?

"You have to go," Reva whispered reluctantly. Dean was stretched out beside her, quiet and very much at home in her bed.

"Why?"

"Because people are watching. Miss Evelyn is surely waiting for your return like an overprotective mother. You've been here long enough for dinner, maybe a movie on television and a little smooching."

"Just a little?" he rolled toward her, kissed her, cupped her breast in one hand and teased the nipple with his thumb.

Reva shuddered. How could she possibly want him again? "Just a little," she murmured.

"I don't want to go," he said, and he proved it to her with another kiss and those wandering hands.

"You can come back," she said. "I'll open Cooper's window for you. You're a cop. You should be good at sneaking around after dark."

Dean went still. His hands, his mouth, even his breathing. For a moment it all stopped. "I'm not actually a cop, not in the sense you mean," he said in a low voice.

"You said…"

"I said I was in law enforcement. I'm a deputy U.S. marshal."

"Oh." She had no idea what that meant. "So what do you do exactly?"

"I'm currently in the fugitive-apprehension unit. The U.S. Marshals Service also handles federal court security and the witness-protection program, among other things."

"Fugitive apprehension. You chase bad guys?"

"That's one way to put it."

She smiled and touched his face. For some reason she loved to touch Dean's face. Hard here, soft there, masculine everywhere. "I bet you're very good at what you do."

"Usually," he said. He watched her face as if searching for…something.

"I can see where it might be very stressful and you would need a vacation now and then."

"Until I came here, I hadn't taken a real vacation in years."

"Well, then, we'll just have to make sure it's a memorable one."

"Already there."

She smiled and rose lazily. Oh, she didn't want to let

him go, not even for a little while. "Come on. Up and at 'em."

He raised his eyebrows and she laughed. When had she ever laughed like this? Never. Not with a man, anyway. "Once everyone sees you go home, they'll settle into their own little beds for the night, satisfied that all is well in their little town."

"And I can sneak back through Cooper's window."

"Yeah." She could handle the gossip if it was only her. She'd been through worse! But she wasn't going to let Cooper's life be tainted by a mother who did not behave properly. She wouldn't give her neighbors anything to talk about.

"You go home and have a nice short chat with your landlady, and I'll call Tewanda and tell her what a sweet and well-behaved date you were, and then you can sneak into the house and we'll have the rest of the night."

Dean did not look convinced. "I am thirty-five years old and I have never crawled through *any* window to get laid."

"You don't have to come back if you don't want to," she said, knowing without a doubt that he would return to her tonight. "I'll just…read the paper." She reached over and snagged the newspaper from her bedside table. She'd started to read it a couple of times, but had never gotten far. It had been a busy week.

Dean looked at the paper in her hand. "What is that?"

"The *Somerset Sentinel*," she said. "Delivered to my door every Thursday afternoon." She showed him the front page, where the huge headline screamed, Two Nabbed For Illegal Deer Hunting.

"Don't you get a Nashville or a Knoxville paper?"

"No."

He was silent for a moment. "Where do you get your news? CNN? One of the other cable news channels?"

She shook her head. "Nope. It's too much for Cooper to handle, all those channels. I have an antenna on the house, so I can pick up one of the Cross City stations."

"What about...news?"

"This is a very strange conversation to be carrying on naked," she said with a smile.

"I'm curious."

How much of herself should she give to Dean? Her body? No problem. Her heart? No way. Her trust?

Maybe.

"Sometimes people come to a small town to hide," she said softly. "To escape from the world you see on the news. The truth is, I don't want to know what's going on in the world. The news is depressing. If anything of consequence happens, I'll find out sooner or later."

"You're hiding," he whispered.

"Yeah."

"From what?"

She laid her hand on his chest and sighed. "Tonight is not a night for sharing secrets, remember?"

"What about tomorrow?"

"There is no tomorrow." She leaned in and kissed him, sweetly at first, then with lips parted and tongues dueling. When she took her mouth from his, she reminded him, "There's only tonight."

Chapter 13

Dean said good-night at the door, mindful of the fact that there were probably dozens of eyes on him and Reva at the moment. They were both fully dressed and illuminated by the porch light for the prying eyes that watched from windows all around the neighborhood.

Reva offered her hand as if for a good-night handshake. Dean took the hand, pulled her to him and kissed her thoroughly. It wasn't a quick kiss, and it definitely didn't qualify as friendly. It was a kiss that made him want to walk right back inside the house and take up where they'd left off.

When he released her, he grinned and said, "I have a reputation to uphold."

"You have no reputation at all here in Somerset."

"I do now."

He turned and walked away, resisting the urge to run. The sooner he got this charade over with, the sooner he'd be back in Reva's bed.

As he crossed the street, he took his cell phone from his pocket and checked for messages. Alan, who had terrible timing, had left a terse "Call me" on Dean's voice mail.

Dean dialed Alan's number as he stepped onto the sidewalk. "What's up?" he asked when his partner answered with a surly "Penner."

"We know why Pinchon came back to his old stomping grounds after he escaped," Alan said. "Rumor is there's money from a deal that went down right before he was arrested. Lots of it. A quarter of a million dollars, we hear, and it's missing. Pinchon's looking for it. If the rumor is true, that's why he's here visiting with all his old pals, instead of taking off for parts unknown."

"Then he should be easy to find." Dean stopped in the front yard. The air smelled of spring, the crickets sang their own tune, and a breeze wafted gently through ancient tree limbs. There was peace here. The kind of deep-down, real peace he had never known. Was it the place? Or was it Reva?

"We'll get him sooner or later," Alan said.

"It's already later." Dean leaned against the trunk of an old oak. He wouldn't rest easy until Pinchon was behind bars again where he belonged. "Reva doesn't even know Pinchon's out of prison."

"I'm sure she'd like you to believe that," Alan responded.

"She doesn't read a decent newspaper, and she doesn't have cable TV. She's isolated herself here."

Alan was silent for a moment. "Let's say you're right and Reva Macklin has no idea Pinchon escaped. If you tell her he's out, I'll bet you dollars to doughnuts she'll run and hide."

"Yeah. I think she's terrified of him."

Alan sighed, obviously disgusted. "That's not what I

meant. If there is money missing, maybe she has it. Where did she get the cash to open a restaurant, anyway?''

"No," Dean said. "That's not possible. I told her tonight that I'm a deputy marshal, and she didn't even blink."

"Did you tell her why you're there?"

Dean's heart sank. "No."

"Trust me, that news will get more than a blink out of her."

He knew Alan was right. Still… "She doesn't have the money, and she's not waiting for Eddie to show up and take up where he left off."

There was a moment of silence before Alan asked softly, "Are you sleeping with her?"

"Not at the moment."

Alan spat out a few curses that would have Boone blushing, then took a deep breath. "Okay, I'll be there tomorrow afternoon. You're getting out of town."

"No."

"I'm not going to sit back and watch you throw your career away over a woman!"

"I'm not throwing anything away."

"You're walking a very fine line, Dean."

That was the truth. "I assume someone is already checking into Reva's finances to see if they can come up with money she shouldn't have."

"Yep. It'll take a couple of days, though. Be careful," he added in a calmer voice. "I don't want to have to break in another partner."

"I'll be careful." Dean ended the call, then turned off the cell phone. If Alan tried to call again, he could leave a message.

Careful. Dean Sinclair was nothing if not careful.

Loving Reva was the least-cautious thing he'd ever done.

Reva sat on Cooper's bed, wearing a rose-colored robe and nothing else. She'd opened the window a few minutes ago. A gentle spring breeze washed over her as she waited for Dean to return.

Like it or not, she was changed yet again. She wasn't the same woman she'd been before Dean Sinclair came to town. Something inside her, the woman she had buried, was breaking free. At this very moment emotions she'd denied herself for a very long time were growing. She could almost feel them, warm and tingling and fragile.

And foolish. Dean wasn't just a cop, he was some kind of federal marshal. She should be terrified that he might find out about her past.

But she wasn't. They had no future, no past. They only had *now*.

An unpleasant thought made her heart lurch. What if Dean didn't come back? He certainly didn't have to, and he hadn't actually said he would. Maybe he was finished with her and didn't feel the need to return.

She should be divinely satisfied and sleeping the dream-less sleep of the well loved. Why did she need and want more so desperately that the very thought of Dean made her body respond in ways she'd forgotten were possible?

Why was she so afraid he wouldn't come back?

The last thing she wanted or needed was an emotional attachment to Dean Sinclair. She sighed as she kept her eyes on the open window and the night beyond. It was too late for that worry. If she had been the kind of woman who could give her body and not her heart, she would have found a man to warm her bed years ago. But that's not who she was. When she gave of herself, she gave everything. Heart, body and soul. Dean could never know this. If he knew, he'd either run from her in terror, or he'd think they might have something beyond this affair.

The first response would break her heart; the second was impossible. Dean wouldn't ever get serious about a woman who had once been involved with a man like Eddie Pinchon.

She tried to write off her old love for Eddie as a foolish mistake of youth, but she knew it was more than that. She'd never known her father, her mother had always been too busy for her, and her stepfather had tolerated her. She had been pretty enough to have men make passes at her all the time, but desire wasn't the same as love.

Eddie had made her believe he loved her, and she had been so starved for that emotion she'd convinced herself she loved him back. For almost two years she'd enjoyed the life she'd always wanted, ignoring the signs that something was not quite right. When she could no longer ignore the signs, it was too late. Eddie owned her; he wouldn't let her go.

That wasn't love.

She wasn't gullible anymore, she wasn't a child. But she was vulnerable and always would be.

Sitting on Cooper's bed with the spring breeze washing over her, Reva finally decided that Dean wasn't coming back. That realization shouldn't hurt so much, but it did. It settled in her gut like a brick, heavy and cold. He'd used her and walked away. He'd taken what he wanted and lied to her. She was a foolish and gullible woman, sitting here in the dark waiting for a man to come to her, to make her believe she could become someone she was not, that she could have, just for a while…

A hand appeared on the windowsill, and a moment later Dean vaulted himself up and into the room. He didn't wear khakis this time, but jeans and a dark T-shirt that would blend with the night.

"I thought Miss Evelyn would never let me go to bed," he said as he turned to her. Maybe in the dark he couldn't see that there were tears in her eyes. "She wanted to know everything."

"I hope you didn't tell her everything," Reva said as she stood.

"Nope. I talked about the food a lot," he said. "And if anyone asks, we played cards. I didn't know what was on television tonight, so I didn't want to go there."

"I'll remember that."

He wrapped his arms around her easily, as if they'd stood just this way a thousand times. When he kissed her, she fell into him, grateful and angry with herself for feeling that way.

"What's that in your pocket?" she asked as he took his mouth from hers.

"An embarrassment of choices," Dean said as he lifted her off her feet and carried her into the hallway. "Condoms in every color you can think of, some that glow in the dark and a few with doodads."

"Doodads?"

"Don't ask."

Standing before her rumpled bed, he very gently eased her down. With large hands that were much more tanned than they'd been when he'd arrived in Somerset, Dean untied the sash at her waist and opened the robe.

A few minutes ago she'd been afraid that Dean wasn't coming back. How could she have doubted him? He wanted her, and he was honest and open. Even if she couldn't admit that she loved him, she could certainly admit that she cared for him in a way she'd never cared for another man.

He undressed himself, joined her on the bed and took her in his arms.

She almost told him that she'd been afraid he wouldn't return, that moments before he'd come through the window she'd been certain he wasn't coming back. But what she'd asked of him didn't require that kind of confession.

Dean found himself kicked out again about four in the morning. Reva seemed to think that a safe time for him to make his covert trek across the street.

He hadn't had much sleep. Maybe an hour here and a half hour there. He was exhausted. Drained. So tired he could hardly stay on his feet.

And if Reva hadn't chased him out, he'd be awake still, making the best of this night.

He let himself into the Fister house, making sure the door didn't creak as it closed. A light from the kitchen burned softly. Was the old lady already awake? Or had she left the light on all night? Frugal as she was, he couldn't imagine her leaving the light on.

So he was extra careful as he climbed the stairs. Reva didn't want anyone to know he'd spent the night at her house, and he couldn't blame her. He'd soon leave the gossip behind, but Reva had to live here.

He made it all the way to the top of the first flight of stairs before a bright voice called, "Good morning! My, you're up and about awfully early."

Dean turned slowly. Damned if the woman wasn't every bit as quiet as he was! "Couldn't sleep. I thought maybe I'd take an early-morning run."

"I suppose a young man of your ilk must work to keep up your figure."

Dean couldn't be sure if she was insulting him or not. He trudged to the bottom of the stairs. Crap. All he wanted was a few hours of sleep. Was that too much to ask? Apparently so.

"When you get back, I'll make you something to eat."

"You know," Dean said as he reached the door, "maybe I'll skip the run and just have a cup of coffee, instead."

"Nonsense." Miss Evelyn gave him a gentle shove that sent him on out the door. "You get your run in, and I'll make you something to eat. It'll be ready in about half an hour. Is that too soon?"

"No, ma'am," Dean said as he began to jog toward the sidewalk.

An early-morning jog. Just what he didn't need. Why was he going to such ridiculous lengths for Reva's reputation? If she was a married woman and their affair was illicit, he might understand. But neither of them were obligated to another in any way. They were both adults. It shouldn't matter. But for some reason Reva wanted to maintain a spotless reputation. The least he could do was run a little bit to help maintain that reputation.

He didn't go far before he noticed, thanks to the street lamp, that one of the windows at Miss Reva's was open. The screen had been propped against the side of the house, and the window itself was thrown at least halfway open.

Dean jogged in that direction, no longer half-asleep but wide-eyed and on alert. Maybe someone had accidentally left the window open, but given the last break-in, he couldn't buy that.

He eased himself up and through the window. The opening took him into a downstairs parlor where a dozen of Miss Reva's guests ate lunch six days a week. Nothing was out of place that he could see, there was no apparent damage, and as far as he could tell nothing was missing.

Dean took a quick and silent walk through the rooms.

All was quiet. Not a squeak or a creak in the old house warned him of an intruder. There were a few papers spread across one of the tables, and in Reva's office a small stack of papers had fallen to the floor. For all he knew, someone who worked here had left it that way.

He made his way to the third floor, every step cautious and silent. Each room was searched quickly, but as far as he could see nothing had been disturbed. He finally ended up in the room where he and Reva had first made love. On the fainting couch. Dean stood in the doorway, wondering what on earth had happened to him. Sex was one thing. Complete surrender was another.

A few minutes later he left by way of the window, making sure it was closed securely this time.

She should be sleepwalking through her Sunday morning, but Reva felt strangely rejuvenated, even though she hadn't gotten much sleep last night. She'd been up early to make her picnic lunch for the raffle. Cooper had come home in time to get himself cleaned up and dressed for church, and they'd arrived just in time to take their places in the back pew.

Louella Vine, owner and operator of the bakery in the downtown area, turned once to glare at Reva. Reva smiled. Louella turned up her nose and snapped her head around, chin high.

Reva had never understood why Louella hated her, but the woman's feelings were obvious. They were competitors in a sense, but their restaurants were so very different. Reva could not imagine why the woman felt threatened. It was time for the services to start when someone stepped into the aisle and past the woman at the end of the pew. Reva glanced up and almost choked on her own tongue when she saw Dean, dressed in his dark-gray suit, blue shirt and striped tie, crossing in front of her and then sitting down at her right.

Cooper, who sat at her left, grinned and waved, and Dean smiled back.

Reva glared at the man beside her. "You can't be here." Her words were so soft no one could possibly hear her. Not even Dean. He read her lips.

"Why not?"

Dinner was one thing. Going to church with her was another matter entirely. People really would talk!

"If I snore, just nudge me with your elbow."

Reva glared at Dean. "Why are you here?"

He grinned. "I understand there's a bake sale and picnic raffle after church."

She shook her head, just as the congregation rose to their feet to sing the first hymn. "Go home."

Discordant but enthusiastic voices rose in song. Dean shrugged and mouthed at her, "Too late."

He should be in bed sleeping. Dean strolled before the table laden with baked goods and perused the selections. Cakes, cookies, brownies. They all looked good. The selections were already thin. Churchgoers had bombarded the table as soon as services let out, quickly choosing the best of the baked goods.

If Miss Evelyn hadn't mentioned the picnic to him when he'd been ready to head to bed, he'd be asleep right now. But the idea of spending the morning with Reva was too tempting to resist. He wanted to see if she still glowed. She did. He wanted to know if he ruffled her feathers at all. He did.

If he was smart, he'd call Alan in to relieve him and get the hell out of town. Nothing could come of his relationship with Reva. As soon as she found out why he'd come to Somerset, she'd despise him. Game over.

Dean was usually smart, but apparently not today.

He came to a huge platter of sugar cookies. He recognized that platter with its pattern of roses. Miss Evelyn had carried it out of the front door this morning. He cast a glance to the end of the table where a gaggle of older ladies stood. Miss Evelyn's eyes cut to the untouched platter of cookies. Was that a touch of panic he saw in her eyes?

Dean lifted his head to the young woman who stood behind the long table of goodies. "How much for the sugar cookies?" He pointed to Miss Evelyn's platter.

"How many?"

"All of them."

She cast a surprised smile his way and began to bag the cookies. He took his wallet from his back pocket and flipped it open to withdraw the correct number of bills and hand them over.

Brown paper bag heavy with cookies in hand, he took off in search of Reva and Cooper.

A small playground had been erected on the church property. There wasn't much to choose from in the way of equipment. A swing, a slide, one of those horses that rocked back and forth on a sturdy spring. He wasn't surprised to find Cooper and Reva there; Cooper was playing with his friends while his mother watched.

"Cookie?" he asked, startling her.

Reva snapped her head around and positively glared at him. "What are you doing here?" she asked in a lowered voice. "Go away."

Ignoring her, Dean grinned and took a cookie from the bag. No guts, no glory. He took a small bite. Apparently Miss Evelyn had taken Clint's advice. The cookies were actually quite good. "Why should I go away?" he asked after he'd swallowed the small bite. "Half the town is here. The other half is across the street. I didn't snore in church and I haven't made any improper advances. Yet."

"People will talk," she said.

"Let 'em," Dean said gruffly. "What are they going to say?"

Reva turned her gaze to Cooper. He and his friends were taking turns on the slide, laughing and shouting. "They'll say a man doesn't sit with a woman at church unless he has intentions of some sort."

"Intentions?" He couldn't help it; he laughed.

Reva blushed. "I'm serious. Just…go home before things get any worse."

Dean was about to argue with her when the sheriff joined them, placing himself at Reva's other side. No way would he walk away while that man was here. Dean reached around Reva with the open bag and glared at the sheriff.

"Cookie?"

Chapter 14

She felt as if she'd just run a marathon her heart beat so fast. Her knees were none too steady, either.

If Tewanda wasn't in charge of this blasted picnic raffle, she'd grab her basket and go home. She didn't like the way Dean and Ben glared at each other, and she didn't like the way Dean looked at *her*. If she thought they had anything more than what they'd enjoyed last night, she wouldn't mind the glint in his eye and the set of his mouth. She'd probably adore what was undoubtedly a very *permanent* look.

Dean looked wonderful in his suit and tie, and that didn't help matters any. His Sunday attire suited him in a way the jeans and T-shirts didn't. He was comfortable in his suit. She had a feeling this man who laid his eyes on her in a way that made her bones melt was the real Dean Sinclair, much more than the sometimes inadequate handyman he had transformed himself into for his vacation.

Her heart hitched. He wasn't wearing a gun today, at

least not that she could see, but as a deputy U.S. marshal a gun was surely a part of his everyday life. If nothing else, she knew she couldn't live with that. Not that she'd ever be forced to make that choice.

Rafer Johnson bid twenty-five dollars for Louella Vine's lunch, and she preened as she passed the picnic basket to him. That was the highest bid so far. Most of the picnics were simple and fetched no more than fifteen dollars. Husbands bought their wives' lunches, sweethearts did the same, though sometimes with a little more flair than the more-settled husbands. Grandsons paid too much for sandwiches and sweet tea made by their grandmothers.

Tewanda lifted Reva's basket, peeked inside and told the crowd what she saw. Lemon bars. Fresh fruit. Chicken salad and potato salad. Before she could ask for a bid, Sheriff Andrews shouted, "Thirty dollars."

Someone in the crowd gasped. Probably Louella. A few other low voices muttered.

Tewanda grinned and nodded at the sheriff. For a moment all was silent, and Tewanda began to step toward the sheriff with the lunch basket in hand.

Then Dean called out, "Forty."

The murmuring of the crowd was not so soft now, but rose in excitement. Reva closed her eyes, wishing she could disappear.

Ben spoke sharply, his voice rising above the crowd noise. "Fifty."

"Wait just a minute," Dean said. All eyes turned to him, including Reva's, as he reached into his back pocket and pulled out his wallet. He flipped it open, looked inside and leafed through the bills.

"Seventy-seven dollars, and I'll build a fort on the playground."

Cooper and his friends jumped up and down and

shouted gleeful *hooray*s, and the raffle of Reva's picnic lunch was over. A very unhappy sheriff stalked away, and Dean collected the basket from Tewanda and handed over his cash. All of it apparently.

Reva made her way toward Cooper, weaving past people who grinned at her too widely. It had been years since she'd been this furious with anyone. How could he? He'd embarrassed her, made a spectacle of her and of himself, and she would never, ever forgive him!

"Come on, Cooper," she said when she reached her son. "Let's go home."

"Not yet. Pleeeeze. We're going to play tag, and Terrance is going to—"

"No," she said. "It's time to go."

She took Cooper's hand and together they walked through the crowd toward the sidewalk. They weren't quite fast enough. Dean caught up with them long before they escaped the church grounds.

"Aren't you going to help me eat this?" he asked, his voice friendly and relaxed and…oh, he had no idea how angry she was!

Reva released Cooper's hand and turned on Dean. "No, we are *not* going to eat lunch with you."

The expression on his face was one of innocence and serenity. It had to be an act—Dean Sinclair wasn't innocent or serene. "I can't eat all this by myself."

"Not my problem," Reva said, turning away and taking Cooper's hand again to lead him home.

"Wait." Dean fell into step beside her. "You're really mad."

"No wonder you're in law enforcement, Sherlock."

"All I did was—"

"*All you did* was make a spectacle of me," Reva declared. "People will talk about this for years. You have no idea what you've done."

Cooper added to the conversation. "He's going to build us a fort! Can it be a big one with a wooden ladder and a swing and a roof so we can sit up there even if it starts to rain?"

"Sure," Dean answered.

"I don't think so," Reva snapped. "Any structure built by Dean Sinclair will probably fall apart the first time anyone tries to use it."

"Ouch."

"I'm sure if you do actually build anything, it won't be fit for the children of Somerset."

"I'm getting better," Dean said just a little defensively.

And that was the problem, wasn't it? Every day, Dean indeed got a little better. A little more appealing, a little more important. Every day, every single day.

"Why did you have to come to town and…and stir things up, take something that worked just fine before you got here and twist it around, and—"

Dean grabbed her arm, gently but firmly, and pulled her to a stop. "Here." He handed the picnic basket to Cooper, but his eyes remained on her. "Go back to the church grounds and find us a picnic table. Stay out of the cookies and the lemon bars until after you've had lunch," he added. "We'll be there in a minute."

Cooper glanced to his mother for affirmation, and she nodded her head. Slowly and uncertainly, she sent him to do as Dean had asked. When Cooper was well on his way back to the church yard, Dean said, "This has nothing to do with a picnic raffle or me coming to church or making a spectacle."

Her heart thudded too hard, seemed to climb into her throat. "It's just all wrong."

"You don't want me to stay."

"You said you wouldn't..." Reva began.

"What are you afraid of?"

She couldn't tell him, could she? "I'm afraid that I like you too much," she said. She was going to suffer when he left. She'd known from the start that he wasn't going to stay here, had convinced herself that was the only reason she could afford to get involved with him. But when he left Somerset, it was going to hurt. To watch him drive away, to know he wasn't coming back...it would hurt forever.

She was falling in love with him.

Maybe the best way to scare Dean away was to tell him part of the truth. "I can't possibly be involved with a man who carries a gun. You know how I feel about them."

"You knew before last night that I have a gun. You didn't exactly push me out the door. Besides," he said quickly when she started to argue, "someday, somehow, you're going to have to realize that it's not guns you need to be afraid of. A gun in the wrong hands is a dangerous thing, but it's the hands you should fear, not the weapon."

She did fear the hands. Not Dean's hands, though. Never Dean's hands. "It's more than that," she said softly. "There are things about me you don't know."

"So tell me," he said.

Dean's answer to her problem was so simple, so straightforward. The words would stick in her throat if she tried to confess, wouldn't they?

"I'll think about it."

They ate lunch at the picnic table nearest the playground—Cooper's choice. Tewanda's youngest, Cooper's best friend Terrance, joined them, declaring that Cooper's picnic lunch looked much more appetizing than his own.

Dean had removed his jacket and loosened his tie in deference to the heat. Reva looked fresh and cool in her lightweight blue dress. Like the others she owned, it had a hemline well below the knee. Her shoes were flat and comfortable, and her hair had been pulled back into a thick ponytail that caught the sun and turned to honey.

She didn't say much as the meal progressed. The conversation was primarily about plans for the fort Dean now had to build in the church playground. Terrance and Cooper each had very specific ideas for the structure. If Dean gave them everything they wanted, the fort would be bigger than the church.

Eventually the boys asked to be excused. The playground and their other friends were waiting.

When they were alone at last, Dean turned to Reva. She sat beside him on the concrete bench, but had managed to place herself on the far end. If she scooted away from him any farther, she'd fall to the ground.

"Okay," he said in a low voice. "Talk to me."

She watched Cooper for a moment, then turned to stare at him. Had she been gathering strength since she'd sat down? It looked that way. "You've never asked me about Cooper's father."

He wanted to tell her it was none of his business, but he couldn't. She didn't know it yet, but Eddie Pinchon was very much Dean's business. "I figured you would tell me about him if you wanted to."

"You shouldn't have stayed here this long," Reva said in an accusing voice. "You should be gone by now!"

"You're right," he answered.

She sighed and turned her head so she could watch Cooper play. Or so she wouldn't have to look at him. "There hasn't been another man in my life since Cooper was born. Not until you came along."

Dean's gut churned. "The kid's six years old!"

She smiled gently, but didn't turn to look at him. "It didn't seem like such a long time. With work and trying to be a good mother, there really wasn't time for anything else. Besides…"

Finally she turned her head to look at him again. "The only thing that matters to me is giving my son the kind of life I never had. He won't ever go hungry. No one will tell him he's so stupid his life is not worth living. People won't laugh at him, turn up their noses…" Her eyes shone bright and she paled. "People won't point and whisper when he walks down the halls at school."

The twist in Dean's stomach turned to white-hot anger for grievances long past. "From everything I've seen, you're giving Cooper a great life. The best."

"If people find out who I used to be, who Cooper's father is, his life won't be so great. I can't afford to bring a man into my life for anything more than…what we had last night. I'm not going to tell you my secrets, Dean, and I can't get more involved with you and go on with lies between us. Where does that leave me?"

"I have a few secrets of my own," Dean confessed.

"Not like this," she whispered. "I swear, if I had known when I—" She stopped abruptly, drew away and lifted her chin. "I thought it would be okay to sleep with you and then watch you walk away. It's all I can have. I didn't know it would be so hard."

Dean leaned forward. Reva had nowhere to go, unless she wanted to jump up or fall off the bench. "You can trust me to keep your secrets, and there's nothing you can tell me that will make me feel differently about you or Cooper. The past is past. It doesn't matter nearly as much as you've convinced yourself it does."

She shook her head. "I can't…"

He kissed her, lightly, briefly. Prying eyes were no doubt watching, but he didn't care. Maybe she didn't, either, since she kissed him back.

When he took his mouth from hers she whispered. "Please tell me again you're not going to stay here."

"I can't stay," he said.

Reva sighed in obvious relief.

She hadn't expected this complication, but she should have. Dean had to go; she couldn't have a lasting relationship with him…but watching him go was going to hurt like hell.

Dean carried Cooper on his shoulders as they walked home, and her son provided the conversation. Dean had made the mistake of suggesting that Cooper spend a nice quiet afternoon, maybe reading a book.

Cooper was telling Dean all about his favorite book, *Elton the Elephant Goes to Town.*

"And *then* Elton went into a candy store, but he was too big and the gumballs spilled all over the floor, and *then* he went to the toy store to buy a game, but the aisles were too small, and *then*…" Cooper continued, almost breathless. There were a number of *and thens* still to go.

Dean listened, commenting here and there on Elton's adventures. Occasionally he glanced at Reva, and when he did she felt that gaze to her bones. A man's eyes on her shouldn't make her shiver. It shouldn't make her want what she couldn't have.

"At the end," Cooper continued, "Elton decided to go back to the circus and…and do you know what happened next?"

"No," Dean said.

"Oh," Cooper said, deflated. "I was hoping maybe you

knew what happened at the end. I forgot! Didn't you read
Elton the Elephant Goes to Town when you were a kid?''

''Nope. Sorry.''

''Now I have to find my book and see how it ends!''

When they reached the grassy yard and turned toward
home, Dean swung Cooper down and placed him on his
feet. Cooper ran toward the cottage and Elton, and Dean
stared at Reva.

''Thanks for lunch,'' he said.

''Don't thank me. You paid way too much for it.''

''It was worth every penny.'' He sounded and looked
completely serious.

He nodded toward the restaurant. ''I meant to tell you
earlier, you need to talk to your employees about locking
up at night. This morning I found that window wide
open.''

Reva's heart sank. Great. Something else to worry
about. ''You don't think whoever broke in last week came
back, do you?''

''I don't know. I climbed in through the window and
walked around. Didn't see anything out of place.''

''I'll talk to Tewanda in the morning. If she's sure the
window was closed when she left, I might have to see
about having a security system installed.''

''Good idea.''

''Good and expensive!'' Reva exclaimed. She sighed.
''Oh well, if I have no choice, I have no choice.'' She
looked Dean up and down. Like it or not, wise or not, he
got to her in a way no other man ever had. Was she willing
to risk everything, including Cooper, to keep him?

No. She could risk her own life and reputation, and she
would. But she wouldn't risk Cooper's.

''Speaking of money, what are you going to do now
that you've spent all your cash on lunch?''

He smiled, that half smile that grabbed her gut and wouldn't let go. "The downtown bank has an ATM. I'll hit it in the morning and get some cash."

"I would hate for you to be destitute because you felt the need to make a spectacle of yourself."

"You're much too concerned with spectacle making," he teased.

"Payday is Friday. If you'd like, I can write you a check early."

His smile faded. "For what?"

"Yard work, hanging wallpaper, fixing my sink, painting. The list goes on and on."

"You don't have to actually *pay* me," he said, sounding almost horrified.

"Of course I do."

He shook his head. Did he think that because they'd slept together she wouldn't pay him for his work?

"You'll get a check on Friday like everyone else," she said.

"I don't want—"

"You'll get a check."

Dean crossed his arms. "You're stubborn."

"You do work for me, you know."

"Yes, ma'am."

Reva shook her head and turned to walk away. Talk about stubborn!

"Aren't you going to ask me over for supper?"

She spun around. "Hungry already?"

"No."

She knew what he wanted, how he felt. Dean was hanging on with everything he had, trying to make the best of what little time they had left. Maybe she should do the same. "Six o'clock," she said. "We're having leftovers."

"I love leftovers," he said without cracking a smile.

Reva headed for her cottage. She knew he watched her all the way, but she didn't so much as turn her head to check.

Last night it had been just him and Reva. Tonight, with Cooper added to the mix, dinnertime had a family feel to it. Family. True, Dean had a family—in brothers and a sister, in-laws and nephews and one very spoiled niece.

But this was different. So different it scared him more than a little. There was a sense of belonging here, a warmth he had never experienced before. Reva and Cooper laughed a lot. They laughed at silly jokes, at each other…at him. Anything was fair game. Cooper found the book, and the fate of Elton the Elephant was at last resolved. He had to show Dean his other favorite books as Reva cleared the kitchen table.

The phone rang shortly after Reva joined them in the parlor. She reached for the portable phone on the coffee table, managing to snag the receiver just before Cooper got his hands on it. Again they laughed, as if racing for the phone was an everyday occurrence.

Reva was smiling when she answered the phone, but her smile didn't last long. It faded quickly as she listened to the caller. Dean sat up, instantly on alert. Was it Eddie? Had he found her? If Pinchon thought he could come here and take up where he'd left off seven years ago, he didn't know how Reva had changed.

And he didn't know he'd have to go through Dean to get to her.

She ended the call and placed the phone on the coffee table. "Cooper," she said calmly, "go put your books away and get ready for bed."

"But, Mom," Cooper pleaded, "I still haven't shown Dean my *really* favorite book!"

In a matter of days he'd gone from Mr. Sinclair to Mr. Dean to just Dean.

"Now," Reva said. Even Cooper recognized there was no room for argument, not tonight.

Dean said good-night to the kid, got an unexpected and hearty hug, and then waited until Cooper was well down the hallway before asking, "Who was on the phone?"

"Tewanda," Reva answered tersely.

A wave of relief rushed through him. "What's wrong?"

She stared at him and sighed. "I should have known it would happen."

"What happened?"

"It seemed like such a good idea at the time, but..." She shook her head. "How could I have been so stupid?"

Frustrated, Dean rose to his feet. "Dammit, Reva, are you going to tell me what's upset you?"

She looked him in the eye. "Someone saw you climbing in Cooper's window last night. Or climbing out at four in the morning, not that it matters. By morning, everybody in town will know that you spent the night here."

Chapter 15

"No one could've seen me," Dean insisted. "That window is shielded by trees on all sides. There's no way..." He went still. Reva could almost see the wheels in his brain turning. "Who started the rumor?"

"I don't know," Reva snapped. "Does it matter?"

"Yes," Dean said, "it does. The only way to have a clear view of that window is to be standing on the side of the big house where I found that open window. Whoever saw me is the person who's been breaking into your restaurant."

"Do you think so?"

"Has to be."

Reva wasn't as convinced as Dean, but she called Tewanda and asked who she'd heard the rumor from. Tewanda, who again teased her about getting caught as if the infraction meant nothing, gladly divulged the name.

Two more uncomfortable phone calls—complete with nervous laughter and a heart pounding so hard she could feel it pounding in her chest—and Reva knew where and how the rumor had started.

She shared the information with Dean, who smiled and nodded as if it all made sense to him. It certainly made no sense to her. He promised to take care of the problem in the morning, not at all concerned about the gossip that was going to run rampant no matter what they did.

In fact, he wrapped his arms around her as if nothing had gone wrong.

"How can you be so calm?" she asked, feeling anything but calm.

"So a few people in town know I spent the night here. Is it really that big a deal?" He stroked one large hand up and down her back. "We're all grown up, Reva. What we do behind closed doors is no one's business but ours."

"I know that, but—"

"You deserve a life," he interrupted. "A complete and full life of your own, beyond being supermom."

A part of her wanted to believe him. Maybe Dean was right. What had happened between them, what still might happen, was no one else's business. It didn't concern anyone but the two of them.

She'd tried to be perfect for so long, doing her best to make up for earlier mistakes, that she had lost a part of herself along the way. Had she unnecessarily robbed herself of a chance at love?

Dean leaned down and kissed her neck, very gently, too briefly. That simple touch was enough to send her insides whirling.

"Next time I spend the night," he whispered against her neck, his breath warm and arousing, "I'm coming and going by way of the front door."

She should tell him that there wouldn't be a next time. Instead, she said, "Then you can do your happy dance all the way home and everyone in town will know what happened.''

''I don't have a happy dance,'' he said solemnly.

Reva found herself smiling up at him, suddenly much less worried about the new rumors. ''Cooper can teach you his.''

Dean's eyebrows shot up. ''I have seen that dance, and trust me, you will never catch me doing anything like that no matter how happy I might be.''

She leaned against him. He was warm and solid, and she belonged here. For now. ''Are you?'' she whispered. ''Happy?''

He hesitated, and his face took on that unreadable expression she had come to expect, on occasion, with shuttered eyes and a firm jaw. But when he finally answered, he said, ''Yes.''

The news that Eddie Pinchon hadn't been seen for a couple of days sent chills up Dean's spine. The escaped convict could be on his way to Somerset. He could already be here.

Dean packed a bag of necessities, after ending the call with Alan. Reva didn't want him too close, but what choice did he have? He would either stay with her or sleep in a room in the big house where he could watch the cottage from a window. This rented room was no longer adequate.

He should have told her the truth days ago, but no matter how he phrased it, the confession would come out, he knew, sounding very, very bad. At the moment it was more important that he stay close than it was to be totally honest with Reva. When this was all over, he'd explain. If she let him.

He put his pistol in the duffel bag with a change of

clothes and an extra clip. He'd prefer to wear the pistol, but he knew that would spook Reva. One of these days they were going to have to work on that. In Eddie's hand, a weapon could very well be evil. In the right hand, a gun was just a tool. Since it was one of the tools of Dean's trade, he couldn't very well spend the rest of his life hiding it from Reva.

The rest of his life? Where had that come from? In truth, it didn't matter if Reva remained frightened of guns or not. He wouldn't be around long enough to cure her of that fear or any other.

Soft, quick footsteps sounded on the stairs and a moment later the door to Dean's apartment flew open. No knock, no call of his name. Reva stood there, much as he had left her. But her eyes shone bright and her face flushed too pink.

Cooper.

"What's wrong?"

Dean realized what had brought Reva here the minute he saw the sheriff climbing the stairs behind her, his ascent much slower and steadier than Reva's had been.

"Is it true?" she whispered breathlessly.

"I don't know what he told you."

"Only that you came here to spy on me," she cocked her head and studied him as if they'd never met, as if he was a monster who'd just sprouted a second head. She couldn't have looked more pained if he'd slapped her. "Is it true?"

"Reva," Dean began calmly, "I can explain."

She laughed at his pathetic plea, running one shaking hand through her hair. "I deserve a prize or something. I have the worst luck with men. The absolute worst." She stepped into the room, her usually soft, brown eyes pinned on him with blatant accusation and anger. The sheriff walked in behind her, calm as you please.

"What did you expect to find?" she asked in a low voice. "I hope I haven't disappointed you. My life is pretty boring. Of course, you did what you could to spice it up, didn't you."

Dean glared at the sheriff. "What did you tell her?"

"I didn't get far before she ran out on me," Ben Andrews said. At least he had the decency to look contrite. "I didn't want to upset her, but after I heard…I couldn't just sit back and let you lie to her that way."

"Get out," Dean ordered.

"Reva?" Andrews asked, ignoring Dean's order. "I can stay if you need me to. I'd be happy to walk you home."

She shook her head and sat in the chair by the window. "Thanks, but I need to do this alone."

Reluctantly the sheriff left the room. Dean slammed the door shut behind him. When he turned back around, Reva was lifting the old photograph of herself from the table.

"Don't…" Dean began. Too late.

Reva stared at the old picture of herself for a long moment. "I was so afraid you'd find out about my past, and you knew all along." Her voice was thin, weak. Dean took a step toward her, but she waved him back. "Stay away from me," she ordered as she studied the old photo. Finally she held it up, facing Dean. "If this is the woman you came to Somerset to find, you're out of luck. She was gullible, easily manipulated, needy. She died the day Cooper was born."

"Reva, I'm so sorry."

"Like hell you are. What exactly did you expect to find here? I haven't had anything to do with the people I knew in my other life since long before Cooper was born. You're wasting your time." She blinked once, stiffened her spine and stared at him, her eyes widening as if something had just occurred to her.

"Honey—"

"Don't call me honey," she demanded.

She was right; it wasn't his place to call Reva honey. To sit on her sofa and laugh with her child. To sleep with her or sit with her at church, to reach for that rare peace she'd given him for a while. It was over, and he had to get back to business. Now. No more excuses.

"Eddie Pinchon escaped from prison two and a half weeks ago. Alan and I came here because we knew there was a possibility…"

Dean didn't get a chance to finish, because Reva turned white as a sheet and then jumped and ran. She threw the door open, rushed out of the room and down the stairs. Dean grabbed his bag and followed her, easily catching up with her as she flew out the front door of the Fister house.

"Slow down."

"I left Cooper home alone," Reva said as she ran. "I have to get him out of bed. We have to get out of town tonight. Eddie can't find us. He was never supposed to get out of jail!"

She was near panic, so he didn't even try to stop her. He stayed right beside her, his pace matching hers as they ran toward home. Her home, not his. His home was a cold apartment in a big city and he dreaded going back there. And he would go back. Soon. Alone.

"I can protect you," he said as Reva vaulted onto her front porch.

"Sure." She swung open the front door. "You've done such a fine job of *protecting* me so far."

She ran down the hall to Cooper's bedroom, held her breath as she stepped into the dark room. Seeing her son there, safe and still sleeping, she swayed on her feet. When Dean tried to steady her, she pushed his hands away.

Retreating into the hallway, she closed her eyes and leaned against the wall. After a long moment she sank slowly to the floor, as if she could no longer bear to stand.

"Were you laughing at me the whole time?" she whispered.

"No," Dean said, dropping to his haunches. He wanted to reach out and touch Reva, but he knew she'd only push him away again. "Never."

She looked him dead in the eye, more accusing and wounded than anyone he'd ever seen. And he'd done it. He'd been the one to do this to her. Nothing he could ever do would make up for this kind of pain.

"So what was it? You got bored waiting for something to happen and decided to see if you could turn me on to pass the time?"

"No," he said quickly. "Dammit, Reva—"

"Don't talk to me like I'm the one who's done something wrong here." Her eyes met his. "Yes, I have secrets. I'm not perfect. But I never lied to you about who I am. Never."

"I wanted to tell you," he said, "a hundred times. I almost did."

"What stopped you?"

"Knowing that when you found out, you'd look at me the way you're looking at me now."

Reva covered her face with her hands. "I don't have time for this. I can't stay here."

"Maybe Eddie won't try to find you," Dean said in a soothing voice. "So far, he hasn't—"

"He'll come here," Reva said. "Sooner or later, he'll come here."

"Do you think someone will tell him about Cooper?

Who knows about him? Is there anyone you can think of who would…''

He stopped speaking when Reva stood and stepped past him. She went to a linen closet in the hallway, opened it and tossed a neat stack of towels onto the floor. A wooden shelf was removed, and when that was done she loosened a panel at the back of the closet and pulled out a duffel bag.

The black bag was faded, dusty and heavy. She tossed it to the floor so that it landed halfway between his feet and hers. ''Open it,'' she said hoarsely. ''Go ahead, Deputy Sinclair. Do your job.''

Dean's heart stopped. He knew what was in that bag. He wanted to be wrong, but one look at Reva's face and he knew he wasn't. He dropped to his haunches again and unzipped the bag to find exactly what he'd expected. Hundred-dollar bills, neatly bound and stacked one atop the other.

''It's all there,'' Reva whispered. ''Every penny. It's the reason you're here, isn't it? You came for the money, and I was just—''

''No. I didn't know anything about the money until last night. Where did it come from?''

Reva shook her head. ''I'm not sure. When I heard Eddie had followed that guy all the way to Florida and killed him and been arrested, I took off. It was my chance to get away. To escape. The money was in the trunk. I didn't find it for days, and when I did…I couldn't spend it and I didn't know how to get rid of it without calling attention to myself. It's dirty money,'' she whispered. ''I don't know where it came from, but I know that much. Two hundred and fifty thousand dollars worth of dirty money.''

Dean glanced up.

"Don't look at me like that! What was I supposed to do—turn it in? I was pregnant, scared and doing my best to hide until the furor died down. For all I knew, Eddie would manage to get off and he'd be back on the streets. Burn it? I almost did a couple of times." Reva ran agitated fingers through her hair. "I would've changed my name, but I didn't know how. My social security number, my driver's license—I needed them. I'm sure Eddie had friends who knew exactly what to do, but I was running *away* from that life." She shuddered bone deep. "If Eddie knows about Cooper, he might come here for him. He might come for me, I don't know. It's been a long time, and we didn't exactly part on friendly terms. But I have his money, and as soon as he figures out where it is, he'll be here. If I'm lucky, he'll just take the cash and leave." She went pale again, swayed on her feet. "My luck has been really crappy lately."

Dean took charge. He did it so well Reva had a feeling he took charge often.

He wouldn't allow her to bolt. There were plans to be made, he said, before she could leave town. They woke Cooper just long enough to move him to the car. Reva packed a suitcase for him while Dean carried the sleeping child to her car and buckled him in.

Tewanda had agreed to keep Cooper with her for a few days without knowing why. Without even asking. She was the best of friends, and Reva would hate to leave her behind most of all. More than the restaurant, more than her other friends and the home she'd made for herself and Cooper here in Somerset.

She needed cash in order to run, and no matter how scared she was, she couldn't make herself take any of

Eddie's drug money. She'd rather risk spending one more night in her home than take so much as a dollar.

Besides, she was scared to take any. Maybe, if she was very lucky, Eddie would be satisfied to have his money back and he'd get out of her life once and for all. But if anything was missing, he'd take it out on her. He'd kill her in a heartbeat, without a second thought, she was certain.

After Cooper was safely tucked in a Hardy bed, Dean drove her home in silence. He would never be a handyman. He would never be content to live in a place like Somerset. Why did that knowledge sting after everything she'd learned about him and the way he'd used her?

"Pack a bag," he said as they stepped from the car and headed for the front door.

"I'll do it in the morning before the bank opens," she said, reaching for her key so she could unlock the door. Worrying about Eddie had forced her to start locking her door again, even when she knew she'd only be gone a few minutes. When she walked into the parlor where the lights still burned, she held her breath, almost expecting to see Eddie pop up out of nowhere.

All was quiet, and eventually she breathed again.

"You're not spending the night here," Dean insisted. "You're going to sleep across the street at Miss Evelyn's."

"I can't—"

"It's a little late to be worried about what people will say, Reva," Dean snapped. "You need a good night's sleep, and you're not going to get it here."

They were alone, the truth was out, and in a matter of hours she'd leave Somerset and never see Dean again. Unless he decided to track her down and arrest her for keeping the money all these years. Reva didn't know what law she'd broken in hiding the money, but she knew Dean would see that mistake as a crime that needed to be punished. What would happen to Cooper if Dean insisted on throwing her in jail?

"Why didn't you tell me the truth from the start?" she asked softly. "If I'd known that Eddie had escaped from prison, I could have gotten Cooper to a safe place sooner, I could have made arrangements to get some cash and be out of town within a matter of hours. Instead, you…" She couldn't say it.

"When I came here I didn't know you. For all I knew, you were still involved with Eddie."

She gave a harsh laugh. It caught in her throat and threatened to choke her.

"I couldn't afford to tell you why I was here. And by the time I knew you weren't involved, it was too late. I had too much to lose by telling you the truth."

Reva managed to regain her composure. "Is seduction while on stakeout a normal investigative procedure for you, Deputy Sinclair?"

"No," he answered sharply.

"Gee, how did I get so lucky?" She swept past him, heading for her bedroom. Tears stung her eyes, and she didn't want him to see. "I'm not going anywhere, least of all to your place. I'll take my chances with Eddie. He's dangerous, but at least you can see him coming. Eddie would stab me in the heart without a second thought. You apparently prefer to go for the back. I sure as hell never saw you coming."

"You're going to Miss Evelyn's," Dean insisted as he followed her down the hallway.

"I'm not going anywhere with you," she replied.

"No, you're not." He stopped in the bedroom doorway. Just last night, it had seemed as if he belonged here, as if he could spend a lifetime in her bed. Now he didn't even cross the threshold.

"No, you're not going anywhere with me," he said in a calmer voice. "I'm staying here."

Chapter 16

Dean sat in the dark of Reva's quiet parlor for a long time after he got her settled in across the street. He doubted she'd get much sleep tonight, but if she did sleep, at least she wouldn't have to worry about waking up to find Eddie standing beside her bed.

If not for the money, he could have hoped they'd never have to worry about Eddie. Pinchon would stay there in North Carolina and eventually he'd be caught. He couldn't hide forever; it was a miracle he hadn't been captured yet. The marshals on duty had come close a few times, but Eddie always managed to get away.

If—*when* Eddie came to Somerset, he wouldn't be so lucky. Not on Dean's watch.

The cottage was too quiet without Cooper's incessant chatter and Reva's laughter. He'd always thought this cottage enchanted, somehow. Warmer than other, more ordinary houses. Blessed. But the place was dead without them, just a house and a collection of mismatched furniture. It was the people who lived in this cottage that made it special.

Dean was nothing if not practical. Reva would never forgive him, and he couldn't blame her. They'd never had a future, so why did that knowledge eat at his gut?

Reva shouldn't have to leave her home, and Cooper shouldn't have to leave his school and his friends. Once Eddie was back in prison where he belonged, they could come back here and pretend that nothing had happened.

Sounded like a good plan. Why didn't he believe it would work?

Reva tried not to look at Dean as they walked toward town, their pace slow and easy as they strolled in the shade of the trees that lined the street. They both needed to go to the bank this morning, and he didn't want to leave her alone. She wasn't going to argue with him about that. Not until she knew exactly where Eddie was.

There was also the matter of the person or persons who had broken into the restaurant on at least two occasions. Dean said he could clear that matter up quickly.

He looked like hell. "Did you sleep?" she asked.

"No."

She shouldn't care if he slept or not. He was a liar and a fraud. He'd made love to her pretending to be… No, he had told her all along that he was in law enforcement; he just hadn't told her why he'd come to Somerset. She wanted to hate his guts.

She didn't. "Get some sleep this afternoon," she suggested, "after Cooper and I leave town."

Dean sighed. Oh, she did not like that sigh. "About leaving town…"

"You're not going to order me to stay here, are you?" she snapped.

"No," he said quickly. "I'm not issuing orders this morning. But I thought about your situation a lot last night, tried to take each option and play it out to the best- and worst-case scenario."

No wonder he hadn't slept.

"I think it might be a good idea if you stay in Somerset."

She laughed in disbelief. "You're kidding!"

"No. I've given this a lot of thought, Reva. Eddie is coming to Somerset, we both know that. What if he finds out as soon as he gets to town that you're not here? If he comes to the restaurant, I'll be there. But if he asks someone downtown or stops at a neighbor's house and I don't see him, and he finds out you're not here, he'll be right behind you."

She shivered. Her bones went cold. She wanted to argue with Dean, but she knew he was right.

"What do you suggest?"

"Cooper stays with the Hardys, you sleep at Miss Evelyn's, and I stay at your house and wait for him to show up."

The very idea of Dean squaring off with Eddie scared Reva more than she cared to admit. When she'd first gotten involved with Eddie, she hadn't known what he was like. She knew now.

"I'm not sure that's a good idea."

"Want to live your life looking over your shoulder?" he asked harshly.

She didn't answer; didn't have to. Of course she didn't want to look over her shoulder for the rest of her life waiting for Eddie to catch up with her! "I'll think about it."

"You do that. Disappearing in this day and age isn't all that easy," Dean said harshly. "You'd have to change your name and Cooper's. Maybe dye your hair if you really want to play it safe. The kid's too. And even then, you could never be sure Eddie wasn't right around the next corner.''

Reva shivered, imagining what hiding would mean to her life and her son's.

Dean didn't head directly for the bank, but stopped at the bakery. Louella gave them her best glare as they approached the counter.

Reva knew, after her short investigation last night, that it had been Louella who'd started the rumor about Dean sneaking into her window at night. Did that mean the woman had been breaking into the restaurant? It didn't make sense. Maybe she wasn't the original source of the rumor, in spite of what Reva had learned last night. She might have twisted the gossip to make it seem as if she'd seen Dean with her own eyes, when in truth it had been someone else who'd told her.... So many possibilities. At the moment a prowler who never took anything was the least of Reva's problems!

Very calmly Dean ordered a cup of coffee. When he asked Reva what she wanted, she shook her head. Miss Evelyn, who had been strangely unsurprised by the new sleeping arrangements, had fed her a hearty breakfast she'd barely been able to choke down.

Dean paid for his coffee, and as Louella handed over his change, he calmly asked, ''What were you looking for?''

Her hand jerked, and coins scattered onto the floor and across the counter. ''I...I have no idea what you're talking about.'' She knelt down to collect the coins from the floor on her side of the counter.

''Sure you do,'' Dean said calmly. ''You've been slipping into Reva's restaurant at night and looking for something. I just can't figure out what it is.''

"That's ridiculous," Louella said as she slapped the coins onto the counter. Her face had gone beet-red.

Dean leaned against the counter. "I figure you slipped the lock on the kitchen door with what? An old credit card? That's an easy trick. After I changed the lock and that didn't work anymore, you had to climb through a window. Was it left unlocked or did you manage to slip that lock, too?" He took a long sip of his coffee. "Doesn't matter, I guess. It's breaking and entering either way."

Instead of a red face, Louella now had a very pale complexion. "You can't prove—"

"How else did you manage to see me?" Dean interrupted. "Even if you were walking late at night, you can't see the window I used from the sidewalk or the street."

"So you admit it!" she said, pointing an accusing finger.

"We're not talking about me right now," Dean said. He took another long drink of coffee. "As for proof, I think if I have the sheriff lift fingerprints off the ledge of that window, he'll find mine and yours. What do you think?"

Louella pursed her lips. "I think I'm going to ask you to leave."

"Not until you tell me what you were looking for," Dean said, not budging from the spot. "I didn't see any signs of maliciousness in the restaurant. Nothing was damaged, nothing was taken. You just rummaged around in the middle of the night, and I want two things. I want it to stop, and I want to know why. Otherwise, I will have to call the sheriff and make this an official visit."

Louella seemed to grow smaller, and finally, for the first time, she laid her eyes on Reva. "All I wanted was the recipe for your fudge pie!"

Dean almost snorted his coffee. "You were looking for a *recipe?*"

"Everyone raves about it, and I get so sick and tired of hearing how marvelous that damn pie is. I thought if I could make a few fudge pies and sell them here, business might pick up."

"Why didn't you ask?" Reva stepped to the counter to face the woman. "I would have given it to you."

"You say that now, but if I had asked outright, you would have found a reason to refuse."

"The recipe is going to be in the next cookbook!" Reva said. "It's not a deep, dark secret. Why would I have refused to share it with you?"

Louella's answer was a flinty-eyed glare.

"And why do you dislike me so much?" Reva asked in a lowered voice. She'd always wondered, and it seemed like the time to ask.

Louella pursed her lips. "You have it so easy, with your fancy restaurant and magazine articles and newspaper coverage, while I just sit here and struggle to get by. It isn't fair."

Dean cursed beneath his breath and set his empty cup on the counter. "Let's go."

"No," Reva said. She planted her hands on the counter. "I struggle, too." She wouldn't tell Louella all her woes, but to accept the argument that her life was easy just didn't sit well. Especially not today. "The first year I was here, I had to take out a loan to keep the restaurant opened. There were many months that after I paid all the bills and the employees, I was lucky to have enough left to feed my child. Yes, things are looking up now. I'm doing better. But I worked hard to get here. No one handed me that restaurant on a silver platter."

"All I wanted was the recipe."

Reva turned away. "You can have it. Stop by the restaurant this afternoon and I'll make you a copy."

Dean followed her to the sidewalk, and they resumed their walk to the bank. He didn't say anything. He surely found it amusing that a woman would go to such lengths for a pie recipe, but he didn't laugh. Not at her and not at Louella.

"Was it really hard?" he asked as they reached the bank entrance.

"Yes."

"And you never even thought of dipping into that bag of cash."

She rolled her eyes. "Of course I *thought* about it, but I never did. I didn't want any part of my life built on Eddie's dirty money. I guess you find that silly or amusing or—"

"No," he said as he opened the door for her. "I don't. And I'm not surprised, either."

She looked into his face as she walked past him and into the cool bank. "You don't know me well enough to say that," she said softly.

He followed her. "Yes, I do."

Dean decided he could grab a couple of hours' sleep during the busiest time at Miss Reva's. He and Reva agreed that Eddie would most likely come at night. It was his style to sneak about in the dark, to hide in shadows and pop out like a bogeyman when you least expected him.

But Reva was not alone. Until Pinchon was caught, someone would be watching her at all times. The sheriff was having lunch at the restaurant today. He would keep an eye on Reva until Dean relieved him.

Dean was still a little surprised that Reva had agreed to stay in Somerset. It was the fear of not knowing where Eddie was or when he might show up that made her stay, he knew. She would put herself in danger to keep Cooper safe.

Dean should be able to go to sleep with no trouble. For the past two nights he'd gotten nothing more than an hour here and there; he was exhausted.

It would be easy enough to get Alan here. Hell, he could summon an army if he told them that Reva had Pinchon's missing money. He hadn't made that call yet. Wouldn't, unless he had no other choice.

All his life he'd lived by the book, obeyed the rules. But he couldn't send Reva to jail for what was in reality nothing more than a foolish mistake made when she was too young and too frightened to know any better.

There were so many ways this could go. The DA might want to press charges on principle, tie Reva in to some of Eddie's earlier crimes simply because she'd been there. It would be a tough case to make in court, though. Very tough. Then again, there might not be a single charge filed against her. It was all at the DA's discretion.

Dean didn't have a single doubt that Reva had been telling the truth when she'd told him she'd never been involved in any of Eddie's crimes. She was no criminal; she'd done nothing wrong.

He finally did fall asleep, stretched across Reva's bed fully dressed. His pistol was nearby, on the bedside table. The doors were locked, but he didn't think for a minute that would keep Eddie out if he was of a mind to come.

There were no dreams. Dean tossed and turned, then found himself in a deep sleep. What seemed like only seconds later, a noise woke him.

In one move he sat up and reached for the pistol, swinging his legs over the side of the bed. The bedside clock read 4:15 in bright red. He'd slept longer than he'd intended and much more deeply. When Reva reached the doorway and saw the gun in his hand, she almost jumped out of her skin.

So did he.

"Why are you sneaking around?" he asked, quickly placing the pistol on the table. Reva looked at the weapon for a moment, then walked to the closet.

"I needed some clothes, and you're supposed to be sleeping."

"Where's Andrews?"

"On the front porch, waiting."

Dean sighed and raked the hair away from his face with both hands, while Reva rummaged through her clothes. Her back was to him, and he couldn't see her face. And still he knew she was tense, coiled so tightly she was about to explode.

He would likely never have a chance to explain how they'd come to this point. And if he did, she wouldn't listen.

"I did what I had to do," he said softly.

"I'm sure you did," she replied coolly.

"I never intended to hurt you." He stood and placed his body between Reva and the table where the gun lay, so that she wouldn't see it.

Reva turned, a pale-green dress on a hanger swinging from her hand. Her cool tension turned to anger in a heartbeat. "Did you think the bimbo in your photograph wouldn't have any feelings? I do. I did, even then."

"I never intended for this to become personal."

"What *did* you intend?" She took a step toward him.

"Reva—"

"Forget I asked," she said, spinning around quickly and stepping toward the door and escape. Instead of escaping, she stopped in the doorway and turned to face him. She stood there for a moment, just staring at him. There was no expression on her face that he could read, no visible anger or disappointment.

"For a long time after I got away from Eddie, I was sure that every man was like him. He lied to me from the day we met. He pretended to be someone he wasn't in order to get what he wanted. It took years, but I finally discovered that there were decent men out there amongst the liars and the cheats. I never so much as dreamed of having one of my own. My past would get in the way— I've always known that. How could I tell a decent man that Cooper's father was a murderer who once tried to convince me to stay with him by shoving the muzzle of a gun down my throat?"

Dean's hands balled into fists.

"And then you came along, and you seemed to be one of the decent ones. Handyman, cop—it didn't really matter to me. I knew I couldn't keep you, but I thought that for a while, for just a little while, I could have one of those decent men for myself."

Dean took a step forward.

"No. Stay away from me," Reva ordered. She held the green dress before her like a flimsy shield.

"I'm so sorry—"

"Save it," she said abruptly. "I don't want your apologies. They don't mean anything. They're just words you think will make you feel better."

Didn't she know that nothing would ever make him feel better about this?

She stared at him for a moment longer, then asked in a soft voice that crept beneath his skin, "Why couldn't you have been a handyman?"

When she turned and ran, Dean began to follow. He stopped well short of the hallway.

He couldn't make amends, not this time. He couldn't

make Reva understand that this mess was tearing him up
inside.

All he could do was keep her safe and capture Eddie.
When that was done, he could do her the favor of walking
out of her life without making things any more difficult
than they already were.

Chapter 17

Over the next two days, they fell into an uncomfortable but workable routine. Reva slept at Miss Evelyn's. Dean slept in her bed. Cooper, who was beginning to ask a lot of questions, stayed at the Hardy house, except in the afternoons when he and Terrance came to the restaurant after school. Reva needed to see her child, and Cooper needed to spend a little time with his mother each day. The afternoons together made perfect sense.

The boys were escorted home from school each day, either by Charles or the sheriff, and if necessary one of Ben's deputies would take on the duty in the days to come. All this was at Dean's insistence. It was just a precaution, he assured her. The boys were too young to be suspicious of the fact that for the past two days someone they knew had just happened to be walking in the same direction.

Either Dean or Ben stayed close to Reva at all times. Ben had a tendency to get underfoot, while Dean kept his distance but still managed to be there. Around a corner, at the end of the street, just outside her window. Sometimes seeing him gave her a start, made her heart skip a beat and her breath catch in her throat.

There were moments when Reva was sure running would be better than this, but she knew that wasn't the answer. If she had only herself to worry about, she'd run. She wouldn't ask Cooper to suffer the kinds of sacrifices necessary to make that work.

She could hope that the federal marshals who were tracking Eddie in North Carolina and Virginia would be successful, and this crisis would soon be over.

Reva had to accept that this crisis might never be over. Dean knew about the money, Eddie's money, and he couldn't just ignore the fact that she'd held on to it all these years. She could see the quandary that money put him in. Knew him well enough to know it wasn't easy for him to sit on the information even for a few days.

Was he going to arrest her? He hadn't said so, but then, why should he warn her of his plans? The fear of going to prison would be enough to make anyone run. Maybe he wasn't really confused about what to do regarding the money. Maybe he was just stringing her along, and as soon as Eddie was captured he'd slap the cuffs on her. What would she do then? What would happen to Cooper?

Cooper and Terrance were not yet home from school, but they would be soon. Frances and Tewanda were in the kitchen finishing up for the day. Reva had been paying bills, balancing the checkbook and making notes in her ledger. Tewanda kept trying to convince her to move her financial books to a computer, but Reva liked the feel of paper in her hands, liked making notes in her small, neat handwriting. Her ledger would never crash or be affected by a virus.

While she worked, she listened to the sounds from the

hallway above. Dean worked on the third floor, in the hall where he could clearly see the door to her office. There was so much to be done up there. Wood needed to be replaced, he said, and the whole third floor needed to be painted—except for the parlor he'd finally finished papering.

A shiver worked up Reva's spine. He'd made love to her in that room. No—he'd had sex with her. There was no love in a lie, no love in raw seduction.

She closed her ledger and left the desk, and when she opened the door, she looked up and saw Dean watching, his eyes sharp, his expression grim. He was prepared to follow her, but he wouldn't have to. She was going to the third floor.

Since she'd been avoiding him for days, he was openly surprised when she started to climb his way. He put down the sandpaper in his hand, wiped dust off his face and his T-shirt. John Deere again.

"Is everything okay?" he asked before she reached the top of the stairs.

"No, not really," she said.

There were times when she thought nothing would ever be okay again, but maybe that wasn't so. She'd survived Eddie. She'd survive Dean, too.

"I have to know," she said, lowering her voice so no one below could hear. "Are you going to send me to jail?"

Dean shook his head. "Of course not."

"The money…"

"You didn't participate in any crime," Dean said crisply. "Yes, it was a mistake to keep the cash, but I think if it comes down to it, I can make a case for not pressing charges, since you're assisting in the stakeout and didn't actually spend any of the money. Even if the DA tried, it would be a tough case to make."

That *I think* Dean so casually threw into his explanation gave her a moment's unease. "It's not really up to you whether charges are pressed or not, is it?"

He hesitated. "No. Not if this goes to the DA in North Carolina or a federal prosecutor."

Like it or not, her fate was in the hands of a stranger who had no idea what she'd been like seven years ago. Scared. Pregnant. Wanting only to disappear—as she wanted to disappear now.

"I was a different person then," she said, glancing past Dean and through the open doorway behind him. He'd finished putting up the wallpaper in that parlor all on his own. If she had the time and the money, this entire house would one day be a real showplace.

Dean wouldn't be around to see it. He'd never lied to her about that at least. "And I didn't know what kind of business Eddie was in. I want you to know that. He told me he was a salesman." She averted her eyes and laughed harshly. "If I am ever again attracted to a man, I'm going to ask for proof of employment before things go too far."

"I'm not like him," Dean said.

She looked at him squarely. "Aren't you?"

He did nothing. There was no protest. No move toward her, no defense of his actions.

"By the time I found out what he was like," she went on, "it was too late."

"It's never too late."

"If I can't hide from Eddie now, what makes you think I could have pulled it off then?" she asked sharply. "I tried to leave. You know what happened!"

"The gun."

"The gun," she whispered. She knew there was one nearby right now. Since Eddie was coming, Dean didn't dare leave his weapon hidden in a drawer somewhere just because the sight of the thing spooked her.

Dean reached out, slowly and cautiously, and took her hand in his. She could've snatched her hand away, and he wouldn't try again to touch her. Reva knew that. But she didn't pull her hand back. A spark twisted through her body from the place where Dean's flesh touched hers. It was warm, exciting and comforting at the same time. She'd missed that contact so much.

"I hate to see you afraid of anything," Dean said, lifting her hand and studying the palm.

"You made that case once before," she said, not quite as calmly as she'd planned.

Dean's argument that the hand was to blame, not the weapon, made perfect sense. To her brain, anyway. Her heart wasn't yet convinced. If they had a few weeks or months or years, maybe he could convince her to one day set her dread of guns aside. Unfortunately they didn't have that kind of time. They didn't have any time at all.

He held on to her hand long past the moment when he should have released it. His hands were large, strong and marred here and there by scuffs and scrapes that hadn't been there when he'd come to Somerset. She ran her finger over one blemish, a new, very small scratch across the top of his hand.

"The other day, you said you wished I was a handyman," Dean said, his voice soft. "For the first time in my life, so do I."

"Don't—" she began.

"But I'm not," he continued. "I never will be."

Her heart sank, just a little, even though she already knew who and what Dean was. Just being close to him made her remember, made her body remember, what they

were like together. The way he'd made her feel, the joy
and freedom she'd felt in his arms. Had it all been a lie?

He tugged on her hand and she stepped closer to him.
Too close. "But I do wish I'd told you sooner why I'd
come to Somerset. I should have, I know that. I just—"

Reva tilted her face up and kissed him. He wasn't expecting the move; neither was she. It just happened, as if
her body was drawn to his no matter what had come between them.

She fisted her fingers, grasping at his T-shirt as he kissed
her back. Gently at first, and then harder. His arms encircled her, and he held her as if protecting her from everything outside this circle. He kissed her in a way he never
had before. Hungrier. More desperate. She had a feeling—
no, she *knew*—that Dean Sinclair didn't taste desperation
very often.

There was unexpected comfort in the kiss. A simple
meeting of mouths, and she was no longer alone in this
hell she'd made for herself. She had Dean with her, beside
her, all around her, and she wasn't alone.

She melted inside. Her knees went weak.

And she wished again that Dean was just a handyman.

Dean followed Reva down the stairs. The kiss had unsettled her; it had unsettled him, too. Just when he'd ac-
cepted that everything between them was over, she went
and did something like kissing him out of nowhere.

Eddie was going to show up here, but when? They
couldn't continue like this indefinitely. Dean was still officially on vacation, though if he called in and revealed
the news about the cash, that vacation would very quickly
be over. He'd stalled for a couple of days, but eventually
he would have no choice but to call Alan and report what
he'd found. Somehow he had to find a way to put a spin

on the revelation that wouldn't land Reva in a world of legal trouble.

Dean Sinclair, spinning. It was definitely not his style.

Cooper and Terrance came through the front door with their usual exuberance. The sheriff was right behind them. When Andrews caught sight of Dean, he nodded, then turned and walked away. The kids were in Dean's hands now. Just as Reva was in his hands.

"Hi!" Cooper said with that brilliant grin of his. "Sheriff Andrews walked home with us again, but he said he couldn't stay for lemonade because he had to catch some bad guys or something. He talked to our class again today, but not about drugs. This time he talked about strangers, and how we should never go anywhere with a stranger or talk to a stranger."

"We already knew that," Terrance said in a calm, almost disgusted voice.

"Yeah," Cooper agreed.

"Snacks in the kitchen," Reva said, and the boys ran in that direction.

"Do they ever just walk?" Dean asked. The boys skipped, ran and jumped everywhere, or so it seemed.

"No." Reva started to follow the boys, but stopped before she got very far. She turned to face him and leaned her back against the wall, more relaxed than she should be, given the situation. "I'd like to ask you something. I've never been able to talk to anyone about this, because…no one knows. No one but you. I love Cooper, and I have tried so hard to be a good mother to him, to raise him right and make sure he has everything he needs."

"You're doing a good job."

"Good enough?" she whispered. "Cooper is Eddie's child. Eddie's blood." She shivered visibly. "He even looks like Eddie, more every day. What if…'' She couldn't finish the question.

Dean moved toward her, but not so close that he'd be tempted to touch her. ''Cooper is not going to grow up to be like his father.''

''How can I be sure?''

''He's your child, too, Reva.'' Dean knew Eddie Pinchon's background inside out. Pinchon hadn't had a stable life, not from the age of four when his father had died. His mother's remarriage a year later had placed her child in the hands of a stepfather who'd abused him as a child and then introduced him into the family drug business at the age of twelve. Eddie had been made bad; he wasn't born that way.

''Cooper is a great kid, and he's going to stay that way because he has you to watch out for him. To love him and show him what's right and what's not. Kids don't come with a guarantee, but Cooper has a better chance than most at having a good life. Thanks to you, Reva.''

''Are you saying that just to make me feel better?'' she asked.

''No. No more lies. Not even little ones.''

She shook her head. ''A little late for that promise, isn't it?''

''Is it?''

He moved closer. ''And you don't have to do it alone. There are decent men out there, Reva. Men who won't lie to you.'' He wanted to be the one to make her life complete, but he'd ruined that chance. ''Cooper needs a father, you need a husband. You need…more kids, Saturday-night dances, romantic evenings, a man to love you…''

''I can't—''

''The right man won't care about your past or Cooper's father or anything else.''

"And where am I supposed to find a man like that?"

Here. The word stuck in his throat. *I'm right here.*

The front door opened suddenly, and Dean turned as a man wearing a baseball cap stepped inside and slammed the door shut. As the man lifted his head, Reva grabbed Dean's shirt and took a sharp breath.

"Hey, baby," Eddie Pinchon said with a widening smile. "Miss me?"

She'd thought seeing Eddie again would send her into a panic, but it didn't. A heavy dread settled in her stomach, though, as Eddie looked past Dean to direct his cold gaze at her.

He took off his cap and tossed it aside, revealing very short fair hair. In the past he'd worn it longer, but she supposed this was a prison haircut. The mustache and goatee were new, and he'd lost weight. But he was still Eddie.

"What are you doing here?" she asked.

"You know what I'm here for." His bright smile faded. "Took me a while to figure out where it was, but since no one else has it, I figure it must be here somewhere."

It. Never *my money* or *the cash.* Eddie was being careful, since Dean stood between them.

Eddie turned his attention to Dean. "Who are you?"

"He's the handyman," Reva answered quickly.

"Handyman." Eddie's smile came back. "Just how handy are you?"

Dean took a single step forward. Eddie's hand slipped behind his back. Of course he had a gun on him. Reva's heart started to pound.

"Why don't you get out of here, handyman," Eddie said. "The lady and I have something important to discuss."

Dean took another step toward Eddie. "I don't think so." She saw the bulge at his spine, where his own weapon was not so well hidden beneath his T-shirt.

Eddie's gun snapped up and around, and so did Dean's. They moved so fast, so surely, Reva didn't see anything but a blur. And then they were standing in her foyer, aiming their guns at each other. Eyes on the weapons, Reva felt her mouth go dry, and a roar filled her ears.

"Reva," Dean said calmly, "you still have a few employees in the kitchen. Why don't you tell them to go home? Send them out the kitchen door. We don't want anyone getting hurt here, and the fewer people who know about this, the better."

"You're awfully bossy for a handyman," Eddie observed as Reva took a step back. "And much too comfortable with that pistol."

Dean waited until she was at the end of the hallway before he called, "Reva, you go out with them."

"You'd better not!" Eddie shouted. "If you're not back here in two minutes, I'm going to shoot your little friend."

Reva ran to the kitchen. The women and the two boys had surely heard raised voices, but they would not have heard the words. The kitchen was too far away from the foyer, thank goodness. They were not concerned until Reva burst into the kitchen, out of breath and on the verge of panic.

"We have a little bit of a problem out front," she said urgently. "I need you all to leave. Now."

"Mom," Cooper began, "what's—"

"Just go with Tewanda and I'll come get you later."

"But why?"

She didn't have time to argue. Eddie had said two minutes. Two minutes, and then he'd start firing. Dean had a weapon, too, but what if Eddie fired, anyway?

"Go."

Reva left the kitchen at a run as the women and children made their way to safety. If she lost it, she wouldn't do Dean any good at all. She might even get them both killed. Calm. She needed calm. How was she supposed to manage that?

Dean had been right. It wasn't the gun that was evil, it was Eddie's hands. In Dean's hands, no weapon would ever be used in the way Eddie's had been. He would never threaten an innocent person; he would never use that weapon to torture anyone, good or bad.

She found Dean and Eddie as she had left them, in a heart-wrenching standoff.

"I told you to go," Dean said when he heard her footsteps.

"Maybe she doesn't want me to shoot you, handyman," Eddie said as he circled to the side.

Reva looked at Eddie's gun. Her heart took an unpleasant leap, but she didn't panic. The roaring in her ears had stopped, and she knew she could hold back a scream.

But she was afraid. That gun was aimed at Dean, and Eddie would pull the trigger if it would get him what he wanted.

"You won't shoot me," Dean said.

Eddie laughed. "What makes you so special?"

"I'm the only one who knows where your money is."

Chapter 18

He couldn't afford to take his eyes off Pinchon, not even to glance to the side to see how Reva was holding up. She stood a few feet away and a few feet back, in a position much too vulnerable. "Go on," Dean said. "Get out of here."

"He'll shoot you!" she argued as she inched forward.

"Not if he wants his money, he won't."

"What did you do?" she asked.

Dean tried to move to the side to place himself between Reva and Pinchon, but she continued to move forward as if she intended to stand before Eddie herself, as if she intended to face him down once and for all.

"I hid the bag," he said. "No one else knows where it is but me, which pretty much puts me in the driver's seat."

Eddie didn't look happy. "You're lying. She knows where it is." He nodded his head at Reva.

"No, she doesn't. I moved it a couple of days ago." The bag of money was no longer in Reva's cottage, but hidden on the third floor of the Fister house in one of the rooms he and Alan had never used.

Eddie's nostrils flared. He had no choice but to accept what Dean told him as fact. "It better all be there. I swear, Reva, if you spent my money on this raggedy old place…"

"I didn't spend a dime," Reva said.

Eddie believed her—Dean could tell by the relief that washed over his face. He actually smiled. "That's my girl. You always were pretty smart. Why don't you drop this stiff and come with me?"

She shook her head. "No."

"You can bring the kid if you want."

Reva took a step that brought her closer to Dean—and closer to Eddie. "Wh-what kid?"

She was the worst liar Dean had ever known.

"Remember old Levy?" Eddie said as if they were having a friendly discussion about old times. "I ran into him last week, while I was out and about looking for my money. He told me he saw you working in a restaurant in Raleigh a while back, and somebody told him you'd had a baby. He couldn't remember exactly when it was—you know how old Levy is—but he said it had been a few years. The kid is mine, right?"

Reva opened her mouth to answer, but Dean beat her to the punch. "No, the kid is not yours. He's mine." The words sounded true enough. They even felt true, gut deep. In a matter of weeks, Cooper had become more Dean's child than he would ever be Eddie's, in spite of any biological connection.

"You didn't waste any time, did you?" Eddie asked, cold eyes on Reva's face.

"It's not like you were around," Dean said.

Eddie glared at Dean for a moment, then he shrugged. "Doesn't matter. Come on, Reva. You can bring the kid, anyway. The cops are looking for me. Traveling as a family man would make a nice disguise.''

"She's not going anywhere with you," Dean said. "Reva, you head across the street." Using the front door would take her right past Eddie. She didn't want that and neither did he. "Go through the kitchen."

"I'm not leaving you here with him." Reva insisted. "Give him the money and let him go."

"Yeah, handyman. Give me the money." Eddie, who couldn't afford to kill Dean at the moment, repositioned his gun so it was aimed at Reva. His eyes remained on Dean. "Why does a handyman carry a Colt .38, anyway?" His eyes flickered down to the gun, then back up again. "Government model. You're no handyman, are you."

"What difference does it make?"

Eddie shrugged. "As long as I get my money, none."

Dean knew he couldn't allow Eddie to leave town, money or no money. But he needed Reva out of the way before gunshots were fired. He had a feeling that before this was all over, gunshots would definitely be fired.

"We don't go anywhere until you aim that weapon away from Reva, got it?"

Eddie shook his head. "No more games. I'm damn tired of you talking to me like you have a right to tell me what to do. You want to know who's boss? I'm gonna show you. I can shoot Reva in a lot of places before I kill her. A kneecap, an elbow, maybe a foot or a hand. She doesn't like pain. She never did." He grinned and his finger began to squeeze. "You don't think I'm serious, do you?"

Dean knew Eddie was perfectly serious in his threat. Just before Eddie pulled the trigger, Dean threw himself to the side, knocking Reva down and out of the way. Eddie fired when Dean was in midair, and the bullet grazed Dean's arm. He felt the sting as he fired back, taking quick aim and pulling the trigger while shielding Reva's body with his own.

His aim was better than Eddie's. The bullet hit Eddie in the chest, dead center, and the felon dropped to the floor.

Moving quickly, Dean rolled toward Eddie and knocked the man's weapon out of his hand. Dean didn't want that gun coming back up on him. It was the stuff nightmares were made of. As soon as the gun was well away from Pinchon, Dean checked for a pulse. There wasn't one.

On the floor beneath the window, Reva sat with her head forward, hair falling over her face, her hands in fists against the floor. She was right where she'd landed when he'd pushed her out of the way of Eddie's bullet. As he watched, she lifted her head and brushed her hair back with both hands.

"You're hurt," she whispered.

Dean glanced at the scratch on his arm. "Not really. We need to call…"

Reva crawled forward, tears in her eyes. She reached him and kept on crawling until she was in his lap. For a moment she sat there, her face against his neck and each breath deep and ragged. Finally she lifted his torn shirtsleeve and studied the wound. Blood ran down his arm, seeping, not flowing. As gunshot wounds went, it wasn't too bad.

But it was ugly.

"I thought you were going to die," she whispered. "For just a split second, I thought you were dead. Everything stopped, and all I could think about was what I hadn't said and done. That spilt second lasted forever."

"I'm fine. How are you?" With easy fingers, he turned her face toward his and studied her eyes. She was scared, yes, but not frantic.

"It's over," he said.

She nodded, and then she laid her head on his shoulder. He held her there, wondering what it was she wished she'd said, what she wished she'd done.

"Looks like I missed all the excitement," Sheriff Andrews said as she entered the room by way of the hallway.

"Tewanda?" Dean asked, not at all surprised to see the sheriff.

"Yeah, she called me. I was damn near to Cross City."

Reva lifted her head and looked at the sheriff, but she didn't move from Dean's lap. "Cooper?"

"He's fine," Andrews answered. "I told Tewanda to stay away from the restaurant and keep the kids well clear, and she said she would." He glanced down at Eddie and scowled. "I guess I have to get this garbage on ice and keep it cold for you federal boys."

"I'd appreciate it," Dean said.

"You look like you could use a doctor," Andrews added without emotion.

Dean shook his head. "I can handle it."

"No," Reva said, her voice stronger than it had been a moment ago. "You need a doctor to look at that." She glanced up at the sheriff. "He says it's nothing, but I don't think it's nothing. A *bullet* did that. Make him have a doctor look at it. Order him to go to the hospital. This is your jurisdiction, right? You can force him to go to the hospital in Cross City if you want to. He can't just put a bandage on it and take an aspirin. He needs medical attention!"

Dean took Reva's chin in his hand and made her look at him. He even managed a smile. "Now I know where Cooper gets his conversational skills."

"I only ramble when I'm nervous." She blushed. "*Very* nervous."

"How about I have Doc Fredericks stop by and take a

look at your arm,'' Andrews suggested. "That should keep everyone happy. Everyone but me, that is. I see a full night of paperwork ahead of me, and I imagine by midnight Somerset will be crawling with feds.'' He glared down at Dean. "I don't suppose you could have just wounded the man.''

"He was going to shoot Reva," Dean said simply.

"In that case you were perfectly justified.''

Reva placed her hands on Dean's face and looked him in the eye. So far she hadn't so much as glanced at Eddie. Just as well. A dead body wasn't a pretty sight. She leaned in slowly and gave him a quick kiss. "You're right," she whispered. "You'll never be a handyman.''

Doc Fredericks, who had officially retired years ago but still managed to keep up a respectable business in Somerset, had cleaned and bandaged Dean's wound and sent him to bed. Dean had tried to refuse the doctor's orders, but since he was exhausted from several nights of little sleep and had, after all, been shot, he finally agreed.

The county crime lab had arrived quickly, taken their photographs and removed Eddie's body. A cleaning service Ben had recommended was currently cleaning the foyer of the restaurant. Come tomorrow, customers would be served as always, and they would never know what had happened there.

Reva knocked softly on the door to the upstairs parlor of Evelyn Fister's house. When she got no answer, she balanced the tray she carried on one palm and opened the unlocked door. The door to the bedroom off the parlor stood open and she saw Dean's form on the bed. He'd removed his shirt, but still wore his jeans. His jeans and a white bandage on his right upper arm. He looked as if he'd just plopped down onto the bed and fallen asleep.

She walked quietly to the doorway. He was long, hard and strong, and she'd been so afraid for him. More afraid than she thought possible. While she watched, Dean opened his eyes.

"What's in the bowl?" he asked.

"Chicken soup." She walked into the room and placed the tray on his bedside table. "I also have sugar cookies from Miss Evelyn—the *new* recipe—an herbal tea Miss Frances swears will cure anything, Miss Edna's famous lemon pie and a book." She lifted a slim, hardbound book—*Elton the Elephant Makes a New Friend.* "Cooper heard that you weren't feeling well and thought you might like something to read."

Dean flashed her a half smile and started to sit up.

"Don't," Reva said sharply. "You need to rest. I just had to make sure you were okay and had something to eat and…basically, I just had to see for myself that you hadn't bled to death up here all alone."

"I'm fine," he said, his face and his voice much more solemn than they'd been a moment ago. "How are you?"

"I'm not the one who got shot."

"That's not what I'm talking about."

Reva sat on the side of the bed. She shouldn't be here. She should be furious with Dean for everything he'd done. So why did she want nothing more than to lie down and bury her face in Dean's chest?

"I'm good," she said softly.

As if he'd just remembered that his gun was sitting on the table on the opposite side of the bed, Dean reached out suddenly to lay his hand on the weapon. "Sorry. I'll put it in a drawer."

Reva placed her hand on his chest, and he stopped moving. "That's not necessary."

Hand on the gun, he turned his head to look at her. "Are you sure?"

Reva nodded, and Dean pulled his hand back. The gun remained on the table, a cold thing, a piece of machinery. And as long as Dean was close, the presence of the weapon didn't make her tremble.

"I guess others are coming," she said. "Other U.S. marshals."

Dean nodded. "Alan will be here in a few hours, and he won't come alone."

She didn't ask about what would happen to the money. Having it out of her house was like having a physical burden lifted from her shoulders. She'd never wanted Eddie's money; she'd just carried it with her from place to place like a millstone she didn't know how to dispose of. Dean would take care of it. She had a feeling he lived a lot of his life that way, taking care of other people's problems.

Weary and knowing she didn't have time to carry a grudge, Reva lay down beside Dean and wrapped her arm around his waist. She held on, because she knew the simple pleasure was a luxury she wouldn't have much longer.

"Are you really all right?" she asked. No matter what Dean said, she could not completely dismiss her worry.

"Absolutely. It's just a scratch."

He would be gone in a few hours. Tonight, maybe tomorrow morning. She'd known all along that Dean wasn't going to remain in Somerset, so why did it hurt so much?

Because she loved him, that's why. She'd been so sure she could guard her heart, but Dean had slipped in. He would always be there, she imagined. He wasn't the kind of man a woman forgot.

She couldn't keep him here, but she didn't want his last

memory of her to be getting shot or arguing about his deception and her mistakes.

Reva raised herself slowly and laid a hand on Dean's cheek. Then she kissed him; he kissed her back. Maybe they had both made mistakes along the way, but they did this right.

She didn't tell Dean that she loved him as she unbuttoned her dress and shrugged it off. There was nothing to talk about, no confessions to make, no plans for the future. There was just his body and hers, his heart and hers. Even if Dean never admitted to it, she suspected his heart was as involved as hers.

He had told her, once before, that she would ask him to make love to her again. As she unfastened and unzipped his jeans, she proved him right.

"Make love to me, Dean," she whispered. "I want my last memory of you to be here, now. Not an argument, not an uncomfortable goodbye as you leave town. Just this."

He helped her finish undressing, moving slowly, favoring his injured arm a little, but not so much that she worried about him hurting himself. When they were both undressed, she left the bed and walked to the wardrobe. She opened the double doors.

Dean sat up. "I can explain," he said as Reva reached into the big box at the bottom of the wardrobe.

She'd found the box days ago as she searched for a place to hang her clothes. At first she'd been furious, and then she'd remembered watching Clint arrive and carry this very box into the house. A brotherly joke, she imagined, something they would laugh about in years to come. Knowing that, she couldn't be angry.

Reva smiled as she stood, a randomly captured condom

caught between two fingers. She read the foil label. "Green. That should be interesting."

"I didn't buy those," Dean said as she sat on the side of the bed and opened the package.

"You don't have to explain. I saw your brother carrying the box into the house on the day he visited. I'm smart enough to figure out the rest on my own."

For years she'd lived without a man in her life, but the sight of Dean, beautiful and naked and aroused, lying before her, seemed achingly familiar to her, as if he'd always been a part of her life. As if he would always be here.

She joined him on the bed and sheathed him in the green condom, then laughed at the distress on his face as she leaned in to kiss him. That she could laugh at something so silly was amazing. Dean could've been killed today. She'd been at the wrong end of a gun herself. Cooper had been mere feet away from meeting the man who was his biological father, a man she didn't want him ever to know about. Eddie had died just a few feet away in the foyer of her restaurant.

And Dean would be leaving soon. She had nothing to laugh about, and still…there was this wonderful moment. She hadn't lived for the moment in so long she'd forgotten what it was like to concentrate only on *now*.

She was ready; so was he. But she didn't want this moment to end too soon. They moved slowly, Dean's hands and mouth on her body, their kisses going on and on until she couldn't stand it anymore, until her body shook with need.

Her fingers traced the shape of the hard body she'd never touch again. She watched her pale hand on his tanned chest, his strong legs next to hers, the desire on his face as he caressed and kissed her. How could hands so rough be so tender?

She rolled atop Dean, guided his erection to her and surged to take him in. He did as she asked and made love to her. Deep and hard, tender and yet without restraint. She made love to him, too, moving with and against him, swaying atop him and finally swaying down to take him deeper than before. Wave upon wave of completion shook her body, and Dean came with her.

Boneless and sated, she gently toppled over him, her legs bracketing his hips, her body and his still joined. If only she never had to let him go.

If she was very brave, she would tell him now. *I love you. Nothing else matters but that. I love you. Stay.*

But she was not very brave. She was a coward.

She waited until Dean was asleep, then she dressed and slipped out the door.

The streets of Somerset looked no different this morning than they had when he'd arrived almost three weeks ago. Something was different, though. Dean suspected it was him.

Alan had arrived last night, along with another team of two. They'd taken possession of Eddie Pinchon's body, taken Reva's statement and then left town.

Dean had slept through most of it. Alan had awakened him long enough to take a statement. After Alan's departure, Dean had fallen immediately back to sleep.

He hadn't mentioned the money. Not to Alan, not to anyone. At his instruction, neither had Reva. The money was his problem now, not hers. Last he'd heard, the authorities had decided the cash they'd heard about was fiction or long gone. Until Dean knew where the money had come from, it was his secret. His and Reva's.

As Dean packed his things into Clint's pickup truck, he kept looking toward Reva's restaurant. He couldn't see the cottage from here, but damned if he couldn't feel it pulling at him.

Reva had told him last night that she didn't want any sloppy goodbyes, and he couldn't blame her. The sex had been good, but they didn't have anything else.

The patter of feet alerted him to Cooper's presence. He looked around to see the kid running toward the truck.

"Are you leaving?" Cooper asked as he watched Dean throw a suitcase into the back of the pickup.

"Yeah. My vacation is over."

"Oh." The kid's face fell, and something tugged at Dean's heart. "I thought maybe you would stay here. I can help you find a job! Mr. Keller at the hardware store, he's always needing help, and I bet Mom would let you work at the restaurant if you asked her, and…and you could work for the sheriff, maybe."

"Thanks, kid, but I already have a job." Dean opened the driver's-side door. Behind the seat of this souped-up jalopy of Clint's sat a quarter of a million dollars.

"But you said you'd build a fort on the playground," Cooper whispered.

"I'll send the church some money, and they can hire someone—"

"But I was going to help," Cooper interrupted. "Remember, Terrance and I had some good ideas for the fort."

"I'll mention that when I send the check."

Wanting only to get out of here before he began to feel

any worse than he already did, Dean climbed into the truck.

He was about to close the door when Cooper said in a frantic voice, "I'll be good. I promise I will."

Dean left the truck and walked straight to Cooper, reaching down to pick him up so they were eye to eye. He was so light, so young, such a baby still…though he likely would not agree. "You are a good kid every day. My leaving doesn't have anything to do with that."

Cooper was trying very hard not to cry, in that way six-year-olds have, as Dean perched him on the edge of the pickup bed. They were face-to-face, man to man. "I can not talk too much when you're around. Mom says sometimes I talk too much, but I can't help it. I can be real quiet if that's what bothers you." With that, he pursed his lips closed.

"I like to hear you talk," Dean said. "I'm not leaving because you talk too much. I'm leaving because I have to get back to my job."

Cooper did not look convinced, and his mouth remained tightly closed.

"If I ever do have a kid, I hope he's just like you."

Cooper's mouth relaxed. "Really?"

"Really."

"Maybe you can come back for another vacation sometime. You never did fix Terrance's dinosaur."

"Maybe I can do that one of these days." Dean swung Cooper down and placed him on his feet. "You run on home now. Tell your mom I said…" No goodbyes, she'd said. Nothing maudlin. "Tell her I said thanks."

"You can come home with me and tell her yourself," Cooper said brightly. "She's awake. She has a summer cold—that's why her eyes are all red and her nose is runny—but if you drink orange juice, you won't catch it. There's coffee!''

''I can't,'' Dean said, climbing into the truck again. ''I have to go.''

Cooper backed away, keeping his eyes on Dean. Even when the truck was well down the street, Cooper remained in place. Dean checked out the kid in the rearview mirror, wishing he'd go home with a skip and a hop as if nothing were wrong.

But Cooper didn't move. He stood there as Dean turned the corner and the elegant houses of Magnolia Street disappeared from view.

Chapter 19

June arrived, hot and humid. Cooper got out of school for the summer, and business in the restaurant remained good. A reporter from Atlanta arrived to do an article on Miss Reva's, and immediately they began to get phone calls from that big city. It was not much more than a two-hour drive from Atlanta to Somerset. Reva decided to hire someone to finish the upstairs rooms so she could add a couple of tables, but she never got around to calling anyone. She wasn't ready. Those rooms were Dean's.

Mid-June she received a newspaper clipping by mail. At first she thought it was the article that had appeared in the Atlanta paper, and while it was from an Atlanta newspaper, the article was not about her business. Instead, it was a small mention of an anonymous donation made to an Atlanta women's shelter. A few days later she received another clipping about a generous anonymous donation that had been made to a drug rehab center, also in Atlanta. Ben had dropped by one afternoon, all smiles. He hadn't even lost his smile when she'd rejected his invitation to dinner in Cross City. And for once he had only good things to say about Dean Sinclair. Apparently Dean had arranged for Ben's office to receive federal money to modernize a woefully outdated computer system.

Reva had filed the clippings away, as she filed away the passbook that had arrived in the mail one day. This time, Dean had included a note.

I conducted a thorough investigation. No claim of any kind has been made, so there's no one to return the money to. You were right. It's dirty money. Might as well do a little good with what Eddie left behind. I've disposed of most of it, as you know, but hung on to this little bit for Cooper's college. Tax man or baseball player, the kid needs a good education. Think about it.

The account was in Cooper's name.

She missed Dean, more than she'd expected. And she'd known these first few weeks would be difficult. Every night, every day and everywhere she looked she saw something that reminded her of Dean.

But no matter how much it hurt, she wasn't sorry she had loved him for a while. She couldn't be sorry. Dean had given her back something she'd lost a long time ago. Her woman's heart.

"Mom!" Cooper ran into her office, breathless and red-faced. "Come see!" Without saying more, he turned and pounded back down the stairs. It was not yet eleven, so no customers had arrived. But the place bustled with activity, as her employees prepared for another filled-to-capacity Saturday afternoon. Miss Edna was excited, because there was one reservation for a party of twelve. A family named Taggert, she said. The woman who had called had requested that Reva be their hostess.

Reva followed Cooper at a distance as he ran down the sidewalk in the shade of the trees. She walked briskly, but did not run. Cooper looked over his shoulder every now and then, to make sure she didn't get too far behind, and even stopped once and placed his hands on his hips in frustration.

"Come *on,* Mom!" he shouted.

He turned toward the church, cut past the sanctuary and ran to the back, where the playground was. Reva noted the black truck parked at the curb, as well as a couple of cars she didn't recognize. Alabama and Georgia plates, she saw as she followed Cooper's path onto the grassy church lawn.

Another truck was parked in the grass near the playground, and four men were busy unloading lengths of unfinished wood. Cooper and Terrance stood close, but not too close, jumping up and down in glee.

At the sound of laughter, Reva turned her head and saw three women sitting in the shade and sharing a blanket that had been spread across the grass. They were surrounded by children. A dark-haired little boy, a strawberry-blond toddler and two babies. Twins. When Mary turned her head, Reva recognized her.

She looked again at the men and saw a grinning Clint in the party. Then Dean lifted his head.

"Calm down, Reva," she said softly. "He's just come to build this playhouse, that's all. He's not here for you."

He walked toward her as if he *was* here for her, a half smile on his face, a hint of uncertainty in his walk. He was dressed, as they all were, in jeans and boots and a T-shirt. Not John Deere, this time, but the Atlanta Braves.

"What are you doing here?" she asked bluntly. Heaven

above, she could not bear to have him come and go, giving her hope every time she saw him, breaking her heart every time he left.

"Paying for my picnic lunch," he said calmly. "I brought some help."

"I see that." Her heart thudded as he drew closer. It almost came through her chest when he draped his arm around her shoulder and pointed. "You know Clint. The guy who looks like he knows what he's doing is my brother-in-law Nick. The guy with the long hair is my brother Boone." He turned his finger to the women. "You've met Mary. The dark-haired woman is my sister, Shea, and the little boy, Justin, is hers. That's Jayne," he said, gesturing to the woman who was struggling with the one little girl in the bunch. "Boone's wife, and his little girl, Miranda."

"You brought the whole family," she said.

"Yep."

"To build a fort."

Dean leaned down and kissed her, not even hesitating even though anyone in his family could see if they looked in this direction. "Among other things."

He took a photograph that had been folded many times from his back pocket and handed it to her without instruction. She unfolded the picture, which was of an older house similar in style to her restaurant. There were two stories, instead of three, and a lovely gallery encircled the second story. The antebellum house was in need of some repair, but was not falling down by any means.

"The house is in a little town not far outside Atlanta."

"It's lovely."

"I bought it," Dean said in a lowered voice.

"You what?" She had known he wouldn't stay, but in her heart she'd hoped...just a little. Buying a house so far away was concrete proof that he did not plan to stay here in Somerset.

"I bought it," he said again. "I've already started fixing the place up."

"So you're a bit of a handyman, after all." She tried not to sound as if her heart was broken.

He nodded. "I guess I am." He drew her away from the others into the shadow of an old tree, where they were hidden from view. For the moment, anyway. "I always told you that I couldn't stay here."

"I know."

"And I can't," he said, taking her hand and holding on, threading his fingers through hers. "I'm good at what I do, and even with all the frustration of the job, I do make a difference. I can't give it up to live here just because leaving town made me feel like I was ripping my heart out."

She squeezed his hand.

"But maybe you can come with me."

Reva opened her mouth to answer, but Dean continued, not giving her a chance.

"The house I bought is on the north side of Atlanta. The trip is two hours, tops. We can come to Somerset every weekend, Tewanda can take over as manager, and if you want to open another restaurant—"

Reva went up on her toes and silenced Dean with a kiss. She had ached for his mouth in the weeks since he'd left, and to feel his lips on hers was like coming home. After a kiss that was just long enough to remind her of everything she missed about this man, Dean took his mouth from hers. "The schools are good, and there's Little League baseball. Soccer, too."

Reva wrapped her arms around his waist. "I was going

to say yes the first time. Whatever needs to be done to make it work, we'll manage.''

"We will." He leaned down and placed his forehead against hers. "I love you," he whispered.

"I love you, too."

"Marry me."

"Yes."

He reached into the front pocket of his jeans and pulled out a velvet box, opening it to show her the ring inside. The diamond solitaire in a white-gold setting was antique in style, and when he placed it on her finger, it fit perfectly and felt very, very right.

"I need a little help hanging wallpaper in the new house," he said just before he kissed her again.

Reva laughed and threw her arms around Dean's neck. He had come back for her. She had longed for him, she had loved him, but she had never dared to hope that he might come for her and ask her to be his wife.

"You brought the entire family with you to ask me to marry you," she said as Dean placed her on her feet.

"I figured you should know what you're getting into." He put his arm around her and looked out on his family. "Being a Sinclair isn't easy. Trouble seems to find us wherever we go."

"You've all managed very well," she said with a smile.

"We have, haven't we."

They stood there, holding each other and breathing deeply, enjoying the moment, the sun and the shade and the feeling in their hearts. The other men continued to work and hadn't yet come to collect the one who'd gotten them into this project. The women chatted and minded babies. Babies Cooper and Terrance were now curious about. After a couple of very peaceful minutes, Reva jumped slightly. "Oh, no. I have to go back to the restaurant! We have a big party coming in, and they asked for me specifically, and—"

"Taggert, party of twelve," Dean said calmly. He pointed to his sister. "Her married name is Taggert."

Reva began to count. The men, the women, the children, and Dean. "Is someone missing? I count eleven."

Dean pointed to the boys, who were now playing with two-year-old Justin. "Cooper needs to get acquainted with his new family, don't you think?"

He'd thought of Cooper, included her son in his plans long before she'd said yes to his proposal.

"Do they know what a good man you are?" she asked softly.

"Just a man, Reva. Good and bad. I did make a few mistakes. I'll probably make a few more."

"Your heart was always in the right place. I imagine it always will be."

Reva had never been part of a family like this one, and suddenly she was a little scared. What if they didn't accept her? She didn't know what Dean had told them about her, but she didn't expect he had spun a pretty tale full of lies. Dean would be caught in the middle if his family didn't like her.

"Come on," Dean said, leading her forward with his arm around her waist. "Let's go meet everyone."

"Now?" Reva dragged her feet. "I should change clothes, put on some makeup, fix my hair…" Dean did not slow down. "What if they don't like me?" she blurted in a hoarse whisper.

"They're going to love you and Cooper, I promise."

"You don't know—"

"I love you. They'll love you. If there's a problem, I know how to win them over."

"How?"

Dean stopped, placed both arms around her and grinned. "In case you haven't noticed, we have a preponderance of boys in the family. Cooper tips the scale even further to the male side. Jayne is worried that Miranda won't have any female cousins to get into mischief with, and Shea and Mary claim the women in the family are getting woefully outnumbered." He leaned in close but did not kiss her. Not this time. "What do you say we work on giving Cooper a sister?"

She smiled and nodded.

"Come on," Dean said, taking her hand and leading her toward his family. "I suppose I should tell you now, there's one more reason they're all going to be happy to have you in the family."

"What?"

Dean grinned at her as he led her along. "You're cooking Thanksgiving dinner this year."

She laughed. "Thanksgiving! Planning ahead, aren't you?"

Dean pulled her close. "Yes, I am. Do you mind?"

Reva took a deep breath and walked fearlessly toward her new family. "Not at all."

* * * * *

Don't miss Linda's next exciting story!
FEVER will be available this January
as part of Silhouette's FAMILY SECRETS series.
Look for it wherever Silhouette Books are sold.

Coming in August 2003

Back by popular demand!

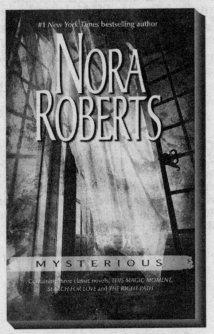
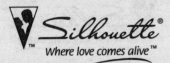

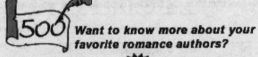

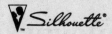

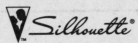

COMING NEXT MONTH